FOR THE LOVE OF
STORMY WEATHERS

BETTY LOWREY

To order additional copies of this book, contact:
Bookwhip
1-855-339-3589
https://www.bookwhip.com

CHAPTER

1

Her sigh was almost audible. It was all the same ol' same o. She longed for a change of pace. Was there anyone in this church building today that had an exciting life? Now she felt ashamed. Stilll, what if out there…beyond the stained glass window God had someone for her. IT wasn't as if she hadn't been waiting all these years and she had given up. Lord, send me someone to love; whole in body, handsome if you don't mind, tall. She almost giggled. She glanced around the room. Not a handsome man in the midst…of course that species would have gone to the lake. She didn't even own a swimming suit. She was pretty dull herself. Maybe even now the Lord was planting someone in her path on her way home. Yeah, sure! And outside it was raining frogs.

Glancing around, Grace noted the summer people were absent. Since beginning attendance at Faith Tabernacle she had heard the expression, summer people, meaning when it was warm outside a certain privileged few were lax in church but loyal to the expensive boats that dotted the backyards in the small town of Haven on the Bluff and regular at the nearby lake where waterskiing was a regular weekend sport. The pastor never mentioned their absence, other than to say, "Things will pick up when school starts."

Grace had come into the hallowed fellowship of Faith Tabernacle by way of Arnel Weather's care. Raped by an unknown attacker, pregnant and destitute, Mrs. Weathers had taken Grace in but not because of the goodness of her heart as many in the church thought. No, Mrs. Weathers knew the truth of the matter in more ways than one but what scored highest on her calendar was that she was undergoing treatment for a cancer that left her weak and unable to do her own work and taking Grace under her wing was the answer to it all.

Before the cancer took complete toll of her body she was able to teach Grace how to run their home. At first she showed kindness but as the cancer progressed her nerves became raw and her patience thin. "I taught you better than that. Do that job over young lady," she would say. "You'll never amount to anything if you leave it like that. Now, hurry there's more to do and we need our clothes pressed and ready for Sunday. You know I'm slower these days." Then she would stand silently, her eyes squinted, studying her ward. "You should be grateful I took you in. Otherwise you'd be out on the streets, with your own parents abandoning you." Those cold eyes bored right through to Grace's soul. "And if you even think you're going with us to church, you better come out of that room dressed in the appropriate color." This was after the baby arrived and Mrs. Weathers had ordered Grace a new wardrobe, in two specific colors. Beige and brown. Grace longed for the joyful colors of her youth chosen by her mother that brought happiness.

Grace wanted to say, "I heard you promise them you would care for me, cherish me as your own child but instead you treat me like your slave. Nothing I do is good enough, though I'm constantly available to your every whim and you do very little in this household for yourself or your husband," but she didn't voice her opinion. The one time she tried her benefactor threw a ladle of hot boiling soup from the stove on her arm. Eight months pregnant, kept from the neighborhood view, Grace neither wanted to be seen; nor was she allowed to leave the house. That night she saw spots of blood on the sheets where she lay and scared went to tell Mrs. Weathers. In her fright she forgot to knock on the door and that was the worst nightmare of her life. On occasion the dregs of ugliness reared up to torment her though she had spent the years since trying to forget.

"We can't take her to the hospital, Reed, no one knows she is pregnant. I doubt they realize she's here."

"What did you think you would do with the baby, Arnel," Mr. Weathers questioned. "Her parents plainly told you she was pregnant." He was on his feet by the bedside, staring at the woman he loved but she was becoming hard to bear. "Let's not fight over this, Arnel." He said her name with a southern drawl. "Just tell us what to do. What do you want done with this baby, it looks like it's coming tonight."

"What did you think we'd do with this baby, Reed? Traipsing around in the dark of night, coming home smelling worse than sin, for all I know it's yours."

What he smelled of, were the chemicals in the medicines his business handled, or those used when a spill occurred. He had slammed the door as he left the bedroom. Arnel Weathers struggled to get out of bed, her ravaged body a string of crêpe skin and failed muscle. "Do you see what you've done? We have enough trouble without you adding to it." She was trying to slip a cotton duster over her thin nightgown. With one hand, Grace tried to help her. "Why are you holding your arm?"

Grace supposed she had forgotten throwing the ladle of boiling liquid on her. She dropped the hand covering the red and oozing welts of flesh. "It's where you…" She began but the fire in Mrs. Weathers eyes let her words drop to nothing, but too late.

"How dare you insinuate I did anything." Arnel's eyes blazed as she began to cough. "Hand me the phone. I have a friend coming here to deliver your baby. In case you don't know, that's what the bleeding 's about," she smirked. "I thought you were going to be a smart one, but you're not." Through coughing and heaving for breath, Mrs. Weathers made the call. "Angeline, it's time, if you could come over and take care of this little business, we'd be so grateful. I know, Honey and I'm going to pay you real good for your time here, and Honey don't bring anyone with you, as I told you for our girl's sake."

The blood flowed faster, Grace trying to keep it from ruining the bedclothes because she had been warned. Not knowing what to do she had saved stacks of papers which were hidden under her bed lest Mrs. Weathers decide to do a search of her room as she had in the beginning. The woman, Angeline, was in her fifties, Grace guessed, thin as a rail, hawk faced with piercing eyes that darted around the room taking in everything. Grace didn't know if her silence was a good thing or something to fear.

The labor pains had begun shortly after the bedroom incident and then her water broke but the hours began to add up, the labor pains wearing her down and the sweat of her body mingling with the blood on the newspapers. "This is not good," Angeline muttered. "It's placenta previa if I'm any kind of nurse at all to make a guess, but she's not dilating enough to birth this baby."

"What do you mean?" Arnel sensed danger and her voice rose. "I promised to pay you highly if you could do this and keep it quiet."

"She's not the first to have a child out of wedlock. Why are you so worried about this? You took her in, for heaven's sake, Arnel. Who would fault you for anything?"

"You don't know the half of it," Arnel replied.

"Then tell me. We've got a few hours here, unless it gets worse and then I'm calling an ambulance."

"I won't let you do that."

The woman straightened sharply staring at her friend and her expression changed.

As worn as she was, Grace saw the hardening of Arnel's eyes, the straight line of her mouth and the determination that this act of God was going to play out according to her instructions. Grace shuddered and moaned so loud both women leaned forward.

"You've always been a perfectionist, Arnel. As a girl growing up, even, but I do wonder what happened to the generosity of your soul. You seem to be void of that trait I remember."

"You should learn not to voice your opinion, Angeline, especially where things are not your business."

Angeline gave a wicked laugh and sat in the chair by Grace's bedside. Taking her hand she began the count, holding Grace wrist just so. "She's lost a lot of blood. I'm going to have to cut her and she's going to have to bear down like there's no tomorrow to get this baby out before it drowns in the fluid."

"You got that, girl?" Angeline leaned across Grace. For the first time Grace considered if there was a dram of kindness in the woman's eyes or was she so far gone she wasn't seeing clearly? "I want you to do exactly as I tell you and we'll have this baby out of there and in your arms in nothing flat."

Trying to nod, Grace realized from that moment on, Angeline ignored Arnel and for some strange reason Arnel sat ghostlike taking in every little movement the nurse made while she kept her own mouth shut.

In time, Grace heard an agonizing scream, followed by the weak sound of a baby's cry, as her whole world went black. She wasn't certain how many hours passed until she felt someone fumbling with the cloth covering her breast and then the attempted suckling sound she could not quite place but felt as cold hands cupped the sides of her face and a voice whispered, "Grace, you must wake up. You've slept all that's possible, now your baby needs your attention."

She struggled from the depths of darkness, trying to rise above the waters pulling her down, the cloth that held her feet captive and her body too sore to move. Words would not surface, her lips felt cracked and dry but she was aware in her left arm she held a warm little body that made a tiny sound. Her baby was alive. She tried to focus on Angeline but it was too much. The woman would have to do what she must to save them both. Grace was certain she was drowning, except for that tiny sound....

The third day after the birthing, Angeline arrived with a bag of baby clothes, four plastic bottles complete with rubber nipples and an assortment of blankets, large and small. Opening one of the dresser drawers she placed the items inside and then took up her usual place by the side of Grace's bed. Looking down at her baby, Grace said, "I named him Joshua. I heard it means salvation." Angeline nodded. "If I didn't have him to love I think I'd want to die. Thank you for the things you brought."

"I don't normally see my patients again," Angeline replied, "but you seem different. Soft and gentle and perhaps beat down by what has happened to you, unless it's Arnel herself has turned you into the cowering piece of clay you are." Her sharp eyes held with Grace. "Your boy seems healthy in spite of the turmoil of his birth. Babies are fighters and you must be, too, in order to survive this."

"How old are you, fifteen, sixteen?" Grace nodded. "You've been to school, previous to coming here?" She smoothed the sheet as she talked. "Arnel don't like your still being bedridden, but I told her if she wants anything out of you later, you must heal now. You understand?" She waited for understanding to dawn in Grace's eyes. "We were friends as young girls, Arnel and me, but life didn't always treat us the same," Angeline's eyes clouded with memory. "We met our men, her Reed and my Joseph. Hers got a degree and became a pharmacist; my Joseph went to war and didn't come back."

Grace reached for Angeline's hand and squeezed it hard. "I'm tough," Angeline continued, "and though I value friendship I don't go along with all I see. There's injustice in this world. I got a feeling you've had your share but you hang in there. Now I don't know what you'll do when she dies," Angeline jerked her head toward the part of the house they could see through the opened door, "But I know what's coming down the road, she's already picked out his next wife. Always was one to make things happen her way." Angeline rose up to leave. "You watch out for you and that baby, if opportunity knocks to give you a better chance at life, you take it. Don't get caught up in lovin' the first old boy that comes along to make you promises. Promises are cheap. It's the reality of life you gotta think on. Better yourself. You hear me?" She peered down on Grace and her baby. "Don't you ever let anyone tell you you ain't no good. You're as good as the next person but you've got to be good. You understand what I'm sayin' girl?"

Though she would like to have seen Angeline again and heard her wise counsel, Grace heard Angeline left *Haven* for a while. She wondered if she returned for Arnel's funeral. She asked Mrs. Hutchens next door to keep Joshua in order to attend. There were few family and mostly church people in attendance. She saws Reed wipe tears from his eyes and wondered that she had no tears for Arnel. She didn't go to the cemetery but hurried home to pack her belongings as she wondered where she and her boy would spend the night for she remembered Angeline telling her Arnel had chosen his next wife.

Coming back to the present she was restless sitting in church, listening to the pastor. "What are the things that attack your belief, your faith, the very Christianity you profess to believe?" Strange he would ask that, as she sat there trying to figure out her own life. "First of all," he continued, "the devil puts doubt in your mind." Yes, he does, she agreed but not shaking her head as those sitting around her were.

"Good to see you, Stormy," Pastor said as she was leaving. She didn't shake his hand as little Mrs. Peterson had him cornered. *The words, my grandson, came across the way, as heads turned.* It was community knowledge her grandson was testing the waters; fifteen and laughing at life. A sobering thought, when did she quit laughing? Was it when Reed died or when her son was killed by a drunken driver that dragged his bicycle into town and left Joshua lying by the side of the road?

She thought she had overcome those tragedies, facing them, all the while tucking them into her subconscious which meant not a day went by but what she remembered both. Thank God Reed had been there when Joshua died or she might have gone down. The loss of Joshua aged him even more than the years he was older than her, so much he gave up his fight against cancer and was gone within the year of Joshua's death. It was hard losing both, for different reasons. Here she was on a Sunday, mourning them all over again while she was barely thirty years old and felt forty.

Whether to grab a burger or join her friends who attended a different church was the question. A sudden step on the brakes cleared that from her mind. What was that sound she'd heard? The car in front had stopped as a man cleared the door, agitation in his stance as he glanced back at her briefly and then stood studying the front left area of his car. The lane was blocked. The cars behind were backing to the nearest exit, except for the two behind her, teenagers she guessed by the blare of a radio, but her eyes were on the man, visibly upset by the movement of his shoulders and wave of his hand as he talked into a cell phone. If she didn't try to back around the teenagers she would be there awhile, and there was no room for another car to pull around or back out in the two lane space.

Grace turned the key, got out of her car and walked forward. Someone's husband, she guessed, on his way home to dinner. Dressed in tan slacks, a white open at the throat polo and a thick head of sun streaked brown hair was all she could see coming up from behind but then he turned, a clouded expression on his face, which would have been drop dead handsome if he hadn't seemed angry. He stared at her as though it were her fault as he leaned into the car and dropped a phone on the dash.

"I didn't know if you were all right, or not," she began, for the first time seeing the tire on the wheel laying to the left of the lane, his car leaning almost to the pavement. "What in the world happened?"

"Good question." He closed his eyes and took a deep breath. "Some dumbo, yesterday in Illinois, said he fixed the problem, evidently he didn't. Sorry, I must have looked the devil I was that perturbed."

"You did appear a bit ruffled," she replied.

"Ruffled?" His laughter was as wonderful as he looked when he smiled. She couldn't help but notice.

"May I help you; take you to find someone to fix the wheel, or anything?"

"I've made a call for roadside service. It will be a matter of minutes, and then if you mean it, I could use a ride to the nearest hotel."

"Sure. I'll just wait in the car."

The wrecker came to pick up his car, crossing the medium as though it was done every day and she supposed if your vehicle was large enough you could. It was as he came around the backside, between her car and the teenagers she heard a scream as her own car moved forward on its own. Her first reaction was to jump out, the second to scold the teenager.

"I'm sorry, Mam, sorry, I accidently put the car in the wrong gear. Sorry," he called out as he backed away, free now because the car behind him had done the same. She wondered why he was in such a hurry, the radio blaring, his friends practically hanging out the window; he hadn't been in any hurry before. It was then she heard a noise and glanced down to see if her bumper was intact. And there lay the stranger, whose car was just towed away, on the ground, writhing in pain, his hands clasp around his left knee cap, his face turning redder by the moment. She dropped down beside him. "What's wrong?"

"That kid pinned me between your car and his and you let him drive away."

"I didn't know you were there."

"You didn't see me walking behind your vehicle?"

"Well, yes, and I wondered why but then my car moved forward on its own and I forgot about you."

"Obviously."

He was miffed and she didn't like it. "Why did you walk behind the car?"

He pointed. She glanced the direction where his suitcase lay a bit crushed with a few items spilling on to the sidewalk. "How did it get there?" Then it hit her, he meant to put it in the trunk of her car.

"Lady, would you just help me up, please, and since you have been so nice to wait, do you think, possibly you could drive me to the nearest ER, or quick stop, whatever this one horse town has?"

"Now you are getting sarcastic. What have I done to bring that on?" She was a bit surprised at herself, talking back to a complete stranger. She'd had fifteen years of being docile. Now she was ready to do battle with someone she didn't even know. He was reaching a hand toward her as the color on his face was changing from red to a slight greenish cast as his stomach seemed to go into dry heaves.

"Don't you dare faint or throw up on me," she warned, stretching a hand and bracing her feet on the pavement as he tried to rise. Finally, she stood behind him; both hands settled into his armpits, giving it all she had, practically trying to lift him to bring him to his feet. His height seemed to create an imbalance. He weighed more than she thought. "Now for the passenger seat," she said between gulps of air. "I figured you at say, one seventy. What do you weigh?"

"Not that it's important at this moment," he practically snarled, "I'm six, three, my pant length is thirty four, waist thirty four, presently, and I'm working on it, and I weigh in at two hundred pounds. I wear boxer shorts size thirty four and shoe size eleven. Is that enough information?"

"More than enough, "she snapped back. "Do you need help getting in the car or do you intend to hobble along beside it?"

An expression of pain crossed his face, as a slight green cast replaced the redness, again. "Don't you dare throw up in my car," she repeated, holding the door as he grimaced and tried to crawl into the front seat. "For heaven's sakes," she grumbled, "stand against the seat, then sit and I'll lift your leg inside for you."

He did as told, backing against the seat, sitting down, his feet still on the pavement as she picked up his left leg and he did a howling scream mixed between pain and anger, the right leg kicking out in protest as she jumped back. Realizing what he had done, he gave a quick guttural "I'm sorry," she could barely hear and with one hand wiped at the sweat that had popped out on his brow.

"It hurts like the dickens and the right one doesn't feel the best," he explained, "It may be broke, too."

Pulling away from the curb, she drove to the first exit and turned left. "The hospital is about three miles up the road." She pushed her foot to the gas pedal, aware now, he was in true pain.

"I hope, you hit a bump back there and I thought I was going to pass out. Do you always drive like this?"

"Only when picking ungrateful strangers up off the road," she muttered under her breath as she swerved to miss a dog chasing a squirrel. He did a sudden tilt her direction, let out a scream and passed out. "Great," she said between clenched teeth. "Now he faints." In five minutes she was watching the medical crew load him onto a gurney.

"What's his name?" She must have looked ridiculous. She didn't know. "Come on then, little wife," the big burly guy pushing the gurney called back, "we'll find you a place to sit while we determine what damage has been done to your husband." She started to protest. "It's okay, Honey," he smiled. "It happens all the time; people under stress don't know where they live, much less their name. It's the reality of trauma in an accident. Believe me, we've seen it all." He let out a huge guffaw of a laugh. "What'd you do, run over him?"

"Something like that," she replied. Who'd believe the truth? She didn't even know the guy.

She must have looked pretty ragged when they called her four hours later. She'd had no lunch and her stomach was growling fiercely, beside that she had chewed her beautiful fingernails into an abrasive mess. Seldom did she pay the twenty dollars for a manicure, but this weekend she had splurged. "You can join your husband now," they said. "We had to set the bone in his left leg, and put a cast on the right one, too, but that one might come off in a week or two. Then there's his arm, sprained and in a sling where he tried to catch himself as he fell."

"But it was his left knee cap," she interrupted.

"He thought it was his knee cap. The broken bone twisted and put pressure on the knee cap, a freak of nature accident made his knee cap feel like it was coming loose and the right leg received damage when the kid's bumper pinned both legs to your car."

"He told you?" She felt such relief that she was weak in the knees. She didn't have to fill out papers.

"Yeah, he managed to talk between passing in and out of consciousness."

"What's that about?"

"Some people can't stand the sight of blood."

"There was no blood," she replied, indignant that he would imply such.

"Exactly. But he thought there would be and his blood pressure was out of kilter, as were his electro lights. Come to find out he was training for one of those triathlon-whatever events where you run races, but you knew that."

"No. I didn't."

"So," the big burly guy shook his head. "I guessed as much. You two are separated."

"No, we aren't," She all but stomped her foot. "Let's just forget this discussion. What's next?"

"He can go home. He's still woozy, but you can watch that and try to keep him still, there's always the threat of blood clot." He turned to leave before she could say another word. "Bring your car around," he called back, "we'll get him in a wheel chair and have him ready at the side entrance with the big blue awning." She considered the information, was it possible not to know if a bone in a leg was broken?

What was she supposed to do?" She would drop him off at the nearest hotel as he requested. But when she pulled under the big blue awning, there he sat looking forlorn; both legs in cast sticking straight out in front of him while the burly guy whispered, "Now take good care of him. We don't want to lose him, do we? Remember? Blood clots." He smacked his hands together. "Just like that." She bit her tongue and turned toward the door. "And, Hon," he said, "Get rid of that awful tan you're wearing. You belong in jewel colors. You're a beautiful woman, but you ruin the whole effect in those suckers."

Suckers? She wanted to jump on his back like a feline cat, claw at his neck until he took back the words.

Another medic came running, opened the passenger door, ran the seat back as far as possible and proceeded to help him in, which was a feat in itself since the legs wouldn't bend. He glanced at her apologetic and she couldn't help thinking the spice had gone out of him. A sort of sorry feeling for him was creeping into her conscience. "Where to?" She asked. He shrugged, closed his eyes and pretended sleep. Some three fourth of a mile down the road she pulled into the Hearthside Inn, drove under the portico and stopped. Once inside at the desk, she asked, "do you have a handicap room?"

"Fraid not, just rented the last one to two perfectly healthy people anxious for any kind of room. Tournaments going on in town and most hotels are already sold out. We have one twin size bed, no amenities with that one." Either he was eyeing her choice of clothing thoroughly or now she had a chip on her shoulder from what the big guy at the hospital said, or she had grown a lump on her body one couldn't miss. "Sorry, nothing's available," he repeated, waiting for her to hit the street and move on.

"I'm curious, why?"

He put one finger to his lips and said, "shh."

"Let me guess, it's yours." He nodded. "And you are making money."

"All's fair in love and war," he said. She turned and hurried to the car where her patient was sleeping.

How was she going to get him into the house? What would the neighbors think? Would they even notice? Did she notice them? She took a deep breath, reached for her phone and dialed the sixteen number to the hospital. "I need to talk to someone in the ER." She chewed on her ragged fingernails, waiting. A familiar voice asked, "May I help you?" She pictured him, the burly guy. "What are you, some kind of girl Friday?" She heard laughter. "How long is this man going to sleep and how do you suggest I get him into the house?"

"Well, the drugs were necessary to set the bone in the left leg; it's possible it's a fracture. I'd say he's good for the night, now the other problem, I suggest you call the police and ask them to help you get him in."

"Are you serious?"

"Try it, but make up a good story. They will love helping you. Good bye, business calls."

"What can that hospital be thinking?" She stared at the cell in her hand, drove a few miles and then made the call. "Hello, yes, please." Waiting, waiting and waiting her nerves were shot and she only had two fingernails left to chew on. "Police? Yes. Yes sir, do you by chance have anyone working the south end of town? You do? Oh, thank goodness. I have a dilemma, shortly after lunch as we were downtown near Anthony Boulevard, this was after attending church, there was an accident, a wheel rolled off a car and as my man thought to help, a car with a teenager driving hit the wrong gear and pinned him between the bumper of our car and theirs and he suffered a broken leg, anyway they didn't keep him. Well, long story short I can't get the poor dear into the house and I wondered if you had a good Samaritan police officer in our neighborhood that might help me."

She waited, knowing he was discussing the matter with a second person. She was down to one nail.

"Oh, you do? That would be the most wonderful thing. Two eleven Chris Street. Thank you so much."

"Sergeant Devon Malloy will knock on your door, shortly. We have to make a Police report on the teenager. Did you get his name and we need the make and model of the car."

"He sped away, sir. I don't know his name, having never seen him before. He was a teenager and I was so alarmed helping my man I don't remember anything about the make or model of the car."

The officer arrived as she pulled into the drive and was out ready to help. Their patient responded to the officer's suggestion, made it inside and collapsed into the big chair by the fireplace. "Is that where you want him?" She was at a loss for words. They both stood there staring at him. For the first time she noticed the bit of slant to his eyes. He really wasn't a bad looking guy.

"It will do," she replied. "I can't thank you enough." She shook the officer's hand, and walked with him through the hall to the front door. "I was beside myself… with him so groggy and both legs in casts he can't put any weight on," she sighed, "not to mention the arm in the sling." The officer handed her a card with his phone number, his badge number and his name on it. "Thank you," she said. "a lot."

She walked back to where he sat, rather sprawled. They had sent him home in hospital gown and draw string pants cut off knee length just above the casts, and she had not the presence of mind to remember his clothes. The growling of her stomach reminded her she had not eaten lunch or dinner and perhaps neither had he. The least she could do was scramble eggs and make toast. In the kitchen she stuck the officer's card on the refrigerator, hoping she never needed the information he had listed on it.

He awakened disoriented and grumpy. Before he muttered a word, he had more than a terrible taste in his mouth and it took a few minutes to remember; they had set his leg, put a cast on it and reminded him it would take some getting used to. His bladder must be stretched beyond imagination; he had an acute need to find a bathroom and quick. He tried to rise, realizing both legs wore cast, the right leg would be released from its prison within a week if he slowed down and treated it right, but whatever they'd rigged up was not conducive to walking anywhere. He couldn't crawl. What was he to do?

She found him wearing that pained expression she remembered when he was laying behind the car.

"What do you need?"

"Do you have a bathroom and how do you propose I get there?"

She thought for a moment. "I'm not sure I know the answer but you can try leaning on me."

Still two shades in the woods, as the saying went, he tried to stand, accepting her help to do so and wrapped his arms around her shoulder. "Let's hurry," he groaned, "else we might have to clean the floor." It was hobble and drag, the walk of a few feet seeming a mile or more. "Can you steady me while I untie this string to my pants waist band?"

"I'd rather not," she choked out. "You are on your own." But when she turned loose, he slipped sideways toward the door facing. Rolling her eyes, she said, "You win. I'll just turn my head. Okay?"

"Clearly you can see I'll fall if I stand, so I'll sit."

Between clenched teeth she said, "All right. I'll be outside the door." Silently she berated herself. Foolish. Foolish. She had brought a stranger into her home and was now helping him to the bathroom?

"I can't get up."

"What?"

"I said, I can't stand. What was I thinking? Will you please…just close your eyes, open the door and lend me a hand?"

"Next, you will ask me to pull up your trousers." She actually thought she heard him say, "Yes, please."

The deed was done. She took his hand, helped him to the bed and turned back to wash her hands while he stared at her in disbelief as much as to say, "really, you touch my hand and have to wash yours?"

CHAPTER
2

It was two hours later she fell into bed, worn to exhaustion. She had scrambled the eggs, sitting opposite him as they ate and though he remained incognito, he seemed to appreciate the food. "Remember there's a bathroom across from the bed that you might manage." She contemplated her last words. "Do you think? Well, wait and see then tell me when you are ready. "Do I sleep in these clothes?" He was trying to rise, his free hand pushing against the chair, the one in the sling as useless as his legs in the cast. "I mean, it doesn't bother me but it's your bed."

"What do you normally sleep in?" she asked, blushing as she realized the answer might be embarrassing.

"An old Tshirt and boxers," he replied, an impish grin hovering around his mouth. "But clean."

She huffed a load of air, and appeared busy, fluffing the pillows, straightening the sheet and avoiding his stare. "You have pain pills. I'll get a glass of water." She was gone before he could protest and back with two pill bottles and a glass of water. "This one," she held up the larger bottle, "the doctor suggests you will need before sleep tonight, and the other is to prevent inflammation."

"Maybe the pain meds will knock me out which would be a blessing. What is the second?"

She read the label, mentally sounding the name, "I believe this one contains steroids."

"Oh, no, I don't know about that."

She was removing the lids, taking out the pills and handing them to him. He tilt the glass of water, and swallowed both medications. "Can I do anything for you before I turn in?" Studying him, she saw the tiny worry lines fanning out from the corners of his eyes and the strange set to his mouth as if he didn't want her to leave."I'll be in that room." She pointed as he nodded and glanced away.

Here she was, lying in a beige huddle on the bed, fully clothed too exhausted to change into night clothes, her mind in a muddle, wondering that as tired as she felt she remembered those macho bits of advice. For a moment she thought of hauling herself from the bed to dig in the bottom drawer of the chest where colorful bits and pieces of clothing chosen years previous were secretly stored. What have I done? For all she knew the man in the room, next door, could be Jack the Ripper. Somewhere between that thought and the next she fell into a sound sleep; startled and wakened to the sound of a crash, outside, no inside, but what? She rushed to the hall wondering if she had forgotten to lock the door and someone was in the house but then she heard the groans coming from the other bedroom.

Finding the switch, the room flooded with light from the ceiling bulb. There, on the floor, surrounded by broken glass sat her cast laden visitor. "I can't get up," he said, "and I've broken your lamp." When she didn't reply, he continued, "I'll replace your lamp." A piece of the glass was between his fingers. "It looks like crystal, am I right?" She nodded. "Do you think I'll find one to replace it?" She stared at him. "Are you angry?" He dropped the glass and tried to snap his fingers. "Are you awake?"

She turned loose of the door frame, where she'd been hanging trying to gain her wits. "I'm awake but I was in deep sleep and forgot you were here, so I guess it shook me up." He seemed to be waiting for an answer. "The lamp is crystal. It belonged to my husband's first wife. Don't worry about the lamp." She entered the room, now. "The question is how to get you out of the floor."

"I was trying to get to the bathroom." His shoulders slumped in defeat. "I can't crawl. I think we'll have to cut the cast off my good leg…if I have a good leg."

"No, the doctor said you needed it on several weeks. Maybe you could take off the sling and use the strength of your arms to pull yourself up. Isn't it worth a try?"

"Whatever you say," he replied, glum. "I think we'll need a kitchen chair…something firm."

She brought in a chair from the kitchen nook and placed it in front of him. "By the way, my name's Stormy." She offered a hand. "Stormy Weathers."

"Peter Daniel's," he replied, reaching up. "Is that your real name?"

"Feels like it," she grinned for the first time. "But no, I have another; I received this one when I was quite young, born to older parents and quite pouty, as I often heard, thus, the nickname stuck."

He was staring, "I'm not sure you look like a stormy, maybe…" He was ready to try the chair, peeling off the sling and gripping the seat on both sides, hoping to rise. "I can't believe I'm in your home with both legs in cast and my arm in a sling trying to get out of the floor. This has to change." Bearing down he felt the pain rip through the arm supposed to be in the sling, as sweat broke out on his brow and the whole world threatened to go black and the effort seemed futile. Momentarily defeated, he laid his head against the wood of the chair. "I can't get on my knees, my legs are stuck out in front like to iron rods and my arm hurts like the dickens. Could you call your friend, the Police man, again?"

"He's not my friend. I met him tonight for the first time, same as you. Our big guy at the hospital suggested I call the police, evidently he knew they sometimes help the citizens if they are in their vicinity."

He was feeling his bladder spasm. "Just call him." The words were terse but he was becoming desperate.

She backed out of the room. "Well, all right." There was fire in her eyes. "I will."

Sergeant Devon Malloy was sitting on the corner of South and Main watching two teenagers make out in a car in front of Walgreens. He knew he had to send them home, it was past curfew. He wondered they didn't see his car, but he was parked discreetly behind the sign that welcomed visitors to town. His cell rang, he answered and listened. "Your man can't get out of the floor, will I return to help you?" He almost smiled remembering the gentleman in double casts. "I'll be there in about five minutes." He turned the key and listened as the engine rumbled, and then pulled out into the street and alongside the teenager's car. "Listen, Buddy, it is past curfew, go home or I'll have to run a check on you and call your folks."

With their leaving, he turned his car toward Chris Street for the second time that night.

She was still in her day clothes. He thought that a bit odd, but not as strange as most things he encountered. This wasn't his usual shift anyway, with the Captain's permission he switched to nights for his friend to take the day shift to be able to spend nights when there was no nurse with his wife who was seriously ill with cancer. In fact, Cal wasn't sure she was going to make it through. Sad. Sad, he shook his head, a picture of Cal in his head. That man loved his woman.

The same lady let him in and he followed her to the bedroom, to find the patient in the floor with his arms wrapped around a plain wooden chair. He wanted to say, "like that chair, do you?" But that was insubordinate and could cause a reason to write him up. She didn't really seem the type to rat on him but then again there was a stormy look in her eye now that wasn't there before. Tired, maybe? They both appeared bent out of shape.

Somehow he had missed the first round of matrimony his friends had already graduated from and found a second playmate to whet their interest. Now they dubbed him the priest cop, and he still wondered where that come from. They couldn't resist tapping his shoulders as they passed by, "still an old bachelor, Malloy?" This woman was interesting, no airs, no come-on's, just weary of taking care of her husband he guessed as he waited to hear what needed to be done to get the fellow out of the floor.

"It's obvious your husband cannot push up with his feet or his arms, the one being in a sling. What's your suggestion?" She stared at him, her green eyes tired and lacking expression. "We've not had much sleep, which means neither of us seems capable of coming up with a plan that works, outside of waiting until tomorrow and investing in a lift of sorts." As an afterthought or perhaps no thought at all, wearily she said, "Right now, let's us just say he's not my husband. Just someone I picked up off the road."

Peter listened to her discussion of himself as though he weren't there and he supposed he didn't present a stable picture, sitting in the floor, his legs straight out and his arms wrapped around a chair.

"Will I hurt him, if I put my hands under his arms and try to raise him and when I get him up you make sure his feet don't slide out or sideways.

I can't believe they'd send him home this way." The man groaned and she gave a deep sigh. "All right, you are nodding, so let's try it."

Peter grit his teeth, feeling the cop place a hand in, under his arm, then a shove upward when he thought his armpits were on fire and he was blacking out, so intense was the pain that ripped up his arm, down again and left him shaking like a baby rabbit in fright. But he was on his feet, he knew because without preamble she was standing so close he felt her breath on his cheek and her feet were placed one on either side of his better leg, making sure that foot did not slide on the wooden floor, the other leg with a mind of its own and nothing to hold it, was sliding nearly bringing them both back down. She grabbed hold of the waist band of the cutoff scrub pants and hung on for dear life while the cop struggled to right them. "Lord," he tried to swallow as pain shot through his whole body. "Stormy."

He'd give him one thing, he was strong. He guessed her at one twenty and his own weight making the cop's muscle rise up like a veined egg, its imprint against the twill material of the shirt, made him feel disgraced and ashamed to be caught alive in this situation. Not that he'd particularly want to be dead. Strange thoughts were popping into his head, just like the time he was on steroids. Steroids? He'd said he didn't want them but she gave them to him anyway. This whole thing was her fault. All of it. Anger pounded in his temples, ran through his veins and stood him up stiff, ungrateful and terse. "If I don't get to that bathroom I'm going to ruin these clothes. For some reason my bladder is active when I'm not."

"I hear you," Cop boy replied. "Let me just walk you to it. It's not far and I won't leave you."

"Are you trying to placate me or do you see me as a person unable to do for myself?"

"The latter, sir." He glanced at the lady. She glanced away. "I'll help get him into the bed and leave," he said in a rather lack-luster way, thinking no one cared. He was now a lump of clay, unneeded.

An hour from the time he sent the teenagers home, he was back sitting on the street corner, rehashing the excitement of the night, an ungrateful baboon of a fellow in two leg casts, an arm in a sling and a ravishing redhead with tired green eyes hanging onto a door facing, not from fear, but weary to the bone. He certainly had no choice but to help her. Wasn't that what Police officers were asked to do?

Remembering the address, he pulled up the information. Reed Weathers, age sixty one, deceased, Grace Henderson Weathers, age thirty, Joshua Henderson, deceased, Arnel Weathers deceased. She had married an older man. Arnel must have been the first wife and Joshua, Reed's son. Was she or Arnel the mother? She was a beautiful woman, the one cast boy called Stormy, and he wondered why the data base didn't mention him. He pondered awhile the cast boy calling her Stormy…or was that a description…..he wondered. So she was thirty. He was thirty three. Cast boy looked about his age. Were they married? Why did he care? Because his biological clock was ticking his mother often reminded him and she wanted grandchildren so why was he wasting time when there were plenty women in the world? He wasn't wasting time; he just had not met the right woman, yet. He thought more about Grace, the red head. She was stunning with that red hair and green eyes. Auburn, he corrected himself. It was a pleasing color, natural he thought but what did he know and he had been as easily dismissed as the trash man, hadn't he? "Thank you. Goodbye." He was on the sidewalk, again. Here he sit, in charge of security of the South side of the community considering widow Grace Weathers, or was it Stormy? What did she mean she picked cast boy up off the street and was she just tired to deny he was her husband?

She awoke to glance at the clock. Seven. One hour until work began. She hurried to the bathroom, turned the water on in the shower and began stripping down; amazed she was still wearing yesterday's church clothes. Then it hit her. She had a house guest. In fact one wearing cast on both legs and an arm in a sling. What? How could she forget something that important? Work would have to wait, today. She stepped into the shower. Had she locked the door? Did it matter, he couldn't navigate without help.

An hour later she glanced at the clock. She had called in and now listened for movement in the guest room. He must be conked out. If the door was open, she would peek in. Tiptoeing, she made it to his room, found the door open enough to peek in and nearly choked on surprise. He was sitting in bed, a towel under what he described as his good leg, sawing away at the cast with a pair of scissors she realized he had found in the bathroom.

"I know you are out there," he called, "You might as well come in."

"What are you doing?"

"Good morning to you, too," he said. "I'm trying to free myself to be able to stand and not topple over every time I do."

"But the doctor said you must wear the cast at least a week, maybe two to give strength back to your leg."

"The doctor is not the one who falls down and can't get up, so the doctor can go jump the proverbial stump for all I care." He glanced at her, now, his eyes filled with warning and anger directed at her.

"What have I done?" She threw her arms wide, embracing the room. "Are you blaming me? I don't even know you."

"No, you don't and you gave me those steroids when I told you not to. I haven't slept a wink."

"I don't recall you saying, don't. I didn't prescribe them, the doctor did." She turned to leave. "Call me if you need anything. I'm staying home, today, but tomorrow I go to work."

"What kind of work?"

"Nothing significant. I'm in charge of Daily's Pharmacy. Your drugs did not come from that facility."

"Hmm." He was too busy sawing away at the cast to further their conversation. She slipped away.

He was worn out when his mission was accomplished, but made himself slide off the bed, roll up the debris in the towel, all the while making a mental note he would have to replace this one with the monogrammed C on it. Immediately he realized he needed a cane, a crutch, a walker, whatever it took to navigate the short distance from bed to bathroom. He didn't dare call to her, she seemed rather disconnected this morning, rumpled in person and in nature, he thought. At least she had clean clothes. He might as well practice patience because the good Lord knew his supply was running very low.

The cut off scrubs were not his choice of fashion. He heard her stirring in the front rooms and decided to take a chance. Opening the door, he hollered, "Stormy, do you have any loose fitting clothes of your husband's you'd let me wear?" He heard her walking his way as he gave the door a loose swing shut.

"I wasn't going to say anything, we seemed to have gotten off on the wrong foot, but yes, there are a few casual twills he wore at the beach on vacation or cotton pajama bottoms if you prefer."

"Sorry about my grumpiness. This little hindrance was not part of the plan and I am grateful you took me in, otherwise I'd be hobbling, maybe even rolling down the Interstate, and I don't like to think I'd be sleeping under a bridge." He thought he heard her chuckle. There was a bit of silence and then she knocked on the door. "I'm dressed," he said, letting the door open wide. She held out a stack of clothing for his observation. "That's wonderful," he grinned. "I'm sick of these cut offs and I've got to figure out how to take a bath."

"Not in the shower, I hope. I don't know if our hallowed Police man is still on duty, or if he'd come back. We got a bit raunchy with him, don't you think?" She cast troubled eyes on him. "Not as grateful as we should have been."

"In my defense, I was worn thin, and you were exhausted. Maybe I could send him a ticket to something. Surely he goes into the center some time, or maybe a month of dinner paid at his favorite spot."

"I see their cars parked outside Maloney's every week, on Wednesday's, the Italian spaghetti place."

"Good as done, if you know his name."

"I'll look. He left his number on some kind of official card." She stepped inside to place the stack of clothes on the side of the tub. "Remember, don't even think of using the shower, I would be too embarrassed to have to come in and help you."

"Really, Stormy, you were married."

"That doesn't count," she grinned, backing from the room and closing the door.

"I wouldn't want to embarrass you," he called from behind the door, "nor myself."

His laughter followed her all the way down the hall.

On Tuesday, returning to work at the pharmacy she was met by Billy George, "I called your house and a man answered," he seemed puzzled.

"My cousin," she explained. "I have a house guest. Think nothing of it. Why did you call me?"

"The order that was supposed to arrive before Christmas came in yesterday and we don't know what to do with it."

"Can it be returned?"

"I don't think so." He motioned she should follow him. "But there's no place to display these," he pulled a package of twelve light up necklaces with matching bracelets from the oversized box sitting in the middle of the make-up aisle. "If they weren't in red and green I'd sit them in the Senior Citizens care center. You know, the canes and walkers and paraphernalia they all ask for."

"Your idea being they could be used for what?"

"Well, they're old. I could persuade them a lighted bracelet on the arm would be an asset. You know how they all ask for me." He was a bit embarrassed to remind her.

"It's because you are cute and kind and no one else takes time to talk with them. It's your gift."

"I'm not sure it's a gift." He sighed. "But I do like them, maybe because I miss my grandma so much."

"Whatever the reason, you are a real trooper." She smiled and left him feeling as though God had touched him. "You decide, Billy. I trust you completely."

"I've already decided then. I'll separate bracelets from necklaces. Box up the necklaces 'til next November and we will display the bracelets in the Care center with my sign that reads, "Billy's suggestion: "See where you are going when it's dark, just wear the bracelet and let it light up."

"Sounds great, Billy." She entered her office, closed the door and slid into the desk chair. The day passed with four thirty arriving before she finished with the vendors. "I must leave," she told Billy. "And you're out of here at five, right?" He nodded. "Then all is well. I'll go home and check on my house guest."

Billy watched her through the doors, get into her car and drive away. "I wish I were your house guest," he whispered. He loved her. His mother guessed as much. "Honey," she cautioned. "She's your boss and much too old for you, your love will come."

But, he replied, "Mom, she's so kind and puts up with so much."

He thought perhaps with the death of her husband life had become more calm and kind to her. Not that Mr. Weathers beat her or anything like that; he expected too much of her. After his first wife died, he seemed to court her with respect and sincerity but once they were married it was as if she must earn her keep. There had come a time of appreciation from the old man as he became more ill in her taking over efficiently and the loss of their son had softened him considerably. She hurt the most, because she and Josh were very close, still, Mr. Weathers doted on Joshua and his future. Joshua's death was more than he could bear. The first wife had not produced a child. Now this one was gone and Billy wondered if Mr. Weathers secretly wanted to die.

She had no parents, then Joshua died and finally Mr. Weathers. Billy stood by her side through the funeral and at the gravesite. She was amazing. "I just want to lay down and bawl for your sake," He said.

She patted his arm. "I'm all right, Billy. By the grace of God, I am standing. I feel as though I have left this body and what I'm experiencing belongs to someone else. I say and do the right thing, at least I hope I do, but I feel as though I'm looking in, the picture isn't quite clear yet and I pray as I go along it becomes clearer." Time passed and she did not fail him. Her example of a Christian was what he wanted it to be. But one day after a customer had left he kept remembering the woman's parting words, "You've lost a lot, Stormy. I don't know how you are holding up." His opportunity to ask her how she was managing to stand firm came quicker than he anticipated.

"How are you holding up? You have lost a lot. Is your love for God really that strong?"

They were stacking a shelf with a new supplier's merchandise. "Come with me," she said. They walked to her office, up a flight of thirteen steps, placed where the owner could view what was going on in the whole building. "Take a seat, Billy." She smiled. "If I never do another good thing in life, I want to tell you about what is pulling me through this terrible time of loss. It is God who is carrying me through. Some days I barely know what I'm doing, especially in the beginning losing Jason, then Reed, and you know he was older and sometimes demanding but always good to me and though I may not have loved him in an exciting bold adventurous way I did love him or else I would not have married him. I don't know why he asked me to marry him, other than the fact he was lonely. At that time of life he was much older. If it were now I can't imagine myself even considering marriage. But there were reasons."

"It was not in our plan that he have cancer that would take him too soon. I had to come to grips with that." She sighed. "Losing Joshua, Reed lost his love for life, and a weakened body cannot defeat the disease of cancer." She glanced out the window, her expression troubled. "I could barely string two words of prayer together, I was that distraught inside, but here's the wonder of it all." She held his gaze now, an amusing expression on her face, "in those few words, whatever they were and I suspect most of them were, "Lord help me," in those words a peace would come into my troubled mind, my heart kept beating and if I had sunk to the floor, somehow I found myself back up on my feet and I would go outside and walk the block and when I returned to the house, I knew the God I feel lives in Heaven had heard my prayer and leaned down to steady me on my feet and touch my heart." She reached across, to lay her hand on his arm. "Does that make any sense? I want you to know this God who I serve, not meaning I'm the best person in the world, nor that I don't make mistakes, because I do, but I want you to know Hell is real. God is real. You've heard the song, He knows my name?"

Billy nodded. "He hears me when I call? My Mom sings that a lot." His boss, the friend he loved, smiled.

"Good for her. Billy, have you given your heart to the Lord?" He let his head drop to his chest for a moment, staring at the floor between his feet. "Billy, if you haven't I want you to think about it. Death has proven it drops in unexpected as in Joshua being run over. Billy, if we died suddenly we should have this matter of knowing God settled. If death happens unexpected, we have no future day to accept him. I want you to think about this. Heaven is real and so is the devil's domain. No one wants to go there."

"But your peace and calm, does that come from God?"

"There's no one else, Billy. You've been to church enough to know of the Godhead, God the Father, God the Son and God the Holy Spirit. When Jesus died he said I go to prepare a place for you and where I go, you can come and later, he said, I send the comforter to you. That is found in the fourteenth chapter of John. Which meant the comforter would comfort us until it is time for us to go to Heaven. That's where my peace lies."

"I've not done anything wrong, yet, Mrs. Weathers."

"Never lied, never cursed, never fought with a friend or family, always do everything one hundred per cent right?"

Billy was nodding agreement. "Billy, we all sin and come short of the glory of God." She smiled seeing Billy's expression. "No one said you did wrong, Billy. I just don't want you to reject the one who can save you."

"But I'm not ready, Mrs. Weathers. I haven't lived long enough to do anything, and I want to."

She rose up. "Then it's time we get back to work. I don't want to bore you with asking you meet your creator."

"I'm sorry," he mumbled as he followed her down the steps. "I know you are disappointed with me."

"I'm sorry, too," she replied gently. "I'm disappointed for you. I really like you and I want to know where you will spend eternity."

His heart was heavy. He felt he had disappointed her, but he wouldn't always be working in Daily Pharmacy and Convenience, he had plans; soon he would began the last two years of his college and he would be moving on. Those two years would bring an opportunity to branch out socially, to meet different more important people. He didn't know what his moral code would suffer, he'd told his mother he would do his best to keep the rules she'd set and how she'd watched over his upbringing when no one else seemed to care, except maybe Mrs. Weathers.

Her words, I want to know where you will spend eternity, flashed through his mind. What was her fear? That he would go completely against the grain, forgetting all his mother had taught him and for that matter what she had? He was moody that her influence always made him want to do his best. No one had the right to expect so much from another person. He was a month short of being twenty, meeting the girl of his dreams was in focus for the next two years and finding a lucrative job that paid bills and left something on the side to advance. He hoped to meet a girl just like he imagined she was, and now that they'd had their little talk he felt unsettled and a bit angry at her suggestions.

Their usual banter and end of day words were missing that night as she locked the door to the business and he accompanied her to her car. "I appreciate your walking with me, Billy," she said. "You are such a gentleman."

"Good night, Mrs. Weathers."

She was exhausted. Should she stop for something to eat or go home? She forgot all together that she had a house guest as she reviewed the discussion between her and Billy. He was at that tender age that any rejection whether by her or someone else would seem a nightmare. She was of the age to care for those God chose and placed into her circle. She decided home was the haven she was seeking, to leave behind for a few hours the rush of the business world. Pressing the radio button she settled in the seat.

Music surrounded her. Susan Boyle was singing I Had A Dream. The words served to ease the tension she had felt most of the afternoon. Sighing, she agreed everyone has a dream but hers seemed to be floating in stagnate water, nothing earth shattering happened to her. Marrying Reed had satisfied a girl's dream to have a home to care for. But there had been no rocket flares, or stars in either of their eyes. It was a satisfying arrangement. He needed a wife and she always wanted to be someone's wife. Here she was, a widow, today feeling life had passed her by; Reed died, and her precious son…oh, and the agony of remembering. Shattered dreams did not bring peace to one's soul, God forgive her.

The clouds were turning gray and it looked like rain. A melancholy day, she thought as she pulled in to the drive, raised the garage door and hurried into the house to a strange but comforting smell. Purse on counter, high heels by the bar, she suddenly realized someone was cooking. Then it hit her, how could she have forgotten? He was here. That Peter Daniel's person was here. Quietly she retrieved her purse, slipped the shoes back onto her feet, and prepared to meet him.

The dining room table was dressed in white linen, the best dishes and silverware complemented the crystal glasses. It was a table set for guests but with only two plates. She heard him hobbling to the door. For a minute he watched her very solemn surveying of the room. "I hope you don't mind," he said. "A person can only stand so much silence and lack of interaction, so I ordered a roast, went through your kitchen and found what I needed."

"You managed very well. It looks wonderful." She turned her head, gathering thoughts. "It has been a long time since anyone did something like this, that I could enjoy. Thank you." Her voice broke, but she was unaccustomed to anyone doing personal or private things for her. "I am surprised you used the china and good silverware."

"If you don't use it who will see it and enjoy it? I may be a man but I enjoy the flash and splendor," he grinned. "You know, building it up until you've made statement." She nodded, yes that was her theory. "Sounds good?" She did not comment. He continued, "These potatoes have garlic sprinkled over them as they simmer in the skillet, is that all right?"

She nodded, suddenly feeling shy. This was her first set down with a man since Reed died.

"A penny for your thoughts." He cast interested eyes her direction. "I saw your countenance change."

"You are very observant." He was waiting for her to reply. "I don't think we've used these dishes since my husband died. It's a very strange feeling. He always sit head of the table. It was quite grand, actually."

"You are a grand lady, Stormy."

"Not really.' She blushed as she lay her fork on the side of her plate. "You don't have to say nice things to me, Peter. I've existed these many years. I certainly know the difference between those ladies and myself."

"No," he said, gently, "I don't think you do. Truly, in my line I see hysterical ladies who come unglued at the drop of a hat."

"Are you saying my work probably does or does not have that category attached?"

He shrugged his shoulders, tilting his head her way. "I don't know what you do in the way of work. I meant you."

"I run the City Pharmacy that has a million supplies for many of the community to purchase."

"And you never experience a break down, life goes on at its own pace, the daily, weekly rituals s thing of confidence each person experiences because nothing new comes along to break down the citizens high expectations?" He turned to give her an enormous smile. "I feel we should leave the subject behind before I really irritate you and you lash out at me like the storm you are named for."

"I'm pretty docile," she managed to mutter. This was all a bit much, especially from one who was her house guest, or not her house guest but a happening one couldn't quite explain nor did she want to explain to anyone. What was she to do in her own kitchen when someone else was in charge? It was a bit intimidating. She watched. He sit bowls of green beans, the new potatoes from the pan into a serving bowl and beautifully browned corn bread . The roast came last, sitting in creamy gravy, where there were small carrots around the meat, chopped celery and onion.

"Ta da," he said, whisking the dishcloth in his hand into a flag suitable to a flamingo dancer, which made her laugh considering the boot on one foot and the sling hanging loose against his side. "Oh, so you find me funny?"

"For lack of explanation, let's say the boot takes away your grandeur." He was sliding into the chair opposite, dutifully examining the table top. "It's all here, I noticed," she said, "What more could we want?"

"Si," he said. "Do you bless the food?"

"I will," she replied, bowing her head. "Heavenly Father, we thank you for the blessings of the day, for this fine food Peter has cooked and we present ourselves to you, asking your watch care over us, thanking you for all things and asking blessing on this food and ourselves as we sit here together; for it is in your name we ask. Amen."

"Amen," Peter agreed and became suddenly quiet, as he said, "I hope the food is to your liking and I thank you for not being upset with a stranger in the kitchen. Shall we do this the old fashioned way and help ourselves?"

They were a bit shy in the beginning, but the absolute perfection of the food made for good conversation. "Do you always cook like this?" She asked.

"No, sometimes I burn the food," he replied, "but I was on my best behavior tonight. I wanted to impress you." They raised eyes and forks and grinned at each other.

"You have," she said.

Thirty minutes later they were clearing the table, he was running hot water in the sink and she picked up a clean dishcloth to dry and put away the dishes.

"I've not done this in awhile," she commented. "I was getting in the habit of picking up food, forget the cooking."

"What did you bring home? I tried that," he said, "But there are only so many hamburgers one can handle."

"My friends claim I'm the salad queen, and Sander's at the bottom of the hill makes the best. It never looks like leftover from the day's luncheon. There's fresh tomatoes, lettuce, a touch of green onion and they know I love the cranberry-crumbled cheese mix. Take out is five dollars and about all you need by the time they add the crackers."

"Hmm, I'll have to remember that. Sanders." He repeated the name three times. "There, maybe it's settled in my memory. They say repeat a word three times and you have it stored. We'll see." He liked seeing her in the kitchen doing household duties. "You look good," He said. "In spite of our stormy night and I should tell you, your police officer came by today to check on you. He said if you need anything; please feel free to call him. You sure you don't know him?"

She began to place the silverware in the drawer's divided compartments, considering the officer for a moment. "No, I had never met him before but it's nice to know he's out there. She changed the subject then. "Due to your work you will be coming through from time to time?"

"I'll have an office here, not a large one, mind you, but substantial enough to entertain complaints, store my equipment and in general hang my hat and listen to what the average client who enters the door has to say."

"Your job is…? I've wondered and meant to ask but we always begin a different conversation."

"You might say I'm an advocate for the family but hired by the hospitals to follow through on complaints, which allows the hospitals to correct any grievance or make right a procedure that offends the general public. You know, "parking is terrible," so what do we do? As most public facilities, we have someone come in and paint stripes, then whoever parks across the line or in the middle of two spaces…" His eyes were sober as he glanced her way, "then it's on the person driving the car, isn't it? I've done all I can do to correct a simple problem."

"You deal with property issues?"

"That's only one aspect, then there's Mrs. Johnson who became quite weary sitting overnight in the public side of intensive care's waiting room and it was cold and no one offered her a blanket, because her husband remains a patient, we see that Mrs. Johnson is in charge of the blanket cabinet, for her stay as others may need a blanket."

"There's more?" She questioned, putting the last bowl in the cabinet above the microwave.

"Actually, that is the part for whence I was hired. 'The people's advocate to the hospital when the bill was charged an item they don't understand or challenge. If we don't make our client's happy, they won't return. I'm the listening ear, the solution guy to put a smile back in their heart and on their face in a time that can be very daunting, a loved one is ill, there's not much hope, but someone has to remind them hope lasts, that's my job."

"Impressive," she said. "I had no idea hospitals had someone as the go between."

"It's a new concept."

"You like what you do? It's a question."

"I do like working with people, the public. If we can make this world a better place with more understanding of each other, what's not to like?" He smiled, sliding down into the first chair by the table. "Me and this cast have to find a spot to rest ever so often. I apologize if it shows bad manners."

"Oh, no, that's fine. I understand." To be courteous, she slid onto the chair opposite him.

"So," he tilt his head, studying her face. "Do you like what you do, your job at the city pharmacy?"

"We have all the rural area to cover with people needing work to make ends meet." She paused, thinking, "I sort of fell into this work. The pharmacy needed a bookkeeper. I was qualified and got the job. That led to purchasing and finally overseeing the whole store when the owner's wife became ill."

"That's how you met your husband? He owned the business, wife dies, you looked familiar and trustworthy."

"Trustworthy, I hope." She smiled. "He needed someone. When I saw the opportunity I ask questions and he as the boss took time to explain the procedure, and then his wife died and within a year after that I married him."

"I suspect it was either marry him or quit your job. Right?" He saw her stiffen and quickly held his hands up. "Whoa, that didn't come out right. Let me rephrase that." A hurt expression on her face told him he better make it good. "I meant," he looked up to the ceiling. "I meant, you are an attractive woman and now he is single, he was bound to notice you and as you stepped up to help with the business he found your presence even more comforting…" She was folding the dishcloth. "I'm not doing too well, am I?" She was rising up from the chair.

"No, you're not. I'm having difficulty following your way of thinking." She started to leave the room.

Forgetting his body was controlled by a clumsy boot on one foot, he started to rise to apologize.. "Please, don't leave. Let me try to correct my clumsiness. I meant you are very pleasing to the eye, how could he not notice?" He had managed to cross his ankles, something he hadn't done in several days and with his body unbalanced he caught himself with his hands coming to rest on the floor. "Well, this is awkward." He was trying to raise the upper part of his body.

"I don't really know what you intended to say," she replied, "but it is plain to see you are only digging the hole deeper. I'm going to help you this time but in the future…you get the picture?"

"Yes, ma'am," he managed to mutter, standing on his head was draining his oxygen supply. She was slipping her hands under his arms, digging into the arm pits and straining to raise him up. Together, they managed a half way position where he started to topple and his arms automatically went around her waist, hanging on for dear life. "Oh, no," he managed, "I didn't mean to do that, didn't think, I'm sorry, please….."

Some flash of warning whipped into her mind. This was a completely unbelievable mix of events that would be hard to explain. She hoped no one was watching through the open blinds and if they were that they spelled her name correctly when they made their report. A nervousness claimed her as she felt the need to turn loose, surely he was the one with the move on and she was a helpless victim. "You're done," she said as she gave a quick yank, thinking his whole stance would fall apart and he'd turn loose of her, but it didn't work quite as she planned.

He screamed in agony as the sudden action threw his weight onto the foot inside the boot. "I can't believe you did that," His voice was almost the whimper of a child. "What evil thing did I do to deserve that?"

"I'm sorry." Her action had thrown her off balanced and pressed upon him, while he bore the weight of them both.

"No, you're not. I see your expression. I tried to be kind to you but you won't accept me."

"There's no reason for your kindness," she snapped. "I think you planned that little fall."

"God as my witness," he replied through clenched teeth, "I didn't. I guess I was tired after…"

"Well, you are on your feet again. The kitchen is clean and I'm going to my room." She back away, full steam.

He watched her go, his anger continuing to hit in peaks as he branded her the ice Lady or…her name. Stormy.

She didn't come out of her room until the next morning when she slipped quietly out into the garage. She had thought about his falling and her obviously unsettled way of dealing with it. They had enjoyed dinner together but in all fairness he probably had been on his feet too long and still wasn't completely fluid in movement. Hadn't he said as much when he sit in the chair after they finished the dishes? She, on the other hand, had been nervous and would have been whether male or female sit across from her. Other than Reed she had never enjoyed a meal with the opposite sex. First her parents had kept her from the other gender based on they were travelers, picking up jobs as they went, guarding her from the rough crowd they frequented until that one day when someone raped her and she became pregnant.

Lost in remembering she was aware he had been waiting for her and had just called to her but she didn't hear what he said, though she saw his expression. "I said the people who are housing my car brought my computer and brief case. Tomorrow I will resume work and before leaving I will reimburse the expenses incurred by me."

As if he was following her, she slammed the car door and turned the key to the ignition. Each morning she put two fingers to her lips, kissed the tips and returned the kiss to the small cross on the gold chain that hung from the visor. Her mother's parting gift held her together when all else seemed to fail. Or was it the cross, she questioned.

"We failed you," her mother had whispered. "We will never change. We like the challenge of traveling the states picking up work as we can. It is better for you to stay with this nice lady who has offered her home to you. She said she will see you finish school and go to college if you wish, but you must help her. She is very ill, maybe unto death. You understand, Stormy?"

Tears were streaming down her cheeks as she nearly choked on her words. "What about the baby?"

"Mrs. Weathers says you can keep the baby. Is that what worries you, Stormy? You will have your baby. The road is no place for a baby. Stay here and finish school, have your baby and help Mrs. Weathers. She's a good lady."

Stormy found other peoples description of good unlike her own. Billy, at work, was a good person. Audrey that ran the cash register and checked out the customer was a good person but Mrs. Weathers was not good. Angeline was a good person and maybe the pastor fell under that description. She often wondered what he thought when she married one of the older members of his congregation. Did he think Joshua was Reed Weathers's child?

She kept their secret to herself. The night of the funeral, he came to her room.

"Grace, are you all right?" His face was etched in grief but showed surprise when he saw the boxes packed and sitting by the door, the drawers still open and empty of content. Even Joshua's diaper bag was ready for departure. "Are you leaving, Grace?"

"Yes, Sir, that was the plan according to Mrs. Weathers. I could stay as long as she was alive but then I must find a home for me and my baby."

He leaned against the wall just outside her room. "Do you know she tormented me, Grace, asking me if I intended to marry you so you'd continue to take care of our home?" Glancing up he met her eyes. "She found great pleasure in saying you wouldn't know what to do with a young girl like that after living with me. Did you know?"

"No, Sir, I didn't know. Mrs. Weathers expected a lot from me and I tried to do my best but sometimes she found what I did insufficient. My punishment was to do it all over again, even if it required my working all night."

"So that's why you were up all night? I once asked her if you shouldn't be in bed, going to school and all." He groped the door facing for support."She said you had nervous energy and couldn't sleep. Well, it seems she was right; you couldn't sleep, could you? Because she told you what to do." He sighed. "She told me; too, Grace, but I had a choice. She couldn't throw me out if I didn't." He held Grace's gaze now. "I loved her, Grace. When we first married she was nothing like she turned out to be after the cancer treatments. Once, they even did radiation on her head and I wondered if something went wrong and the effect changed her nature. How was I to know?" A terrible deep sigh came from within him, a groan of sorts attached to it. "I always hoped the girl I married that was happy and carefree would return and leave behind that one that demanded everything be just so-so. Only as she died did I see a glimpse of her younger self. She looked at me and said, I love you Reed, always have."

He turned to leave but stopped half way. "Grace, where will you go? And, will you call me each night, please?"

CHAPTER

3

Now as she drove to work she remembered all he told her through the years about this young woman he fell in love with, who seemed to love him in return. Whatever the reason for her change and illness, he clung to the past when life was easier and happier. As promised Grace had called each night to tell him, there were no low dives available to her due to the child in her arms. She was turned away. "You cannot work," they'd say. "We do not need you." She had found Angeline's name in the directory and was allowed to spend the nights there.

She thanked God it was warm enough Joshua was not suffering from lack of a home to go to. On the fourth morning, leaving her baby with Angeline who was now retired, she began the walk to school. When Reed pulled alongside her and simply said, "get in the car, Grace," she did, though she remembered the atmosphere before she was raped as a child when she was thrust into someone's car and held tight between two male bodies.

"This isn't working, Grace. I'm dying of loneliness, I miss Joshua. I even miss those quaint times of seeing you around the house and it isn't working for you, either, if I understand your phone calls each night." He was quiet for the next three miles, as she wondered if he forgot she was with him. Finally he said, "How about we do Arnel's plan, Grace. Could you stand to live accordingly?"

"What was her plan?" Grace swallowed hard. "She didn't like me, Mr. Weathers. She only wanted her home to run as she knew another could make it happen, but she wanted me gone as quickly as possible. I am trying to honor her wishes but I feel Angeline is wearing down taking care of Joshua, for you know he's a hand full."

"Come back, Grace. Joshua can attend the Day Care down from us. I'll pay. For now, there are no toddlers, just new born babes and then the age skips to five year olds, plenty old enough not to cause problems."

In her head, she could hear Angeline's advice. "When was the last time you heard from your parents, Grace?" In her heart she knew the girl's parents were never coming back. Like everyone else they had sold Grace a bill of goods. "Better yourself, Grace." She said, "No one else can do it for you. Whatever it takes, you can do it."

"Did you hear me, Grace?" That troubled expression was on his face again, sadness in his eye. She shook her head; she had been deep in her own thoughts. "I ask you Grace, to marry me and let things go on as they are now."

She was stunned. "But I'm too young to marry." Her voice sound weak and despairing even in her own ears.

"And I'm old. But I will treat you right. You and Joshua will have a home you will never have to leave." Her silence made him uncomfortable. "Go back to Angeline's tonight and talk to her, then let me know." He seemed reluctant to close their conversation. "I'm glad Angeline came back to Haven."

She hurried home that afternoon, hoping her child was awake. She needed to hold him, to feel the return of her love only he could give. There was no one else in the world. Angeline watched, knowing there was a problem but one she had very little hope of helping to reconcile. An hour passed and Grace had rocked the child back to sleep. "Lay him down, Grace," Angeline advised, "here, I'll move and you can lay him on the couch." Reluctant Grace rose to do as she was told. "Now, Grace," Angeline said, "What is troubling you. You haven't spoken a word but you continue to sigh in such a mournful way that I'm aware today you are not happy. Has someone hurt you?"

It was difficult to begin but once Grace began the words boiled up and poured out as fast as she could speak and when she finished Angeline was sitting on the edge of her seat. Her fingers threaded the loose knit afghan on her lap as she studied what she had just heard and as she considered this young girl, she raised her head toward the ceiling and closed her eyes. Grace was close to tears when finally Angeline spoke.

"I've had many trials, Grace. Some I made for myself, others I felt inflicted upon me by uncaring people. You have suffered the same. I would not advise you carelessly, for in you I see a part of my own life all over again. Arnel was a hard taskmaster to you, difficult with her husband these last years, but it was not always so. I don't know what happened but she changed, when Reed's work became productive and the money began to flow, Arnel took on a new demeanor I certainly didn't understand, but then she said I was a hard woman to deal with." Angeline gave a deep sigh, "I think that was because I didn't always agree with her and we were at odds many times."

Angeline rose up to pace back and forth the length of the room as she talked, perhaps, Grace thought she is working this out in her mind as to what I should do, even while she walks back and forth. Grace waited. Her own future felt bleak and she could not quite wrap her mind around becoming Mr. Weathers's wife; to follow in his wife's footsteps was beyond her. She had neither the desire, the strength nor ambition to be Mr. Weathers's wife. Why would he even ask her to consider such a tryst? He was old. She was a teenager about to graduate high school with a baby to add to his life. No, it would never work. She wished the plan had never been put before her.

"Grace, is there anyone you feel you love, the father of your child, perhaps?"

Shocked, Grace replied, "Did Mrs. Weathers not tell you? I was raped." Grace shuddered. "I don't know who it was, I was grabbed and shoved into a dark room and the only thing I remember was the sound of the bed. It was a metal bed, cold to the touch. I tried to picture something that was not attached to what was happening to me."

"All Arnel told me was that you were expecting a baby and they were hiding you from society for your own good. She thought they could pass you off as an overweight girl in order for you to continue school, but you were earning your keep by doing odd jobs around the Weathers home."

"That's true. No one knows I have a child. I have no friends. I don't trust anyone, anyway. Why would I need them?" Grace shook, suddenly cold and Angeline pulled from the arm of the chair a crocheted wrap.

"How would you feel about being an older man's wife?" Angeline peered hard at this girl she realized was innocent in the ways of the world. Why would she be sheltered when her parents, according to Arnel, were modern day gypsies, according to Arnel's interpretation they lived a life of travel. It was in their blood. But Angeline's question was, "Could you live as a wife to an older man?"

Again, Grace shuddered as she swallowed the lump in her throat and tears formed in her eyes. "What would I have to do?" She whispered, fear raising in what she was afraid she would hear. "I don't know what I'd have to do."

"More than clean the house, I'm afraid," Angeline muttered beneath her breath, but aloud she said, "Being raped was not pleasant, was it and the result was the child there, asleep on the sofa." Angeline's words felt heavy, but a decision was to be made and it need be based on truth, not whimsy or ill gained knowledge. She waited for the girl to reply. "Do you understand my question?"

"Yes, ma'am. No, it was not pleasant. It was night, I had been sent to buy vegetables at the corner store when I was grabbed from the street, two boys pushed me into a car and threw a blanket over me and held me tight between them. I know the car traveled a distance and they carried me into a room and told me not to remove the blanket until they were on the outside of the door and if I tried to leave they would hurt me. You are to be with this one person, they said, but if you try to escape there will be a dozen more, so if you know what's good for you…" Her words faded away as her body went into a spasm of remembrance. "It sounds like a lie, but it is true." Now the tears spilled down her cheeks as a great sob wracked her body and filled the room. "Why do I have to tell you this?" There was torment in her voice. "It was not what I wanted and yet it happened and my life has been nothing I thought it would be since." She gulped for air as she hugged her body, wrapping her arms as tightly around herself as she could in her mind to prevent anyone hurting her again.

"And your parents did nothing?" Angeline said, resigned that no one had come to the girl's defense.

"What could they do? Who would believe them? They travel. All those years they kept me from harm and then in one minute someone destroyed the safety they had managed even as they traveled. People looked at us and thought we were not good. They didn't want us in their towns, but my father was a good worker and my mother a good woman willing to work to make a way for us. The only problem was me, I slowed them down."

"They said that?"

"No." Grace reply was more a wail as her baby moved on the couch and Angeline place the afghan she held over the child. "My mother saw that I was educated, by night studying with me and making it interesting to learn but Mrs. Weathers said there would be no home schooling and she enrolled me in Haven after I took the test and my own mother showed them the plan she had used to teach me as we traveled and they accepted it."

Interested, Angeline leaned forward to ask. "How did you do on the test they presented? Here at Haven on the Bluff?"

Sniffing, Grace replied, "I excelled." Angeline smiled as she leaned forward to pat the girl on the knee. "Now, back to the original question, can you be a wife to Reed Weathers?"

"Why would you expect me to marry him?" Fire rose in Grace's eyes. "I'm young. He is old. We don't know each other." She let her head sink, her chin against her chest as she closed her eyes. "I've relived what happened to me a million times and I've wondered would I know who did this to me? If I by chance met him, would I know who he was? It goes around and around in my head but I have no answers, only sadness that it happened."

"You remember nothing?" Angeline shook her head. "I shouldn't ask that, Grace. It is none of my business."

"He was not old," Grace replied. "I could tell by his body, he was not old and his body was firm. I'm not sure he wanted it to happen, but the two who grabbed me threatened him, they said to him, you're not leaving this room until the deed is done." Fresh tears fell in huge drops onto her folded body. "I begged him. I think they had given him drugs but it wasn't alcohol because I could have smelled that, but something wasn't just right. And he was strong…but when he finished he just got up and left. They opened the door and let him out and left me."

"He didn't talk?"

"He tried, but it came out slurred. All I remember, he said, Be still. I don't want to hurt you. I made that out."

"Do you want to sleep on the answer you must give Reed Weathers?" Angeline asked as Grace nodded. "Do you want me to tell you what can happen if you decide to become his wife?" Grace sat numb and wadded up in the afghan as she stared hard at her sleeping child on the sofa. "I will give you a scenario and a guide line you must present should you agree to marry a man three times older than you. There will be advantages and disadvantages and should you decide to marry Reed Weathers, I expect you to tell him of our discussion and that I will always be in the background of your life as long as I live and I will not stand for you to be mistreated because I have told you, you are as good as the next person. Your journey this far may seem unfair to your young life, but it will be what you decide to make of it from this point on and you can make it happen. It is up to you."

"I'm afraid." Grace pinned her eyes on Angeline. "No matter what you tell me, I don't know what to do. Aren't you supposed to love the one you marry?" Closing her eyes Grace visibly shrank into the chair where she sat. "I didn't like Mrs. Weathers but I knew my Momma had an agreement with her and the one time I disagreed, she said I had better get in line with what she expected or she would have my parents picked up on charges they had stolen from her, and they didn't, I'm the one worked for her." Angeline stared hard at the girl, from her expression she knew the girl told the truth. Arnel was a hard person, but she hadn't known how hard until now.

Stormy blinked, she had driven past her own house. Now she must circle the block. It all looks perfectly normal she thought. Only a complete stranger is in my home. I go to work each day, what does he do? His very presence brought back memories she had hoped to forget, but instead they sprung up as from nowhere to attack her.

She thought she had lain to rest the strangeness of her life with Reed Weathers but in resurfacing it was claiming her waking hours when she needed to concentrate on work and how to deal with this man she didn't know. If the neighbors saw him they would come out of curiosity to meet his acquaintance. What must she do?

Leaving her car sitting on the concrete drive near the street, she entered her home noting a light was out in the garage and she must replace it or forever grope in darkness if she were to leave the house unexpectedly by night.

Stepping from the back foyer into the kitchen her eyes came to rest on the stack of clothes she had left for him in the bathroom. "What do you think?" He asked as he was coming from the utility room. Glancing his direction she was immediately startled to see once more there was a boot on the very foot he sawed off that first night and though he balanced himself at the moment a pair of crutches lay angled floor to chair. "How did that happen?" She pointed, realizing his austere expression, more than explained why the form was there.

"Can't we make exceptions this one time? I was….stupid. Today it hurt to the point I called the doctor's office. They sent a couple here." He held his hands up, shaking his head. "Let me explain, there is no mess and I apologize for my inconvenience to you and your home…but if you allow, they said I must stay at least two weeks, possibly three and if you will allow them, they will come here to check on my progress to healing."

"Why?" Already she was reaching for the phone, dialing the sixteen hundred number. Could there be any truth to his words, the whole thing reeked of fabrication but then why would he want to be in her home, precisely? "Yes, may I speak with your team that cares for patients outside the hospital who have," she struggled to find an accurate description, "those wearing casts on their body." She listened and presently a strong voiced male came on line. "Yes, you will help me immensely if you can confirm coming to my home today to reapply cast to my house guest's foot." She listened. "Yes, his name is Peter Daniels. You did? Well, thank you. I needed to know."

She gave Peter a blank stare. "Why would he end our conversation saying, he said you would call?"

Peter shrugged. "Well, you did, didn't you? If I may, this stack of laundry belongs to you. I'm sorry I'm not good yet, carrying things, I'm too busy balancing myself. Fear of falling has become prevalent in my thoughts. We can't depend on your friend the policeman to come every day, can we?"

"You did my laundry?" Embarrassed she glanced at the underwear, all pieces in the palest hint of peach, Flesh, the tag had read. What harm was there to allow herself the enjoyment when no one would ever know? The straps of two bras peeped from between the towels. Evidently the situation was a bit embarrassing to him, also. "Why would you do my laundry?" Suddenly she felt worn beyond reason. She was home from work, needing rest for tomorrow. "I'll take care of my laundry and you can do the same with yours." He was standing there, wearing a puzzled expression while she angry with him was even more so with herself.

"Lady, do you never bend? It was a small thing. I found your utility room, and I thought you wouldn't mind." As though wiping his hands of the whole deal, he spread them to the ceiling; he was trying to please one who would never be pleased. "I needed to ask if I could stay on, indefinitely, of course." He paused, "I don't mean to intrude and I'm extremely grateful for the amenities your home offers that a hotel does not." He reached for the crutches and placed one under each arm. "If you will follow me, dinner is only a matter of shuffling around the table a bit. You said you liked Sander's Salads, I ordered two and a small spaghetti casserole."

Her stomach rolled about that time, siding with Peter Daniels. What else could she do but follow him? He seemed quite familiar with her home by now as he opened the refrigerator door to chilled glasses already filled with ice, the salad which he passed on to her, a bowl of shredded cheese and last the salad dressing. 'You might save my dumping the casserole if you brought it from the oven to the table," he said, grinning. "And there's garlic bread." She realized the plates and silverware were already in the center of the table.

Sitting the casserole on a woven trivet, she asked, "Are you married, Peter?" She was making room for the plate of bread. Rising up straight she waited for his answer. "Or did you have a mother who taught you?"

"Did I dream we covered this earlier in my stay? No, I'm not, for some reason to my mother's dismay I keep avoiding that commitment." He was waiting for her to be seated, his hand on the refrigerator door. "Wine or iced tea?" Retrieving the pitcher of tea, he said, "Why do you ask?"

"Tea," she replied. 'You seem to know your way around the kitchen and have a good command of what foods to serve together, so I wondered…." She let the words drop aimlessly. "You were never a chef?"

His laughter filled the room. "My parents own one of the most popular restaurants in Springfield, not a chain mind you, but a beautiful stone front structure of art that sprawls over two blocks of Sunshine Blvd, parking lot included, bearing the family crest and quite simply called Lily's, named after my mother. She taught me everything I know." He watched as Stormy removed her jacket and washed her hands at the kitchen sink.

"I'm guessing your mother taught you more than the grace of serving others, but very subtlety the art of allowing your guests to eat at their own pace and certainly not to hurry their selection." She settled in her chair.

Bowing his head, he said, "Go ahead Grace, bless the food and then if you wish we will discuss my mother."

"Father," Grace began, "In this troubled world, we come to you to thank you for this day of life and the goodness we've encountered. Now we pray for those we love and we thank you for this food as we ask blessing on it."

"Aww," Grace closed her eyes to savor the flavor of the food. "I don't know what makes their salad different, but they are." Comfort was closing in, chasing away the worries she'd felt earlier. "I admit after a busy day with a few problems, this is nice. Does it strike you strange that we are comfortable though we are strangers?"

"Is this as good a time as any for your answer whether I may stay in your home another two weeks? Forget the third week, I intend to be healed and ready by then to drive and keep my mind on my business." Shaking his head a bit wearily, he said, "I have to admit, the two boots back on does cramp my style…but they said it is the difference of walking later."

Taking a deep breath, with her fork poised mid air, she had to think quickly and make the decision. "I hope I don't regret this, but yes, two weeks and then you will be on the road, again. Since you take care of yourself it's no problem and you do produce great meals." She grinned as under the table, she slipped the heels from her feet.

"Hey, that smile is worth my doing the dishes by myself." A mischievious look rearranged his features. "I did wonder if you would remove those high heels. They must be murder to walk around in all day."

"Not necessarily, if you pay enough and get the right shoe but I'm home, let comfort reign." She tried the spaghetti. "Oh, it's wonderful. Now, tell me about your mother."

"It's a love story," he began, selecting a piece of thick garlic bread. "My dad was a soldier in Vietnam but for a brief period of time he was stationed in Cambodia, one of the countries that backed U.S. intervention. My Dad said he was a church boy lonely and not too keen on the usual boozing the guys did on weekends, so he would go to the local market or the nearest garden park where the foliage was different from our country and he was interested in those things and that's where he met my mother. He described her as a tiny wisp of a woman who could cook delicious food, wore colorful clothes compared to the neutral hues of beige and brown of her family and he said she had a laugh that could cure a thousand heart aches."

"I like her." Grace could imagine his father in uniform, his mother a small beauty in colorful garments. "My own mother sounds much like yours. She wears color and with the color of her hair and olive skin it suits her." He glanced up, interested in her description of her mother. "It's auburn and it's real. My folks main gypsy trait would be the traveling. Most gypsies I know are Catholic faith, but not me, I guess I deterred. Is that a word? My mum says it's still in their blood, being gypsy, but not mine as far as constant traveling. Anyway, there are red headed gypsies. Now, your turn, did your parents marry in Cambodia?"

"Actually, no, my father was sent to Vietnam to work the front lines and she was left behind. About the third month of their separation, my father received her letter. She was pregnant, he had shared the concern but there was no proof. Whether or not he was inattentive in his work that day since his mind was overwhelmed by the info received from Lily, he was wounded and eventually flown back to the states. Lily was still in Cambodia. Things weren't going well for either of them, my father thought he would be returning to the war site but due to inflammation he almost lost his leg. Long story short, bad leg and all he did return for Lily. I was born in the United States. I may have been born out of wedlock as they say, had my mother remained in Cambodia but here I had Dad's legal name and it didn't matter; they told me I was five months old by the time they married."

"And that left no stigma as you went through school?"

"Why would it, I was a child loved and well cared for, that counts more than anything else, doesn't it?"

"I don't know. Society frowns, church people have rules and families bear the brunt of it."

"You sound as though you know first hand." She didn't reply and he let the topic of their conversation go.

They finished dinner and cleared the table together. "Let me carry things across and you won't feel you have to leave the sink." She said."I'm afraid you will fall with your double troubles." She glanced down at his feet.

"Double troubles, huh?" Smiling suddenly, he twirled the dishcloth in his hand. "That they are." He sensed a change in her attitude towards him. "Can we be friends?"

She paused, placing the spoon from the dish of Spaghetti in the sink. "I hadn't really thought of being friends. Yes, you're here, but you will be heading out and I'll never see you again," she shrugged her shoulders.

"Never is a long time," he replied. "Any woman that will let a crippled man stay in her home is certainly worth getting to know as a friend." Now he met her eyes, a serious expression in his own. "In my book."

"I've never had many friends."

Why is that?"

"It's complicated."

"Try me." Letting the water drain from the sink, he dried his hands and turned to her, waiting for an explanation.

"I'd rather not bore you, if you don't mind."

"Stormy," he said, gently. "You are a beautiful woman, and I suspect in all things very giving but you don't trust people. Have you suffered greatly at the hands of others?" His complete goodness of the moment was evident but..

He saw the flash of her eyes. "You have no right to pry. People come and go and you are one of those. If I choose to keep my life private, that is my right." A chuckle escaped his lips as an amused expression came across his face.

"What, may I ask is so funny?"

"I think I just saw why someone nicknamed you Stormy." He leaned against the counter. "What is your real name?" He was enjoying watching the emotions play across her face. "You really don't trust anyone, do you?"

A bit contrite, she replied. "No, I don't and in my life's history there's good reason for it."

"Try me," he said, leaning forward. "It can't be that bad can it? Try me."

"I wish I could," her voice lifted just above a whisper. "But you are a stranger." Her eyes were moist with tears And as quickly as the tears, there followed a straightening of the shoulders, a look of determination and the old fire snapped back in to her eyes. She was mercury, agony, victory all wrapped in one to be dealt with as needed.

Realizing his indecision as what next to say, she thought in her usual habit to explain her fraility of the moment. "I doubt someone of your background could understand what one less fortunate has experienced."

"You might try me," he said quietly. "You cannot look at a book's cover and know what is inside, people are…" He could tell she wasn't buying it, "I thought the pain would never go away."

"But to want to live but wish to die is that not unbearable, when something so traumatic has happened to you as a young child and no one cares?" She turned her head toward the wall. She would not let him look on her pain.

Peter found himself suddenly quiet. What could hurt so much there was no trust? At this moment they were old souls, while she remembered and he waited in silence. Here was to be the foundation of their friendship, coming quickly and unexpected they had fallen into a depth of conversation they neither had considered. Now, either they would begin to build a friendship or let it drop. It was obvious she set boundaries. What was stirring inside himself? He wanted to comfort her, tell her there's hope, you don't have to carry that sadness that just caught you off guard, that you seem to think will be with you the rest of your life. You don't have to be alone.

He was amazed. Stranded here in this little town, his feet in molded boots, no doubt part of an old time surgeon's plan to heal broken bones, something was building within his body to erupt at last and make her feel even more troubled, or was the troubles from the past and not now? If he could reach out to her but he'd meant once to touch her in reassurance and she shrunk from him. What was that about and why was he lingering for an answer, there would be none and she would go to her room and he to his. Why did he have that urge to kiss her? He was dimly aware a phone was ringing somewhere.

"I'll get it, for some odd reason I have left the phone in my bedroom."

Grace couldn't explain it, she wasn't even sure what was happening, but it had. He was looking as though he would like nothing more than to kiss her and she was feeling that was what she wanted. She headed for the door to the hall that led to her bedroom. She had made a complete mess of things, bringing a complete stranger into her home. She had brought in someone as though she was willing to risk it all for the sake of what? Time passed and she had thought that at least he was someone to talk with but it didn't work that way. The phone continued to ring and she answered. "Hello?" A male voice spoke.

"Stormy," he began, "I was wondering if you would have dinner with me? I mean, well I'm off next Friday."

"Who is this?"

"Devon Malloy." The silence was deafening. "Your Police man that helped with your," he cleared his throat. "Er, your friend, or maybe he's your cousin?"

She gave an embarrassed laugh. "Oh, yes, how are you? We meant to send you a thank you card but we didn't catch your name. I'm sure it was on your badge. Or your shirt. I didn't mean to insult you, by not remembering."

"No ma'am, you didn't and it was a card I gave you…but I was wondering, would you have dinner with me? " Silence held him captive, he couldn't think of anything else to say as time seemed to stretch between them.

"When did you have in mind, Damon?"

"Devon. Devon Malloy." He felt like crawling under the rug. She didn't remember his name. Who else did she know with that name?'

"How about Friday night?" By then he hoped her house guest would be gone. "Seven?"

"That's really nice of you Devon. I'll look forward to our dinner date." She hung up the phone and turned toward her bedroom.

"Why did you do that, Grace?"

"What?" She was puzzled that he had followed her to the hall. His expression was one of hurt and that made her defensive. "You heard the Policeman ask me out on a date?"

"No, I couldn't hear." He paused, thinking. "But I know you are trying to get away from me and it makes me sad."

"Don't be ridiculous," she said. "We walk paths around each other but we neither have any kind of hold on the other."

"No, we don't," he said quietly, passing behind her. She watched him move on down the hall. At the door to his room, he turned before entering and met her gaze. "Have a nice evening, Grace."

There was nothing left to do, Grace decided taking a shower and going to bed would settle the unrest she was feeling. Why had she practically forgotten her own discomfort when she became aware of his? Too many times her past rose up to haunt her and she found herself trying to ease another's pain while ignoring her own. And then one day, out of the blue, her feelings would throw her into such despair she felt the need to run, but where?

She thought about Devon Malloy. She remembered he was nice enough but thus far no bells were ringing. And why did she think she was betraying her house guest? From a cabinet she took down a bottle of pain pills. Sitting on the tub surround she wondered why she was hiding out in the bathroom of her own house when she had done nothing to merit the discontent of her soul. Swallowing the pills she ran the tub as full as she dared, and slipped a handful of her favorite bath salts into the water as she slid into its depth. By the time she washed and rinsed her hair the room was as fragrant as her hair was wet. Toweling it dry she slipped into a pair of cozy pajamas, a matching chenille robe over them and realized she was starving when in fact she had eaten only a couple hours before.

Opening the door, she listened for sounds of movement and hearing none, moved out into the hall of darkness. Feeling despairingly alone, she wondered why tonight there were suppressed emotions at war inside her body. Why? Grace sneaked to the kitchen, had she the power she would have wrapped herself around the doorpost, slid down the wall, so strange were her feelings in her own home, what was it that always made her think she was wrong? By the appliance light she poured a glass of milk and found two cookies lying erstwhile on the countertop and tiptoed into the living room to the high backed sofa whose arms seemed to curve around her body in protection. She had sit here when Reed was alive, long hours into the morning as she heard him pace the floor in the night, his own demons controlling his memory of Arnel. "God help me, I can do nothing with you," he said after their marriage and the time of trial. "She governs me from the grave. I loved her that much, Grace and only God knows if she loved me."

Grace knew he longed for comfort. She became the one who said the right word, the wisdom he sought whether she believed what she said, or not. "I'm sure she did," she would reply and watch the light come into his eyes for a time. "You could go to a counselor to search out your thoughts." His eyes would snap in defiance before he remembered he was the one ask her to marry him. "Things will be good between us," he had said. "You will have a home for you and the child. I'll never mistreat you as…" His words stopped. He would not lessen his dead wife's hold over them. The love he had for Arnel would never be replaced, most certainly not by one so young.

Once more, she realized just as her parents had not truly loved her or regretted leaving her; this husband who chose her would never want her. She was a child when Arnel died, not so much in years of age but inexperienced in ways of the world. She longed for creature comfort, someone to put their arms around her, hold her close when times were difficult and the world outside beat at her heart's door. With her mother gone she was enrolled in public school. "You the girl married that old man?" Taunted by class mates, she wondered who told them of her private life. She was glad when graduation came. "You can take two years of college right here, Grace, from this house, on the computer and on the side when the child begins school I will teach you what you need to know to run the business when I'm gone."

"Where are you going?" Her heart had lurched in her chest. If he left, could she maintain the household?

"No, no, Grace, I merely meant as the years pass and I join Arnel."

There had been that day, one week before graduation, a time she wanted to forget; when the Banes ganged up on her in the hall, "You need us to teach you what it's like to be loved by a young buck," Bonnie Bruce taunted. "Lock the door, boys and give us some room, we got work to do." His grin was as sadistic as his face was grim, as leader of the Banes gang he demanded his group all wear black and they each had their lips died a permanent grape color, so their teeth took on a yellowish hue when they opened their mouth. He began to unhook the silver chains that hung from a nail studded belt around his waist, handing the chains over one at a time to his boyz as he called them. "It's a ritual," he said. "I'll show you how it's done."

She had been taken to what they labeled the boiler room, but it was really a huge furnace and an even larger water heater than she had seen before. At the top was a numbered valve she assumed showed the pressure as it built and someone must check it during the winter days, why else would it be there? Any minute she expected to hear the hiss of steam coming from those bent pipes on the top surface. Bonnie was backing her to the wall, his eyes becoming slits as his tongue increased in swiping his upper lip. Could it be he was nervous? She felt the wall behind her back, and there it was; the switch a small red lever beneath a clear glass case, the only thing she could hang on to. She tried to block the present from her mind, she had been here before, but that person now she realized had been different, drugged, docile, not wanting to hurt her, locked into the room as she had been, unlike Bonnie who would take pleasure in her pain. He grabbed her hair, holding it in his fist close to her scalp as he bent his head and came toward her face, his mouth practically salivating, grinding his hips as the low waist pants fell to the floor and his boyz rushed up to aid in freeing him. She knew without seeing he wore no underwear. She gripped the lever behind her back and heard the piercing sound of an alarm going off in the hall, echoing down the length of it as feet came running, the soles of leather shoes slapping the tile hard and someone was pounding on the locked door screaming, "Open this door, you know you're not supposed to be in there."

His disappointment obvious, he pressed against her, his intent to hurt her and leave an imprint on her memory. Grace kicked, aiming for an error where it mattered but for some reason Bonnie had stooped and the force of her feet landed squarely on his mouth. Blood flowed from the corners, his yellowed teeth appeared bent at odd angles. Had she actually scored and hit home? Stunned, Bonnie slapped a hand over his mouth to suppress the scream of pain. His other hand drew back, hatred in his eyes as he meant to back hand her as she stared back, her own anger so evident there was no cowering, while outside in the hall someone was beating on the door demanding entrance.

"You will pay for this. If one tooth is missing, I swear when you least expect it, I will be standing over you demanding justice for what you have just done…you hear me?" With that he turned to his boys.

Bonnie was quickly clothed, but he wrapped the chains around her wrist and drug her to the pipes now visible from behind the water heater, motioning all the while for his boyz to open the one long window. "Boost me up," were the last words and then she heard a sound as if something was falling. Whatever it was made contact with its victim as Bonnie Bruce screamed, a sound filled with pain accompanied by a sickening shuffle of feet. Someone was coming toward her, as loud agonizing words poured out of Bonnie. He was hurt bad. Bent double and bleeding he staggered toward her; malice in his eyes, the eyes of a stalking animal. And then one of his boyz slapped her on the head with a two by four retrieved from the window sill. She thanked God for the blackness that surrounded her.

For now she was safe and next week she would be free of Bonnie and his boyz. She later realized the school had not called anyone to aid her. They wanted Bonnie Bruce out of their hair and covered up his ugly deed. The school's records were clear. No harm done. No one cared about her. But she still remembered the blood on the window ceil and on the strange looking blade or gate on chains that had fallen from above; A device she surmised intended to descend slowly to cover the window exit but it had not fallen slowly. There had been a defect and in her mind she believed it carried a mountain of pain.

She had walked home, nervously watching every street corner, aware of every bush and running when there was too much land between houses in the empty lots. They could be watching her every move and she was afraid. That night she woke up crying, making her boy whimper in his sleep and once he was soothed she padded down the hall to Reed's room and crawled into his bed, hearing his even breathing as she scooted her back next to his, wishing he would put his arm around her just this one time. She had no idea how long she slept there, at peace for once from the bad dreams that turned into night mares but she would never forget being pushed from his bed and hearing his scathing words, "You harlot, why would you tarnish Arnel's bed. Go to your room," and her broken sobs did not lessen until the morning broke.

"I need to tell you," she said as he came home the next evening, but he put his hand up, stopping her.

"I don't want to hear it. Now stay away from me. If that happens again, I will kill you rather than kick you out."

It was months before he spoke civilly to her. "I will not tolerate your wanton ways," he barked that fateful night, his words piercing her as surely as a pointed knife. "Never speak of this and neither will I," and her memory served well to remind her, no matter a kindness he might show thereafter, she must not weaken and need his consolation.

As though it happened yesterday, Grace began to cry, soft whimpering sounds at first, deepening as her body became cool from lack of cover and she in sleep did not know when he came to study her curled form on the sofa. He tried to determine how to handle the broken sobs that reminded him of her sadness and possibly the loss of her child. He could not know the rejection she felt, nor the fact she was left behind by parents who said one thing but in truth meant another. Tainted, soiled, unwanted, though she was now a grown woman there were times Grace felt the lash brought to her sensitive innocent soul as though it were happening now, by selfish uncaring adults who should have known better than to treat a child with such unkindness and humiliation. He thought to pick her up and carry her to her room, when the stab of reality sunk into his peevish mind, he wore two molded boots on his feet, it was all he could do to walk, let alone think of carrying a body, even a child's.

Looking down, he saw the space where she had sunk into the softness of the sofa, her head on one lone pillow, her body in fetal position and he did the only thing he could think to do, removing a soft folded cover from the sofa arm, he allowed his body to claim that empty space, managed to lift his heavy feet up onto the matching tufted ottoman that sat next to the sofa and gathered her into his arms and somehow hooked that quilt like piece over their bodies. He held her until the whimpering ebbed to a gentle hiccup and her breathing became soft and regular. As the warmth of their bodies meld together he slipped into blissful sleep, his head against the high back of the sofa, the arm supporting his effort and her body peacefully resting next to his as she was wrapped in his arms. When next she awakened to the dark room, a soft glow of earth stirring outside the window, she knew nothing of the previous turmoil of her soul but the warmth of someone's caring and it felt right. She slipped back into gentle slumber. She was thirty years old and she had never experienced the warmth of another's body.

He awoke, his feet sticking straight up into the air, the only way possible when wearing a boot on each foot, but his legs seemed to have lost all feeling. Evidently circulation was at its minimum to his extremities, even his hands were numb. He glanced down, thinking she looked peaceful in slumber but he could bet a million dollars those eyes would open stormy and mean as she tried to place some kind of blame on him for being in the position he now found himself. As gently as possible he tried to unravel their bodies and blew a huff of relief when it was done. It was best he go to his room and stay.

She awakened, a moment of apprehension coming as she thought she was late to work but then it was Saturday, the teenagers would be running the shop. She could stay in. With the regular crew in charge of the shop, it didn't matter that it was the busiest day of the week. This was her effort to show young people there were adults who had faith in them. Some of them were childhood friends to her son and they loved her. Grace wasn't aware the whole network of workers at her dead husband's shop cared for her. There was no inside conspiracy to protect a woman of weakness because they learned early on, Grace was not weak. Though they had never understood her marriage to the elderly shop owner, they accepted it based on Grace being a lady. Of course Gerald, the Pharmacist over saw the young ones. With three teens at home, he was the most experienced in what they might consider doing and then there was Billy who would bow and scrape to please her, but he didn't have to. A smile crossed her lips as she considered Billy. His mother confided, "My son is in love with you, Grace." You mean he loves me, Grace corrected to see a frown on Mrs. George's face. "No, he loves you and I keep telling him there's someone out there for him, down the road of course," she fumbled with a night cap she was purchasing. "my hair just goes to knots from those pillow cases," she had explained, "and the beautician suggest I buy a night cap. Anyway I don't mean to insult you, but do you think, perhaps you could maybe suggest he save his attentions for down the road…you know, when he's older and ready, with these additional college hours he's in to be finished?"

There hadn't been opportunity to discuss Mrs. George's concerns with her son. Now, Grace shook her head. The things mother's worried over and if she'd had the opportunity no doubt she would too. Sometimes she thought no one remembered she had a son. Joshua. Her lips moved as she repeated his name. Joshua. But there was no sound. Reed had loved her boy. He had not loved her, nor ever made love to her but he loved Joshua, the child was the right age to take his mind off losing his wife and gave him purpose for each new day, otherwise in grieving she often wondered if Reed would have taken his own life, he loved Arnel that much. No one would believe their unholy union, or was it unholy? Wed in name only, relieved beyond understanding that they neither wanted the marriage consummated. She made the one mistake…going to his room for comfort, not for a wife's duty, but a girl needing someone to help her through a terrible time after the gang dragged her into the school's boiler room and would have raped her, except she set off the fire alarm and they escaped out the window. But the need grew from the nightmares and days when every walk alone to the store was filled with dread and fear the Banes Boyz would come for her again as they promised it was not over. "When you least expect us," Bonnie said, "We'll get you, won't we Sammy? Sammy, was the one who stuck the needle in her arm and made the situation float, real life in a bubble but it didn't erase the hurt and humiliation. Why had they threatened her, Bonnie with his mean eyes looming over her, "you say a word, ever, we will come for you. You won't know what pain is when we are finished with you. You understand? Ever."

Her life story would appear tragic to those who heard it for the first time. For fifteen years she thought she was loved and wanted by her parents to finally realize they took the first excuse presented to leave her behind. Fifteen years and they did not return for her. She didn't know if they were dead or alive after that one phone call from her mother. "It's better for you not to be on the road with us, Stormy," her mother whispered so low she could barely hear. "I know Mrs. Weathers is so good to you; that dear lady who loved the Lord and was so in need of your help. How is she?"

"She died."

"Oh, Stormy," her mother replied as the phone clicked and the line went silent. Fourteen years later, Stormy wished her mother had asked about the baby. Joshua was alive then and the one thing she and Reed had in common was their love for him.

"I want my child in church," she told him when Joshua was learning to walking, her chin firmly set and her eyes unflinching. "I'm going whether you go or not." It broke Reed's heart to see the child waving goodbye to him, tears streaming down his little cheeks. After the first month, Reed broke and went with them. When the Congregationalist looked at the strange little family of three, they failed at first to see the oddity of age difference; what they saw was two people who loved a little boy and a child who grew in favor with the church under the guidance of that love. If they questioned the reason they assumed Reed Weathers in a moment of weakness and his terrible grief of losing his beloved wife had dallied with a young inexperienced girl and was paying the price, but they were said to whisper, "together the two are doing what is right for the child."

Taking a deep breath Grace slipped into the folds of the soft throw, not remembering when she reached for it, but thankful it was there. In truth she felt more a person named Stormy than her given name Grace but Reed insisted if they were to attend church then there would be a modicum of respectability. He was older and wise enough to know they would be scrutinized due to the secrecy of their beginning. Arnel had kept the girl hidden and now he had married her. Either he was a man with no scruples or so deep in grief he never knew what he was doing; he got off lightly and the girl received the blame but before he died he realized by her very nature Grace had turned their minds to better thinking. She was a jewel, a woman to be considered pure and deserving by the church. Reed's friend, who was an elder of the church, had shared this with her as he came for one last visit with Reed on the day he died. She heard his voice, husky and dry, "He said he couldn't love you, Grace, but he greatly respected you." Herbert had looked down his thin nose, studying her and then continued. "I doubt you care whether he loved you. I take you to be a woman that desires kindness and little else. Don't worry; anything Reed has told me goes to the grave with me." Reed died in the winter and his friend, Herbert died the next spring. She supposed his word was sterling.

She shuddered now, remembering how cold it was the day Reed was buried. Angeline stood by her, holding her hand. Angeline had become the closest person she could identify with as a mother figure. She was the only person ever to baby sit Joshua and was there through his funeral, as grief stricken as she and Reed, along with the whole church.

"These people," Angeline said, watching them minister to Grace, "They're good to you, Stormy. I'm happy to see that. I'm afraid my view of the so called Christian community has always been jaded."

"Why is that, Angeline?"

"No one was with us, when my man died. I thought no one cared."

"But, Angeline, did they know you. Sometimes we don't know other's problems if we haven't met them or heard about them."

"No, they didn't know us," she agreed "We never attended; we thought we didn't fit in. They were all better'n us."

"Oh, no, Angeline." Tears welled up in Grace's eyes. "The church may be filled with people, but it's God's house. And," her voice trailed softly away, "God is not contained by the walls of a building."

"Is he here, now?" Angeline glanced around. "I see his people but I don't see him."

"Yes, you do, in these people, Angeline. He lives in our hearts." She knew Angeline was watching as she placed her hand over her heart. "I feel him, otherwise I would be lying on the floor, sobbing. Maybe in truth not for Reed but that he has gone on to see our boy and I'm alone again." The tears ran down her cheek. "At least Reed stood by me at church. Who will stand with me now?" They were comfortable in silence, each considering her words.

After the funeral and last minutes at the cemetery in winter's cold the late afternoon meal was served by the church to those attending Reed's funeral, Angeline was leaving and kissed her cheek. "I'll see you Sunday," she said.

"I'll be home after services," Grace replied.

"I know Stormy. I'm coming to church to stand by you. You'll have to teach me how to act."

Grace hugged her friend so tight, cheek to cheek, their tears meld together.

Beneath the soft throw, she thought she was awake but part of her napped, as she seldom took time to rest or think. She had stayed busy to keep her mind from grieving the loneliness of life. She had dreamed she was being held. Dreams were such elusive things, or else the two pain pills had thrown her into deep sleep. She seldom took anything but the last week had been filled with unusual situations, maybe it was wearing her down and she had been unsettled by last night's happenings. It would not leave her mind; the stranger in her home had wanted to kiss her. How had she known? That was the mystery. She had just known.

It was ten o'clock when she awakened, refreshed and ready to face the world. The sound of metal scrapings came from the kitchen. She sat up straight. He was cooking again, she knew when the spatula rounded the pan, the chime of glasses being set on the table and then he was standing in the doorway. "Hey, you, got any interest in a top ten casserole?"

"What in the world is a top ten casserole?" She climbed from the cocoon of the sofa, folded the throw, placed the pillow on one end and stood back to view her handiwork. No one would ever know she spent the night there, but the ottoman was slightly askew, with her foot she scooted it just so in line with the sofa. Turning to greet him, she smiled. "I had the best sleep I've had in years. I might give up my bedroom for this sofa."

He grinned, avoiding that subject. "A top ten casserole, my dear, has ten ingredients in it, according to my mother." With one hand up, the fingers spread he touch them, calling off the ingredients, eggs beaten just right, chives, bacon crumbled to a fine crumb, ah, yes, a cup of fine crumbs, a dash of this and a dash of that, you get the picture?" With a sweep of his hands toward the kitchen, he said, "This way, Madame." As on second thought, he reached out one hand, the other in the air and she placed her own in his. "Breakfast waits," he said, bowing at the waist, "you first, I find my booted feet a bit awkward to my dancing spirit…and we both know we don't want me falling down."

"No, we really don't. Let me see…" She peeped around the corner. "I knew you were placing the glasses on the table and you are using the fox stone ware."

"Ah, yes, warmed too."

"Warmed?" She eyed him a bit suspicious. "What does that mean?"

"Warmed?" A twinkle in his eye told her he was as usual ready to laugh at her question. "You know, turn the oven on low, place the plates on the middle rack and warm them, which avoids having cold casserole for brunch."

"Brunch?"

"Exactly. Defined by Webster the meal between breakfast and lunch. Brunch." He was passing a very small carafe to her. "My secret ingredient, to lace over the casserole and then you will never want again."

"Promise?"

He laughed. "Of course, I promise." He studied her with pleasure the smile on his face proof he liked what he was seeing. "Your laughter is wonderful. You should laugh more often."

"One needs something to laugh about…"

"True." He picked up on that, quickly. "We've all been through times laughter was scarce, our joy suppressed or short lived."

"Tell me about your experience."

"If I do, then will you tell me yours?" He saw her hesitate. "Remember, a deal's a deal. Proceed with caution." She nodded. "You're agreeing but something tells me you will couch your words to the point you tell very little."

"I admit, I do that." She sighed. "I've just had the best rest I've experienced in years…I don't want to ruin it. You go first."

"Did I tell you I was an only child?"

"Let me think." She held the fork in midair, remembering suddenly they had not said grace. "Ah, Peter, we forgot to thank God for the food. Shall we?" He nodded and she bowed her head. "Dear God, thank you for this day, thank you for the rest of the night and for this food. Help us to be not so selfish but to thank you for life, itself and Father, according to your word bless Peter and heal the bones that were made weak and take away the pain he suffers."

"Amen," they said together.

They had eaten a while when she commented. "All right, Mr. Judith Childs. Tell me your life story. You are…or, you are not an only child?"

"I had a sister who adored me and she died. Thus, I became an only child. I think after the heartbreak of losing my sister, my mother, especially could not bear the thought of losing another…."

"You were the oldest?"

"No, Lala was the oldest. She was around long enough to help spoil me. I'll never forget her special kindness. It was as if she knew she wasn't long for this world." Without asking, Peter was spooning a second portion of casserole on to her plate. "I will never understand why children die." He saw the pain wash momentarily into her expression and then it was gone as she listened to him. He realized she had not explained her son's death. "My mother was young enough to have another child, but as she now explains, she saved herself the heartbreak."

"But she still has you. My arms are empty."

"Yes, she said she decided to concentrate on the happiness she would find in raising me." He shrugged, "I don't know if that was the better thing to do, or not." He tilted his head, staring across the table at her. "Now, it's your time and don't be so reserved. Whatever you tell me, I promise not to share…if that is your wish."

She studied him for a minute. "I don't share my life with anyone. For the life of me, I don't know why I would with you."

"Because, in this short time we've known each other, I think you feel as I do that we connect." His voice was gentle, the expression in his eyes kind. "Your faith in God must tell you this is not just a chance encounter," he smiled. "I've thought on this, there were a thousand other places God could have allowed me to have an accident when the wheel rolled out from under my car….but it was here with you." He leaned forward, "so now, tell me." He leaned across the table, his small finger crooked, "Pinky promise." She grinned and hooked her finger with his.

"Not even those I attend church with know I was raped at an early age, which resulted in being pregnant as a teen." He didn't flinch as she thought he might. "You understand, it was not because Joshua was Reed's son I married him. My marriage to Reed came much later." She sighed. "I think I was a hindrance to my parents. They were modern day travelers; containing gypsy traits…because that is our heritage and they love the challenge of living off the land." She was lost in reverie. "This is harder for me than you can imagine."

"Take your time. We are not rushed." His eyes lingered on her face. "I think if you have never voiced it, you need to tell your story,"

"You major in Psychology?" She guessed. He nodded. "How would I know that?" An amused expression appeared. "And no, I didn't pick the pockets of your clothes when I washed those cut off scrubs, which by the way your good clothes are still at the hospital."

Hands up and shoulders scrunched, he didn't reply, waiting for the rest of her story. "Go on, I'm waiting to hear."

She wanted to say, "I was grabbed off the street, shoved into a car, driven a distance and then pushed into a room with a boy that seemed either drugged or innocent of wrong doing...I don't know who he was and I doubt he would ever know me." Throwing her head back she stared up at the ceiling. "All these years I have wondered if he knew and then I wonder who he was, and had my son lived, perhaps I would have pursued it to know the characteristics he might possess." That was what she wished to say as she looked at him and said, "My son's life was cut short by a hit and run driver who carried his bicycle into town beneath his vehicle and left Joshua dead or dying along the side of the road. That's it."

"No, that's the beginning," he replied, softly. "But there's what happened before and after, how you became acquainted with your husband, the part of marrying a man at least twice maybe three times older than you."

She spread her hands. "This home, the business was his. I had nothing. Sometimes, even now there seems to be a stigma attached to my life. I had to earn my way."

"We all have to," he replied. "We cannot rest on the laurels of those who went before us. You loved Mr. Weathers?"

"No and he never loved me." She registered the surprise on his face. "He loved his wife."

"No one could resist loving you, Grace."

She blushed. "Perhaps, there's the real story. My mother had been hired by Mrs. Weathers as a house keeper. She knew my mother's teenage daughter was pregnant and my mother was anxious to move on." Blowing out pent up emotions, Grace relayed, "Long story short. They left me here believing Mrs. Weathers took me in out of the goodness of her heart but I soon learned Arnel Weathers wanted my services to keep her household intact as she was struggling with cancer."

"How did she explain the baby to the community? Were they led to believe..."

"I was kept secret, not allowed to go anywhere. My condition was too awful to explain in that day. Fifteen years."

"Let me guess, she was afraid they would think your child was sired by her husband. Am I correct?"

"I don't know. I never thought about that...in those days. He was a lot older than me." She thought back. "Once when her mind was clouded with pain, she accused him, but she knew that was not true."

"How much older was he than you?"

"When she died, he was forty five. I was fifteen, but when he died...or, when Joshua died..." She let the words hang. "I guess there was nothing he saw in me that appealed to him. He loved his wife even in death. I was a child, starved for love." She gazed at Peter. "Can you fathom a person so in need of love, nothing else matters and the terrible things that happened...I often thought it was the end of the world...my parents gone and not staying in touch, Mrs. Weathers only needing my services and I looked on him as a benefactor of sorts, never as one would in needing a lover but needing love." She bowed her head and cupped her face in her hands. Her voice was whispery as she said, "I didn't realize I felt so hopeless at the time. No one has ever asked or wanted to hear...me."

He ached to reach out to Grace, but he had already learned those eyes that yearned for understanding had been suppressed all these years and would turn stormy as her body tensed and she turned away; no, she ran away. Did she think she was unlovable? Unattractive? What really beat in her heart and pressed through her mind? Whatever his intention, she would not allow his attention. He felt a moment's apprehension that his time was too short to know Grace's return of his interest in her. And, he questioned, why was he drawn to her? There had never been a shortage of female friends to form a relationship and wasn't that what his mother had encouraged. Now he thought of his parents and their love for each other and he realized what they had was the real thing and he decided he would never accept anything less.

"I am suspecting when his wife died, in his loneliness, he began to focus on your son?"

"Yes," a slight smile formed around her lips as her eyes lightened. "Who can resist a toddler learning to walk and reaching out? As surely as Joshua claimed my heart he claimed Reed's." Her sigh was filled with contentment. "We began to go to the park, take walks in the early morning and then late afternoon to teach Joshua…and you know what happened?" The smile spread across her face. "We began to enjoy those times, where in the beginning things were a bit awkward we loosened up and in time Reed, who often refused to attend church after Arnel's death now decided he couldn't stand to see Joshua cry when we left him on Sunday mornings… and he joined us."

"Mr. Weathers attended church with you? You became a family?"

"Yes."

He loved the whispery quality of her voice. "A child leads the way."

"Yes," she agreed. "Joshua's life was not in vain, though it was short lived." She stood up; beginning to gather the condiments then stacked the plates and carried them to the dishwasher. "Can you make it down the garage steps? I want to show you our town, the places we walked and why?" A new excitement was racing through her veins. "You know," she said, "I don't remember sleeping as well as I did last night, in a long time, it was as though someone held and comforted me."

Peter, by now was wiping the table top clean and glanced away, quickly staring out the window. "I believe I can make it down those steps. Do you plan to wear your housecoat?"

Her laughter floated back as she hurried down the hall. "No, give me a few minutes and I'll be ready. I'm glad you reminded me or I might have. There's a joy in my heart I had almost forgotten."

By the time she aided his entry to the car, she wore a thin layer of sweat on her upper lip and the back of his shirt was wet. With the seat set as far back as the mechanism allowed, they still had to maneuver his practically sitting on the center console and if his leg hadn't been able to bend a bit at the knee he could not have gone. "Did we have this difficulty, bringing you home?"

"Yeah, we did," he replied, "at that time I was not an asset. I think you considered me a liability; let's just say there were other things on your mind, like my not finding a room and you taking a complete stranger into your home, of the male gender at that." Wiping away the sweat that had run down his cheeks, the last few minutes, Peter nodded as she held his gaze. "Here's where I thank you again. By now in that lone hotel room I would be going nuts." Just when he had thought to decline the outing, they had figured out how to get him into the car. Still, it had taken its toll on both of them. "I guess we could just sit here and rest awhile, then go back inside."

"Not on your life," she quipped. "We may be whipped but we're not beat, yet." She put the car in reverse and backed out of the garage. "This is a quaint little town." She pulled out into the street.

"First, I'll show where history began." Within five minutes they were on the outskirts of town, the ancient court house behind them, and the hospital that had been renovated into rooms that housed Senior Citizens while lending them the necessities of a grocery store, a five and ten that was outdated but still existed, both within walking distance of the Housing Center and the Police Station that gave them a certain amount of false security.

"It is recorded that the French held control over this land into the late seventeen hundreds when it ceded to Spain. Mostly Native Americans inhabited the region, but white settlers were beginning to notice the lay of the land and had heard its river was prime for fishing. Then…" She let the words draw out mysteriously. "Then, there were my people. Tinkers by trade, searching for a way to live off the land, they filtered into the settlement. Not a lot of the new inhabitants were excited in a good way over my people."

"What do you mean your people?" He had wondered; Auburn hair, olive skin and hazel eyes made it difficult to guess. "And what was your maiden name? That should give me a clue."

"It won't." She almost giggled. "Before I married the older illustrious Mr. Weathers, my last name was Henderson. I was called Grace Anaelesa Henderson."

"Analesa?"

"An-nae-le-sa." A mischievious grin claimed her. "I can't believe I said that. I have never disrespected Reed Weathers and I shouldn't now." She shook her head, a slight shudder rippling through her body as she filed back into the line of cars going into town a different route. Almost lost in reverie, her voice dropped low. "Then to think I was called Stormy Weathers, the community must have had a chuckle." She glanced across, he was listening. "I never intentionally made waves…but being unmarried and pregnant…although, I was hidden away." She stopped, as suddenly as the traffic in front of the car. "How in the world did I get back on that subject? For a few minutes I felt happy being out of the house."

"I ask your maiden name and I guess you knew I was trying to decide what your ethnicity was?"

Now she did giggle. "My family were said to be the Roma." When he appeared puzzled, she explained, "Gypsies. I might add a generation or two removed, but evidently good enough for my parents to leave me." This time the shudder was full blown. "Can you imagine the whiplash that brings... never understanding your parents left you?"

"But Henderson doesn't feel gypsy, does it?"

"I touched on this, before. Did you not believe me? I once heard my mother's family discussing the justification of taking a family name to deter the community's dislike of the group coming through and disrupting their stable lives...you know, door to door salesmen carrying their strange wares, dressed in flamboyant clothing, playing their musical instruments while they danced." Her eyes lit up again, the hazel deepening into a joyous storm of emotion.

"I like it," he said. "I wondered why you dress in almost monotone layers of clothing. With your auburn hair, skin tone and those eyes...those stormy eyes..." He grinned. Hands in the air, he protested her squinted gaze upon him. "I'm not saying you aren't attractive. In fact you are beautiful but color, turquoise, coral and yes, maybe purple, I can see those colors coming alive on you...I was mystified." He was quiet for a moment. "Do you dislike color?"

"I love color but I don't want to stand out. Mrs. Weat... Arnel, forbade it and he enforced whatever she decided."

"It was...like...a..." He considered the older couple's demands. "It was a decree."

"Like Caesar Augusta," she agreed. "Off with their heads...and I'm not saying that to be crude, there were times..." She shook her head. "We have to get off this subject. Just ahead, see that red brick building; they have built a new façade on the front to represent, let's say something comparable to a Southern Plantation Home, the many steps leading to the wide landing are used in the summertime for musicals because it is adjacent to the River and though it can be a heat and mosquito infested nuisance there are times it is absolutely wonderful when a soft breeze blows in from the water and there's this fragrance we can only believe due to the wild roses that grow so profusely along its banks."

He found himself enthralled by her voice, light and airy, ascending to peals of laughter as she related something humorous to the city's history and Peter realized she had spent many an hour studying the history of Haven on the Bluff because there was nothing else she had been allowed to enjoy and in so doing Grace or Stormy as he truly wanted to call her, had a repertoire' any founding father would be glad to acknowledge. She lost all intimidation; her very being expressed the riotous colors of the South she spoke about, the people, the time and the surrounding, until they became alive. They were real and Stormy was real.

"I've lost you," she said. "I apologize. I don't often get carried away like this; actually no one understands I've studied our town."

"You love it," he said. "It is home."

She was quiet and then she added, "I never thought about it that way, I guess it is home. What do you think of our city?"

"I like it, Stormy. So much so, I'm thinking I would sit up my main office here and the surrounding towns will be satellite stations. The problem is, I have to find a location and not being able to drive, in my allotted time I have left, that seems near impossible."

"I will drive you," she offered, her eyes shining with life. "It would be my pleasure."

His spirit groaned within him. In all truth, Peter Daniel's was beginning to accept the fact, he had fallen for Stormy Weathers, but she in innocence and inexperience due to her sheltered life neither recognized nor would know how to deal with that fact. What was he to do? He had come to like the way Stormy prayed for them both as she blessed the food and sometimes when she said simply, "Lord, I'm asking you to heal Peter's bones that he can go about his everyday life as he is accustomed to doing." In the stronger moments he was happy and blessed as she ask, thinking he felt his bones leaving behind the ache and weakness he had suffered. In the weaker minutes he wondered if she wanted him out of her home so badly her prayers were the only tool she in her goodness felt allowed to achieve that goal.

In the next days, Stormy as Peter had come to think of her went to work, he did the household chores and after work she drove him around the city looking for a building suitable for his office. "There on top of the hill with its sphere reaching to the heaven's sits the First Baptist Church of the city, I'm told the organ pipes reaches the depth of a thirty foot height and the sound is as melodic and majestic as angels singing," she grinned, quickly glancing his way to see if he was buying her story. "You know what? I've always wanted to attend just to hear the organ and the music. This building with its tall sphere is known far and wide."

"Then, let's go, this coming Sunday? Because I'll be leaving the next and it would be a delight to have such a grand memory, attending church services with you."

Her mouth fell open in surprise. "Do you mean it? You would attend with me?"

He shuffled his booted feet on the floor mat of the car. "Well, of course. It isn't rocket science is it? It's attending what…a landmark and worship at the same time."

"But those steps up to the entrance," She said, "you can't push your body this soon…can you…to climb stair?"

"Stormy, I assure you a worship center of that structure surely has an elevator, the founding fathers would want to take care of their elderly members, wouldn't they?" He grinned. "We'll make a deal, if I have to walk every step up, the thing to do going back is this, I'll lie down and you give me a push and I'll thump all the way to the street."

She threw her head back as joyous laughter peeled forth. "You really thought that one out, didn't you?"

"I have all day to think," he replied. "Some days I think I'll go crazy, thinking."

"But," she turned serious. "At least you are able to go on with your business. It's not that I'm insensitive to your situation, I just don't know what I can do about it." Her words ebbed into silence, "I would never have dreamed we, you and I would be out riding the streets looking for an office."

"Thank you, Stormy, I sincerely appreciate your doing this…otherwise it would be more of the doldrums." He sighed. "So where are you and your police man going on your first date, together? Tomorrow night I believe."

She was caught off guard. "Actually, I haven't thought beyond his asking me out to dinner…I really don't know."

"I wish it were me," he said, glancing down at his booted feet. "I would take you dancing."

"Dancing?" She smiled. "I've always wanted to dance in the arms of a fine gentleman, you know whirl around the room?" Her eyes became hooded as she imagined the scene, "I would wear an apricot ball gown, not stiff and unbending material, but soft and full and swingy, the material swirling around my body as the man of my dreams leads and we circle the room."

"Apricot?" He was stymied. "What color is apricot?"

"You've seen an apricot?"

"Well, yes, but tell me the hue of color, pink?"

"Kind of," she replied, the smile deepening as crinkles appeared at the corners of her eyes. "Peachy pink, maybe."

She began laughing, "I cannot explain why I can tell you such silly personal things I've never before told anyone."

"I'm honored." He bowed from the waist up, sweeping his arm to the roof of the car. "I feel so special that you shared your favorite color with me. Apricot." He began to hum, "Somewhere, over the rainbow, apricots fly....and the dream you are having belongs to you and I....If happy little apricots lift their heads and smile ...then we shall dance around the room...awhile.....just me and you...that's where you'll find me." His eyes twinkled as she began to hum along. "Happy little blue birds sing and.. and I hope the song plays on for a while."

"Nice voice, Lombardo," she quipped and glanced quickly toward his feet; "I can see us dancing...except your "troubles" keep making you stumble." For the life of me, why did you have to mess up your feet? Such conflict."

"Careful, Stormy Weather, apricot might conflict with the color of your hair." He laughed. "Can't have that."

"Drat! I hadn't thought of that...but somehow blue just doesn't fit."

"Then peachy pink it shall be and you shall wear apricots on your feet."

They found several places to rent but the one they agreed on was not on the commercial level, but a more homey atmosphere of houses set back off the road, easily recognized as someone's beloved home. Making one call, the realtor came to give them a guided tour and waited patiently in her car while they discussed the pro's and cons of his sitting up shop in this residential area, if it was allowed.

"True," she said, "You will be traveling, most of the time, but an occasional stop here to let your body catch up might be what's needed in this sweet little house. The way the hall closes the office off from the living area is a definite plus."

"How far is it from your place?" He asked, following her to the window, leaning in close as she pressed her cheek against the window pane and pointed. "Oh, yes, I see the tower at the far end of your street, so you are five or six blocks to the West. Right?" She turned her head to find herself peering straight into his eyes and what she saw was that longing she'd seen the night she fled to her room, the same night the Policeman called and asked for a dinner date.

He smiled, leaning to kiss the tip of her nose. Thinking that was all he was allowed, but then it struck him it almost seemed as if she waited for more and then his lips moved down to meet hers. If he felt at a loss for words when the kiss ended… she appeared stricken and rooted to the spot. Her expression was not troubled; more surprised if anything and all right with what had happened.

Stormy was registering what she was feeling, stretching it out as far as possible. This was her first ever kiss from someone who was not ready to strip her of dignity and pride. He leaned in and kissed her again. Finally, pulling away and groaning as he stepped back, "Sorry, Stormy, I…" He fumbled for a word, "I…liked kissing you. It was nice."

She stared at him searching for words, "I don't know what to think, or say. Is this proper, or even all right?" She placed her hands on the sides of her face, "This hasn't…I mean…I." She was blushing. "I'm sorry, I don't know what to say and it suddenly came to my mind what someone else would think." She glanced around for a chair. "I think I need to sit down." The blush was receding, the heat leaving her face. "I'm very inexperienced in this, Peter. I know you can't understand…I don't either, but for me, this was my first kiss."

"Stormy, have you not realized… anyone aware that I'm staying in your home has already concluded we are lovers? In this day and age, few can regard our relationship as anything other than that. You and I know the truth and God knows I've tried to keep it light." He eyed her with a growing suspicion that she was probably right and he wondered how many had questioned his motives and suddenly he wondered if he'd been harboring ulterior…no, he wasn't guilty of that but he had wondered what it would be like to kiss her and now he knew. It wasn't in his power to make a maiden dumbstruck, as the old saying goes, but why was she so subdued?

"I would like to go home." she said and with that she was out the door. Following, Peter managed the three steps best he could because he had walked up the steps holding her arm for support. It seemed necessary to thank the realtor for showing them the house.

The ride home was void of the animation they'd previously enjoyed. Conversation was nil and a glance one to the other was completely out of question. Once parked inside the garage, again she left him to fend for himself going up the steps as she mumbled goodnight and hurried to her room, locked the door and braced herself against its wood panels as he shuffled down the hall, the molded boots making a strange swishing sound. Quickly she undressed, uncertain as to taking a shower now that she pondered his words; anyone aware I'm staying in your home has already concluded we are lovers. What was she thinking bringing this stranger into her house, only he was no longer a stranger. He had kissed her. She fell on her knees by the side of the bed and silently prayed. Lord, am I so inexperienced, so vulnerable that I forget society's rules and ruin my own credibility in the community? Words surfaced in her brain, so real she opened her eyes to see who was with her. No one was there but she felt someone's presence, as the words resounded, I, too, enjoyed and was questioned concerning my fellowship with certain people. And then there was laughter. Stormy jumped into the bed and pulled the covers over her head.

Down the hall, he forgot to close the door, as he stood frustrated and confused in the middle of the room, staring at the one papered wall behind the bed. Funny, he'd never noticed the paper before. He must be losing his mind; he was always aware of his surroundings. True, at home he never worried about anything, someone came in to clean his bachelor existence, he ate with his parents at their restaurant every night and the small postcard patch of grass he took summer pleasure in was in the hands of a competent lawn service. His was an organized life. But to not even notice the paper on the wall behind the bed? He walked closer, studying the theme, Paris, the Eifel tower, writings in flowery cursive, black on dark beige. Had she longed to travel and Paris was one of the places she wished to visit, or did women bow to whims of the day? Interesting. Now, he let his eyes roam around the room, mahogany furniture, a coverlet and curtains that matched the wall paper, large checkered pillow shams in alternating blocks, black and beige with a tailored bed skirt that touched the wood floor.

It was very well done, down to the small leather recliner by the window, a round two tiered table with a glass top that held a black veined marble lamp and the throw in muted brown and gold on the arm of the chair. And he had broken the lamp on the bedside stand. A great sigh left his body. When had he become interested in the trappings of a room? He liked it. He felt at home. Was this what his mother had tried to tell him? "You will know when you meet the right girl, Peter. Your mind won't turn loose of her, day or night, in your subconscious you will examine the possibility that she is the one and then, when you kiss her, you won't be happy until you kiss her again."

"Gee, thanks, Mom." Her giggle had saved them both embarrassment. "So that's how it was with Dad?" He stood there savoring the words between them. His Mom was his main encourager. Setting up the new business had its stress points. "Shush," she said often, "God will lead as you proceed. Don't forget that. In all things." He hoped, but presently it wasn't his business he was hoping progressed. The stormy eyed beauty that probably locked her door held him in a spell, and now she tells him her ancestors were gypsie, but that would be so far back there couldn't possibly be any power left, could there?

Stormy slipped out of the house, quiet as a mouse the next morning. She would pick up coffee on the way. Let him waken to a quiet house. He surely wouldn't cook that evening since she had a dinner date. Mentally she recalled a salad and a stored bowl of spaghetti from one of their mills in the frig, thinking now of her dinner date with Devon or was it Damon. She had to call the man by the correct name, it wasn't as if she heard the name every day.

"You seem lost in thought," Billy interrupted around four o'clock. "Everything all right with you and that cousin at your house." Momentarily distracted, she stared hard at Billy. He repeated the question.

"Oh, it's nothing. I have a date and I was wondering about a good place to dine, I guess." She lied, she had wondered if he would call. Not the Policeman, she sighed, but Peter Daniels and why would he?" It was then the phone rang. She glanced quickly at the number. What a strange number. Three two one, one-two-three-four. She supposed stranger things happened but what a number. There must be a reason behind it; without another thought she answered. "Weather's Pharmacy, Grace speaking."

"Did you have opportunity to view that ordering list I gave you? We need to close that deal today?" She nodded as laughter came across the line. She frowned and then the voice said, "Grace? I know this woman as Stormy Weathers. I must have the wrong number." She recognized Peter's voice as she laid a hand across the phone. "Yes, Billy, I have it ready. I'll bring it when I've finished this call."

"May I help you, Sir?" She motioned for Billy to close the door as he was leaving. She turned in her chair to stare out the window. "And…?" She waited, but he was silent. "Peter, did you call for a reason or just to say hello." She wanted to ask him about the strange number. How could he do that, but she didn't.

He loved listening to that airy quality in her voice. "Hello is nice. I miss hearing you all day long. I was thinking if you canceled your date tonight, I'd rip these molds of trouble off my feet and take you dancing…I tell you what…promise to be honest with me on this…my kissing you disturbed you and I apologize, it just seemed right. Now here's the other part…if he kisses you, I get to put on a record, you do have a record… never mind, we will use my phone.…we will play a song and I'll hold you in my arms and we will sway to the music.…only sway."

She was laughing. "You are crazy."

"But my kissing you disturbed you."

"Something like that."

"Why?"

She couldn't tell him she was thirty years old and had never had a boyfriend, her son was birthed out of rape and the second boy that tried to kiss her was under the same mind set and she began to think of herself as damaged goods and that was why love had never come her way. She wanted to say I liked your kiss but she couldn't and if he held her in the same esteem as he said others who knew he was in her home…then she didn't have a chance.

"I don't know," she finally replied. "It was a spur of the moment thing and I'm sure you didn't put much importance into it."

"Oh, but I did," he replied and when she was silent he continued. "You left an envelope on the table marked Important." He looked closer. "You have a personal remark, it says Billy's ordering list."

"Oh, my goodness," she replied. "I thought it was in my purse. Billy needs that, I'll run home for it. See you in a few." She sighed. "Bye for now." His reply seemed a bit forlorn if you could read one word. She picked up her purse, and met Billy in the hall, "Seems I left the invoices at home, Billy. I'll run home for them right now."

A strange car was in her drive. She parked out on the street and walked inside to the sound of a woman's laughter. A second joined in as she walked through the house and then she came to the hallway. Two women were on each side of Peter walking him down the hall, one wore a floral uniform while the other was dressed in bright blue with a white doctor's coat over it and a stethoscope hung around her neck. With their backs being to her, Grace stood still, listening.

"We just may have to keep you. You say you'll be cutting out of here, come Sunday."

The other added, "I bet you can't wait to get back into ciruclation. "Is there a Mrs. waiting or a significant other?"

"Gloria, you have been wanting to ask that every trip." Now she spoke to Peter, "This girl, has wondered every single visit and I said, Gloria, just ask and then we'll both know."

Peter's laugh echoed down the hall as he said, "Well, why didn't someone tell me. I've been here so long I've dusted every noon and cranny, gone stir crazy for someone to talk to and for once happy to have paper work to do." The women joined his laughing. "Shoot, we could have played checkers, or something."

"I think it's the something, Gloria's interested in. She's out of a long drawn out divorce and just needs something or someone to help fill in those empty hours."

"I understand empty hours," Peter replied, "Come next week I will have my hands full and Gloria I hope….." He turned at that time to see

Grace standing at the end of the hall. His face spread into a wide smile, "Ladies, here is my benefactor. Talk about a Good Samaritan. Sto…Umm, Grace, I would like for you to meet two of my therapy team."

"His favorites, of course," the one she recognized as Gloria, said, "Glad to meet you." She began to expound on Peter being a great patient. She glanced his way, "Of course, right now, he is pretty well beat as we try to finish up." She noticed Grace's eyes on her where her hand was laying on Peter's sleeve, perhaps a little too friendly."He mentions every trip how grateful he is to you for taking him in."

Reluctant to admit it, Grace realized the woman was doing a bit of sucking up on her behalf, while she could only think of one thing; these women came to her home twice a week to care for him. Resentment stung. She could throw them out, Peter too. As quickly as that thought came it was pushed back. Grace realized she had been a fool to think Peter Daniel's gave her any consideration. She had no rights, but she felt the stirring of resentment threatening to overtake her senses. What was wrong with her? She was behaving as a jealous shrew.

"I came home for the report I left."

"It's on the kitchen table." He gave Grace a benevolent smile as Gloria placed her hands on his shoulders and turned him away from her view. "Guess Gloria is ready to finish this task."

Grace felt the sting of dismissal to gather her papers and leave. She was neither needed nor wanted.

Back at the office, she busied herself with work but the image of the two women, familiar with Peter would not leave her mind. This was date night and she was hard pressed to look forward to seeing Devon Mallory again. Time to leave arrived with Billy waiting at the door. "Are you all right, Miss Grace?" She gave him a puzzled glance. "Uh, I mean, you seem a bit distant, is all…." Billy was quiet a moment. "I mean, you left, your cousin didn't die, did he?"

Stunned, Grace suddenly burst out laughing. "That bad, Billy?" She was amused but surprised to know her reaction to seeing Peter with the women had carried over into the work space enough Billy was suspecting bad news. "Oh, no, Billy. Remember, I went home for the invoices…" her voice drifted…"I just have things on my mind, I'm sorry if I concerned you."

"No, ma'am. Uh, yes, ma'am. I mean you've just looked sad and I thought the worst. I guess, your cousin has left now."

"Actually he is leaving either Sunday or this coming Monday, I'm not certain."

"That's good." Grace studied Billy's serious expression. She was beginning to understand the meaning of his mother's words that Billy cared for her. "I mean," he was saying, "you're used to being alone. That's good, I guess."

By now they were standing by her car. Billy opened the door. Grace rose up to peck a kiss on his cheek. "Billy, don't worry over me. Go find yourself a sweet young lady and have some fun. Surely there's things to do here, aren't there?" He waited, always the perfect gentleman as she got into her car.

"Not a lot," Billy mumbled. "Have a nice evening, Miss Grace." He watched her pull away from the curb and he felt a strange dismissal from her. "I don't think that's her cousin. I believe Miss Grace has found herself a man," he whispered and the feeling of being abandoned hovered over him like a dark cloud.

Grace entered the house expecting to find Peter in the kitchen as usual but he was nowhere in sight. Suspecting the therapy had worn him out and that he was taking a nap, she left her purse and keys on the table and went on down the hall feeling strangely exhausted, herself. She would bathe, put on make up to be ready and if there was time, put her feet up to rest a few minutes. The soak in the tub was exactly what she needed and the heady fragrance of the bath salts relaxed the previous thoughts of the afternoon. Maybe she could enjoy having dinner with Devon after all.

She wondered as she lay a simple off shoulder black dress on the chair, it's wispy material light to the touch if it was right for dinner in the town's best restaurant or too much and she remembered Peter saying, "I would take you dancing." Perhaps she should save that one... but the questioned surfaced, why should she? Simple pearl earrings and a drop pearl on a silver chain, were her only accessories but for the high heeled black suede pumps. No, she didn't think she could dance in those six inch wonders but dinner would be nice. With that, Grace sank on to the inviting leisure of the bed and was asleep in a matter of seconds .The next sound she heard was a gentle knock on the door.

Coming awake, Grace slipped into the pink satin robe she kept hanging on the back of the door and opened to find Peter. He stepped back. "Grace, are you all right? Isn't this your date night?"

Catching her breath, she glanced at the clock. "I have thirty minutes."

"Ah, yes, but I didn't hear you moving around and I was afraid you might have gone to sleep," his eyes were troubled, taking in the robe, her make up already applied. "I guess you are almost ready?"

"Yes, thank you." Her voice was whispery and she had that same distinct feeling again. Peter Daniels wanted to kiss her and she….well, she had a question in her mind concerning the women that day, Gloria in particular. She stepped out into the hall. "Peter…." Her voice trailed away. She couldn't voice it, she stood there…trying but couldn't ask.

He leaned forward, as he had at the showing of the house he had chosen to be his future office, unknownst to Stormy, and he kissed her. Gentle and searching at first but as she responded his arms came around her and Stormy's arms were on his shoulder, one resting around his neck as he pulled her close in the most natural embrace either had ever known.

"Oh, Stormy," Peter whispered, "How am ever going to leave you? And yet, I must." At that moment the phone rang. Reluctantly Grace pulled back, to step away and answer the phone. She barely said hello, when the voice began.

"Peter, this is Gloria. If it is all right with you, I'll take you up on that offer. I would love to help you. Just call me back, please."

Stormy handed the phone over to him and turned toward the bedroom. She had a date to go to but the question was in her mind, why had he given his therapy team her phone number when he had a phone of his own?

Devon Malloy arrived, his emotions in full swing, troubled, elated and nervous. She was in his thoughts, beautiful with that auburn hair and translucent skin. Her weariness from the night she took in the patient and her patience with a whining man stayed with him. He waited in the car he had polished to a shine, until three minutes necessary to walk to the door and ring the bell. He would be prompt. She would be ready, waiting breathlessly in the foyer for him, her eyes shining with expectation, her lips moist and ready to kiss. Lord, help them all, those were the words O'Mally had spouted, teasing him. "You never date, Malloy, what makes this one different that you broke your code and you're takin' her out?" Devon wished he knew. Something deep inside responded to this woman.

He spent an occasional hour or two with lady friends from the station. He had dated the divorced classmates through the years but no one replaced the memory he held forever in his mind, soul and conscience of one he would always search for but never know. In the silence of his heart and soul, memory led him down the path to wonder if things had been different could she care, would she have forgiven him for something he would not have done except at that time of young and inexperienced he thought both their lives depended on what he had done.

"Shake it loose, Malloy," he said out loud, opening the car door, reaching for the small clump of roses. He was ready to walk the path, knock on her door and change that dismal memory to one of brightness and hope. He rang the door bell. She answered, looking stunning in a wisp of a dress. "Hello, Grace." He hand her the flowers. "You look lovely."

"Thank you, Devon." She smiled as he gave her the roses. "Come in and sit a minute while I put these in water, or better still, follow me through." He followed, noting the cleanliness and order of the home. Even then he was wondering had the patient left? From a top shelf of the cabinet she took a clear round container, going to the sink to run water and bring back to sit on the table. He had removed the cellophane wrap. Deftly she sank the bouquet into the water and stood back to admire their beauty. "Oh, they are nice and smell heavenly, don't they?" She touched his hand. "Thank you, I've not had roses or any flower, in years."

Surprised, he said, "But you should. I'm happy you like them." It had seemed the thing to do. She deserved flowers. "Shall we go?" She led him back through the room that lay between, a formal dining room with the table set in front of the window, a piano on one wall and a huge formal painting of an older man and woman he suspected her parents. "Your parents?" He wanted to ask, but they appeared so formidable, so unlike her, he kept quiet.

"I have reservations at Dalton's," he said, as he waited to close the door and she was getting in the car. "Is that all right?"

She smiled. "Why wouldn't it be, Haven's number one."

"You know it?"

"I have a friend works there on weekends. It will be a treat. I've never been there."

"They have dancing." He hurried around to the driver's side. "Do you dance?"

"My people dance," she replied, thinking of her parents love for music and dancing. "But I've not really had opportunity to dance these last years."

"Your…friend…doesn't dance? The one with bad feet." He shrugged. "I don't know how to explain him."

Grace chuckled, "Neither do I. Of course right now he can't dance but yes, he does dance."

"Will he live with you after his feet or leg….whatever the problem heals?"

"No, he leaves this coming Monday and then life resumes order. My existence is rather mundane."

"You own the Pharmacy down town?"

"My husband owned it. I'm afraid I came into it by way of marrying him. Did you know Reed?"

"No, I didn't. I Iive on the other side of town and even as a kid we didn't come over here to the more influential side." He glanced her way, "I don't mean that hateful, just that we recognized the difference of the have's and the have nots."

"I understand. My family were modern day gypsies, truly." She turned in her seat to watch his expression. "My mother worked for Reed's first wife. That's how we became acquainted and then she became ill and in time Reed ask me to marry him." She did not elaborate on the private areas of her history. It was not necessary.

"I never met the man. Perhaps I was in training and delegated to a different area of the city. I'm only on this side of town when something happens or in my case I'm trying to help out a friend whose wife is very ill and he needs to spend time with her, so several of us signed up to help him during our time off and he keeps the benefits."

"That is so nice. I'm happy to know who you are deep down." She turned to study Devon. "Are you divorced?"

"At my age? Right." He grinned. "No, I've never married, not even come close to my Mother's dismay."

"You are an only child?"

The grin widened. "Not hardly. My mother has five boys. The teasing in my direction is ridiculous. You know, they call me monk, Father Devon, the spinster. You get my drift?"

"I believe I do," she replied. "Is there a reason…you signed off on women, obviously you don't hate women. Here you are dressed to the nines, a pure gentleman presenting a bouquet of flowers. Who does that, anymore? A real gentleman. Thank you."

He wanted to tell her the real reason but that would ruin their evening together. "Time will take care of everything," he said. "I guess I've not met the one for me. My brothers tell me I'll feel fire in my soul when I do, electricity, one said. I feel foolish telling you their expressions….but where there's four more males you hear everything."

"I bet you do." She sighed. "I was an only child, as far as I know and if there were others my parents were up in years and I'm sure that was a surprise."

"Your parents live in another state?"

"I was fifteen years old when my parents left me with the Colton's." She saw him make the connection. "Yes, you are guessing correctly. "Mrs. Colton convinced my parents it would be better if I stayed behind. She would be my benefactor….and …" She glanced out to the passing landscape, not one to associate intimately with others she had not told her story and as the years passed few would remember when she came to live at the Colton's.

"I sense a bit of sadness in your history with the Colton's. Were they kind to you?"

"Kind?" She studied the design on the small clutch purse she was carrying. "I don't think I could classify their reaction to me. Mrs. Colton was ill and needed a house keeper. She was very strong willed and demanding, not mean, just cool and impersonal. Her husband merely existed around me while she was alive, probably not speaking ten words all that time until she died. He was a man floundering; he loved her that much but he didn't want to be alone. It seems she had told him he must marry me when she was gone. She was that kind of woman; who made all the plans and he never questioned."

"It was a marriage without love but respect, I hope?"

"Yes," she sighed, "Few people know my story and I wonder why I have told you."

"Seems I have that effect on people," he admitted. "Don't get me wrong in the way I say that, it's just that other people sense I've had a few troubled spots in my life."

"But you are a Policeman, what could you have done that would tarnish your name or draw others to you?"

He laughed. "I ask myself the same question." The grin faded as he said, "I wasn't always this age nor a policeman." She was waiting for more of an explanation. "My problem happened when I was a teenager. Therein lies the most precarious years, don't you think? When we hover between being an adult and leaving our youth?"

"That was certainly true for me," She agreed. "So did you help any needy citizens today, you know weak dames accompanying a guy with both feet in molded boots?"

"Molded boots?" His laughter sounded pure and joyful. "That's a good expression, I never thought of it that way.

She told him the long story, starting from leaving church to her attempt to drop him off at a nearby hotel but it was the wrong weekend. "what are you supposed to do? I know he was a stranger but I figured I could outrun him and since he couldn't stand without assistance…surely he was harmless but I won't ever do it again."

"He's that bad?" Devon caught her amused expression. "Sounds like you've received a surprise out of your visitor."

"You might say that." A smile hovered around her features as she thought about Peter. "I've actually not taken time to access the man. I'd say he is high energy and very unused to being tied down or shall we say handicapped. He is running his business from my home by his computer and actually did my laundry which embarrassed me and I've not had to do an ounce of housework since he's been there…" She sighed. "Yes, Peter Daniel's is a surprising man."

"Hey, I know how to do laundry and dishes but I'm not that great at housework which I say comes from being one of five boys and our Mom didn't like the way we did it. You know, using the leaf blower to sweep the floors was good enough for us but she said it sent dust flying everywhere then we had to dust the fan blades, wipe off the top of the frig. The tasks that episode created went on and on. In one day the five of us had that house shining clean."

"You're funny. I bet you have a wonderful mother."

"Yes, she is. She still puts up with me." He saw her expression, raised eyebrows. "Yeah, I live in the garage apartment over my parent's home. I don't have to check in or out, I'm too old for that but the parent's are aging and I'm there to help if they need anything and my brothers all have families of their own."

"Are you the only one in law enforcement?"

"No, two others, Sammy and Eric. Eric is younger than me and Sammy is son number one. Dad was a Policeman."

"You were born to it." She smiled. "Your family sounds nice and I'd say you are exceptional."

He was making the turn in to Dalton's. "See that sign?" He pointed up to a small blue lettered sign that said, Dancing Tonight. Let's have a nice dinner and see how good we are on the floor."

"I'm really out of practice," she replied.

"I've heard it's like riding a bicycle. You never forget." He went around opened the door and tucked he hand under his arm. "Who cares if you can dance, as beautiful as you are tonight no one's going to be watching your feet."

"Thank you, I feel better all ready, it's when I step all over your toes you'll begin to get the picture."

They were shown to their table and given a menu. "What would you like to order?"

"I'm not sure. What are you having?"

"I think the Prime Rib, now that my stomach has settled and since I haven't eaten all day."

"Oh, you didn't feel well and still you kept our date?" She tilt her head to one side studying him. "You could have canceled."

"That wouldn't have helped. I was nervous or anticipating our date, to be perfectly honest." He grinned. "I was thinking you might cancel and somehow the only person I told let it slip to my brothers and if they found out the date was canceled I would never hear the last of it."

She was puzzled. "Who did you tell?"

"My Mother." He rolled his eyes. "She never lets me down but in this instance, mercy the bets my brothers placed."

"Oh, my," She tapped his hand. "Then have your steak and later we will snap a picture to prove our date." She picked up the menu again. "What if I have the petite sirloin and Caesars salad?"

"No baked potato?" He questioned. She shook her head. "It feeds your brain, you know." They laughed together.

"You have joyful laughter," she remarked. "I like it."

"Doesn't cast boy laugh?" Devon couldn't help asking. "He was kind of out of it in pain, last I saw him."

"He does laugh and he jokes and he hums. When he heard I was going out with you, he said if it were him he would take me dancing. That was a bit humorous, considering he can hardly walk a straight line with those cast on his feet, but he is in therapy." Her words drift away as she remembered the incident in the hall.

Their order was taken and then picked up their conversation. "I sense there's more to this therapy bit?" He was filled with curiosity at the change in her voice.

"They say he is progressing, I don't know if he is or not. They come three times a week and one of the girls is struck on him."

"How's that, I need to know in case it ever happens to me. How can you tell?"

"She can't keep her hands off of him."

"Lucky guy. I feel better about him all ready." Devon grinned. "Usually I'm trying to get someone in the Police car and they are fighting me off."

"Is it difficult, the training to become a Police Officer?"

"Not if you are really interested and committed and your past history is clean."

"So you always knew you were going to be in law enforcement?"

She saw him pause, seemingly to look into his past before he spoke. "I always hoped to follow in Dad's footsteps, but something happened when

I was a teenager, something beyond my control that I worried I wouldn't make it. It was just a teenager's digression caused by a few uncaring rowdies and I thought my hopes were shattered. Have you ever experienced something you thought possible to have it snatched right out of your hands?"

"Have you heard of the Banes Boyz," she asked. When he didn't reply, she took the strange expression on his face to mean he hadn't. "Bonnie Bruce was the leader," she continued, "and he made our lives miserable, so yes, I do know about broken dreams and my parents leaving and never returning was disappointment to a young girl."

"Well, we must be tough," he said, rising. There was a new investigation on the Banes Boyz in connection to Haven on the Bend's missing persons. Possibly three women were on record, but he wasn't allowed to speak of the case, at all. "How about we put the past behind us and make a happy future with a spin around the floor until they bring our dinner?"

She gave an embarrassed laugh, as he took her hand, "you may have been dancing all these years but I assure you, Reed Weather's never danced, therefore neither did I past my teenage days." Her laughter was sweet as she remembered, "But my parents helped create the steps…so we shall see."

He led her to the side of the establishment where the five piece ensemble was playing and other couples were dancing. "Your parents loved dancing?"

"They did, she agreed moving into his arms in a modern two step. He was smooth and easy to follow. After three dances they returned to the table as the maitre'd was sitting their plates. He was a perfect gentleman pulling out her chair and then seated across from her waiting…"Oh," she smiled, "it was fun. I had no idea I could still dance."

"I thought we were magnificent together." His smile flashed across those white teeth and she thought him handsome. "You are beautiful, Grace and light as a feather in my arms. I could get used to that."

She smiled. "That's a nice compliment, Devon, but you should date a lot of girls before you say those words."

"At my age," he protested. "Truth is, I haven't wanted to date and then by chance I meet you and I'm drawn to you."

"Kindred spirits with stories to share, I guess," she said, softly, glad that she hadn't told him the facts of her life. They ate in comfortable silence, the ping of metal against glass, the music playing in the background and their being together felt blessed. To her dismay she yawned, trying to hide the fact behind her hand but he glanced at her amused.

"You had a long day?"

"I did and I have full schedule tomorrow. She forgot it was the weekend, remembering quickly but not correcting herself. "Please, forgive me that yawn. It just slipped out. I've enjoyed our evening together, but I believe it is time to take me home."

"Maybe we can do this again?" His expression was one of hope. "I'll call. Will you answer?"

"Of course I'll answer." She smiled as he tucked her hand in his.

They rode home listening to music. He walked her to the door, leaning to kiss her on the cheek and he was gone. She let herself in to a room of darkness, thinking she had left a light on. She had gone only a few steps when she heard Peter's voice. "Home safely, my Pet?" The lamp by the sofa came on but it was diffused as though someone had put a smaller bulb in and there sat Peter.

"Are you waiting up for me?"

"Not really. I was just envious that it wasn't me taking you to dinner and dancing. You did dance, didn't you?"

She was puzzled. "Yes, did you do your homework on Dalton's? Before you ask the next question, may I tell you, you are not my daddy."

Peter's laughter filled the room. "My next question was, did he kiss you and how was it?"

She bristled. "That is none of your business." But he had risen and with that look on his face he was coming toward her. Why, she wondered did he have a way of defusing any anger that flared within her when he wore that endearing expression that made her feel she was special to him?

"May I say, you look truly lovely tonight?" He was so close he was touching her hair, his finger tracing to the pearl earring as he stepped back just far enough to view her whole body. "Ah, Stormy, I am going to miss you. Stand right there." He walked to the old fashioned stereo that had belonged to the Weathers and pushed a button and as they waited for the music he took out his cell and snapped a picture of her. Music flowed through the room as Peter took her in his arms and sang, "you are lovely tonight…if I'm not mistaken you are heaven sent…you're the light that brightens my path, you are every breath that I take, you are lovely tonight…I thank my lucky stars that I found you, what we have found is no mistake..you' the sun and the moon, you are my world..you are lovely tonight." The fact they were dancing in such harmony was almost startling until she realized why."You removed the casts." She pulled away to see the expression on his face. "Should you have?"

"They were going to remove them on Monday as I was on my way out of town. "What's a couple of days? I wanted to dance with you." He suddenly became quite serious. "I have to do something to make you remember me. When I leave I'll be on the road for a month, maybe two, catching up and making contact with my people and then I'll return to the office we viewed together…and it is very important to me….I want to know you will not forget me."

She buried her face against his chest. "You would be hard to forget, " and for some reason the first day of their acquaintance flashed through her mind and a slow chuckle built until she found herself laughing uncontrollably. "It's nerves," she mumbled through the laughter that was slowly dissolving to make tears in her eyes. "You kissed me before I left to go on the date with Damon. I mean Devon. That confused me, so, I didn't know what I should do." She peered at him through the tears. "Was that to undermine whatever good might transpire…how to say this…our relationship getting off to a good start? I mean, why would you kiss me?"

"In my behalf," he said, "I believe you wanted to be kissed, you just seemed ready, was I wrong?"

"Yes," she sighed, "I mean, no. It was very pleasant. I'm sure a fleeting thought wondered what it would be like. It seemed right but I always remember you telling me what people might think your being here in my home and all those things come into play…and I'm confused further."

He led her to stand staring at the sofa. "Stormy, do you remember the night you slept there on the sofa and the next morning we ate breakfast together and you said you slept so good as if someone held you?" She was quiet, thinking. "I held you, but you had such an aversion to someone touching or reaching out to you, I kept quiet." The first songs had ended but the words to the third drew them together.

Whenever you need me, when you think your heart is breaking, when the world seems to keep on taking, your spirit, your will, the goodness that is you, think of me…call my name…hurry to me…feel no shame…for I am yours, you are mine, whenever you need me…

They danced, in perfect unison, their bodies blending as one, as their minds found solace in new found knowledge, could he love her, did she love him, where did the date with Devon fit in? Devon who was nice and comfortable to be with but did not make her tingle and aroused no emotion in her except kindness and cordiality. One wanted more than that, didn't' they? And most of all, considering her unstable introduction to marriage and no consummation, was it too soon for these deep feelings to surface?

As if he read her thoughts, Peter was saying, "Stormy, I don't want you to make any rash decisions, but I've fallen for you. You are much more experienced in the ways of love than me, if you don't feel what I feel," he sighed. "Then it is my loss. I just want you to know before I leave. I truly appreciate you, the woman I've come to know. Yes, it is a short time… but," he laughed here, "My mother always said I'd know when the right woman come along."

"But you don't know me. I am not experienced in the ways of love. How can you say that? Your mother sounds pure and good, she might not like me or think I'm good enough for you."

"You were married, Stormy. Isn't it better going through life with someone, especially someone who loves you?" He placed his hands on each side of her cheeks. "Why don't you come meet my Mother?"

She could stand it no longer. "I was married in name only. Don't you see?" Her voice rose in agitation. "I was not desirable enough for a man who had lost his wife to want me; Me, the person starving for affection who felt abandoned and worthless. Do you know me?" Her voice became sarcastic. "Do you know the longings of a child left behind, whose parents were so willing to leave her behind they didn't check out the character or integrity of the woman they left her with? Can you imagine years of listening to people tell you of her goodness when you knew there was cruelty directed toward you every day of your life and you had no recourse but to take it and do your best? You keep telling yourself this, too, shall pass, it cannot last forever. And there my guilt comes into play. After those thoughts the child in me grew into a woman with a child and through that child I saw

God's mercy. Maybe God used Arnel Weathers taking me into her home that I would live to bear my child and be a good mother to him, my son."

Pulling away, Stormy sank onto the sofa, leaning forward her arms propped on her knees, her face in her hands staring down at the floor. "Only God took my son, too," she said in a miserable voice, void of understanding. "A drunk driver ran over him leaving him to die on the side of the road and we found out where he was when someone noticed Joshua's bicycle stuck beneath the frame of that person's car. "Ohhh," she cried, the sound filling the room with anguish and suffering. Peter knelt beside her placing his arms around her. She tried to shrug free but he would not turn loose until finally worn and weary, still in his arms she grew quiet, her head on his shoulder. His shirt was wet from her tears and his head throbbed with her pain.

Rising from the cramped position he settled at an angle across the seat of the sofa, pulling her with him, thankful the same comforting afghan was on the arm of the sofa as he drew it over their bodies and the same ottoman placed near enough for his foot rest. She, dressed in her wispy black dress finally sank into sleep, snubbing like a broken hearted child while he realized he must leave without her come Monday morning; but he resolved as promised they would attend church together on Sunday.

Time passed the ticking of a clock in the nearby room the only sound and Stormy's ruffled breathing from crying. Finally summoning strength, he carried her to the bed to lay her fully dressed upon the pillow mercifully released from memory's hold if only for a while. Seeing a light blanket folded at the end of the bed he pulled it over her sleeping form, wishing he could lie down beside her and hold her but that was not to be. She was in no shape for misconceived notions,

Peter turned off the light and trudged quite sluggish down the hall to the room they called his. He stripped to slip into the old T that was once Stormy's older husband and then the cut-offs. What kind of man could pass up loving a woman as desirable as Stormy for a dead wife who had probably treated him miserably while she was alive? His mother's words came into his thoughts. "We can't help who we love, son. Let us pray the woman you fall for one day will be a woman any man would be proud to wear on his arm."

"Ah, Stormy," his silent thoughts cried out. "Why is life so complicated?" And he knew if she could, Stormy would right the wrongs of her past and be the joyful and trusting soul God intended her to be. "Stormy." He whispered her name, wondering how many nights he would lie in his bed thinking of her.

Sleep would not come now as he lay on the bed with its tan colored sheet, the curtains at the window reminding him they matched the comforter and while his mind was filled with more important things for some reason unknown to him he wondered why the room was decorated so noticeably different than the others? Here was a modern touch whereas the remaining rooms of the house spoke of the previous owners. Had they made her promise to leave them so? As he thought, the headache he had felt coming now pounded at his temples like a roofer's hammer.

He stumbled from the bed to the bathroom, searching behind the mirror in that cabinet for something to relieve the pain, finding nothing, in desperation he searched the shelves below, pulling away towels and washcloths to find a tissue wrapped box, thin, the size of a book resting almost hidden in the crevice between shelves. Could it possibly contain medication to ease the throbbing of his head?

Unsteady on his feet, Peter turned the tap for water in a small glass he took from the holder and carried it and the box back to the bedside. Unwrapping the piece of mystery he found a small book with a piece of lace tied around its middle. There was no title to reveal the contents. Why would it be stuck in such a private place? People only hid what they did not want others to see. Dare he? This room did not remind him of Stormy; it must have been shared by the Weathers. He sank onto the bed and untied the lace to open the book and began to read. He had seen her handwriting on the papers she left on the table. It was Stormy's.

Where are you God? Have you abandoned me as my mother and Da? I think I shall die in this cold place. Mrs. Weathers says I am not to write notes or keep any kind of record of my life here under her roof. She has removed the fine coverlet from the bed and tore the beautiful wispy curtains from the windows. I am allowed only the blinds, a rough set of sheets she said she purchased by mail order that I would not ruin those that felt like silk beneath my fingers which reminded me of the ruby red wrap my mother wore. Where is my Mother who loved me as a little girl, now that I am tarnished, raped as only evil allowed. The gift you gave to me to save for marriage was taken away, does my mother look on me with shame? For she has left me behind, with nothing to call my own and does Da know? Does he care this woman is mean; with a wish to strike me though she does not for fear I will run away? Then, who will keep her house, wash her clothes, iron and lay them out on Sunday as pious looking as she? The man does not look my way. It is as if I am unclean, something he tolerates on his property though he despises me and wishes me gone. It is she who frightens me most. How can I last? Will I live to see this baby? The food she leaves for me after I have cleaned her kitchen sickens my stomach, why can I not have the same food I prepare for them? In the sin that happened to me, are you blaming me, when I had no say? I did not expect this terrible thing that has happened leaving me to myself, alone and forgotten, despised and pitied. I am alone. I want to die and if she finds me writing perhaps I will. Then I would be out of this misery that is filled with mean people who hate me and truly do not know me, nor do they want to know me. Where were you, God when they threw me in the room and that drugged boy raped me. Will he ever realize what he has done or is it some elusive dream suffered from the drugs for him? Does he know? Where are you? I miss you, Ma. I miss you Da. Please come back for me. I will take care of my baby. I will work hard.

Page after page Peter read on growing more miserable in his soul when he read about the birthing of her baby and then there was the mention of one named Angeline who showed her first kindness received in the Weather's home. The episode with the Bane Boyz angered him, his heart running cold as to their punishment and then he came to the growth of the child coinciding with the death of Arnel Weathers, the terror her husband brought to her life, his threats and hard treatment of her while he was falling under the spell of her baby boy. Did she have the heart to keep her son from one who was so mean to her? She had written and realization was she would not tolerate Joshua witness her being mistreated if indeed he was beginning to care for the child. When he thought he could endure no more he came to her loss, that innocent life taken by the side of the road and her child left to die alone, finding him with the breath of life already gone and having to accept the twisted heap of his bicycle beneath a rented car no one claimed she had questioned would Bonnie have come back to make good his threat from years past, was he now a warped adult that still spewed hatred toward others? Her questions often dipped into a smear upon the page and he realized she had been crying. A girl in her twenties with a dead child and a husband in name only who would not offer words of comfort nor offer himself for support but went instead to his room to be alone and wrestle with his own demons asking God to allow him to die while she must negotiate the expense of the funeral that would haunt her for years to come. Finally he closed the book laying it on his chest, gripping the edges, wondering about Bonnie's threat and the young man she thought drugged and threatened who was told he must use her body or he would be maimed for life and a laughing stock to the community where he lived. Peter could only imagine what the Boyz threatened to do to a young man in his prime. Had Mr. Weathers come upon her writing in the book and taken it from her and hid it? Peter could not think she would have forgotten the book and searched for it…but Mr. Weathers would not tarnish his wife's name no matter how much he cared for her child. Peter shook his head in despair, Stormy thought the book destroyed, some things would never be explained.

He lay there his heart twisted with pain, a mere semblance of the pain a young girl had known when no one was there to hear her cries, her fears or her sadness. No one had cared the unrest she must feel or the grief in her heart. He knew he must rest but he could not knowing there had been no one there to comfort Stormy. The trauma she experienced had been enough to make her doubt life its self and where she questioned God; it was God she found brought the only peace she was to know for she was bound by the secrecy of adults who cared only for each other and whose selfish act formed the evil she received. Finally, Peter rose up to sit on the side of the bed, needing to pray but he could not. The thoughts passed through his mind, returned, and were considered until he was worn and unsteady mind and body. Why could he not turn loose the thoughts?

Head in his hands fully aware now of the years of struggle she had kept to herself, letting no one in to share she had learned not to trust. How had she stood through the loss of her child and how had she been willing to love a man who could not see her goodness for the overpowering hold his dead wife had on his life? Peter felt sick at heart and nothing could assuage the truth. Stormy might never trust a man enough to turn loose of the past. She appeared as normal as anyone and if she was there was only one who had brought her through such trials. It was her right to question but it was with wonder he realized if she did not trust in the Heavenly Father she prayed to Stormy would never do lip service. She was a woman of great price, the pearl the Bible spoke of, the one who did her best in spite of life's beatings for as surely as Stormy walked through the troubles she had secretly written in her forgotten book her God walked beside her.

Now the question pounded in his head as steady as the hammering of the ache that kept him awake. Was he doing what God wanted him to do, helping the hospitals in their new venture, the bridge between patients to their doctor and doctor to facility? Or should he return to practice? How many more were out there like Stormy? Who were those adults who seemingly held their world together in spite of past hardships but brittle to the point one day they could snap and want only to sacrifice that life in view of a better one or take wrong road to end it? Many, unlike Stormy had not found solace in the one true God, instead pills and alcohol or depression had pulled them away and turned them into lonely shells that neither felt nor wanted to feel anything. The sad conclusion was that often families never knew a loved one needed their support until that final letter or fatal bullet. God, forgive me, he prayed, show me the way, I'm only one person but am I doing what you want.

She stirred during the night to realize she was fully clothed in her own bed and without a memory of going there. In the dark she slipped off the black dress and snuggled deeper into the covers but her dreams were coarse with luminous clouds and lightening slashing across the ground as she ran, not knowing the way and losing the path. It was relief when she felt a comforting hand on her and the warmth of a body on the bed next to her.

Peter heard her cry out, thinking the crying would stop but it continued until he could stand it no longer. Somewhere in her subconscious, he wondered, did she become the child again alone and forgotten or was it the indignity of being raped and no one cared when she was a young girl left to bear the shame alone? Or, had his presence in her life uprooted old memories and when he left she would settle into some degree of normal sleep. God forgive me if it's my fault. He asked, silently within himself, is it my fault? There were times he wished he had never studied the many faces of human nature. Wasn't that why he had made a change to his career?

He knew when she turned and moved away. He thought he felt her leave the bed and go into the bathroom but by now he had been awake all night and the weariness of wrestling with both problems, hers and his had worn him thin and the medication he found in the most obscure place of all, his own suitcase, had kicked in and he slept. He a master in Psychology should have known ever the subconscious remembers at the most in opt times and he became awake, his eyes snapping wide, startled that she might have found him in her bed and begin the rage of crying of the previous night all over again.

Allowing his eyes to come down from the ceiling which revealed nothing, walls of a room where there was nothing, he let them slide on to where she lay on the other side of the bed staring at him from her pillow. Staring as if he were a rock or an inept piece of nothing that neither affronted her nor brought anger to surface. She merely stared, her eyes clearly set on is face. "So you are real," she whispered. "You came when I was in such need, didn't you" My dreams were terrible and I could not escape. People from the past caught me and held me doing as they wished and I had no strength to ward them off." A lone tear dropped on the pillow. "I know I called out. I think to my Ma and Da but they did not come, only Mrs. Weathers gaping at me ready to pounce with those hard cold hands reaching out for me and I was running, the wind tearing at my hair as it began to rain great drops that splashed in the dirt making the soil rise in tiny little puffs. I could not run fast enough and then I felt your arms and I heard someone saying, "shush, shush," in the dark and I knew it was someone kind that was not going to take advantage of me and for one time only I was safe." She paused to moisten her lips. "I'm so dry," she whispered in that hoarse voice. "I think this is one of the longest nights I've known…other than when I was living that life."

"I did not mean to invade your privacy but your moaning and terrified crying awakened me and I could stand it no longer."

"It's all right," she whispered. "You have been very kind." She closed her eyes, momentarily. "No one has witnessed this. Is there any hope for me?" She sighed, glancing away as if studying the bedpost. Will I go mad and one day hurt myself? I have wondered will the day come that I cannot handle the dreams; my despair?"

"Why would you hurt yourself, why would you think the time will come? What has kept you going to this point?"

Grace shuddered, remembering. "There was a time it was very bad and then I found Jesus, the one good thing that came out of all the years of turmoil. The Weathers attended church and though they kept me hidden during my pregnancy for some reason it was their thought I must attend church but keep my mouth shut. Through it all in my childlike innocence I was searching for hope, needing something to cope with despair and the pastor said God's love covered me there with his hand?" A faint smile dawned on her face. "You know, like the song?"

"And covers me there with His hand." Peter hummed the song. "A wonderful Savior is Jesus my Lord, a wonderful Saviour is he. He hideth my soul in the cleft of the rock where rivers of pleasure I see. He hideth my soul in the cleft of the rock that shadows a dry thirsty land; He hideth my life in the depth of His love and covers me there with His hand…and He covers me there with His hand."

Stormy smiled. "Something like that," she said. "You have a nice voice. I hear you humming, occasionally. Do you realize you hum or sing a lot?"

"When I'm happy." His eyes met hers. "I'm happy right now in your husband's cut off sweats and old T shirt."

"Really?" She extended one arm from the covers. "Me, too. All I could find in the dark to put on was this and I wasn't even sure but it felt like the old granny gown I keep for times I'm cold. Yes, I was right. It's my granny gown." Her grin was filled with humor, for the first time the light came back into her eyes. His smile widened. "What?" She asked, "Don't you like my granny gown?"

"I love your granny gown."

"You are going to make some woman a very nice companion."

"Companion?" He raised up on one elbow. "I don't think I can settle for companion, for me it will be husband."

"That will make your mother happy."

"It will make me happy," he stated, settling back on the pillow. "If you have any forms to fill out, I will find a pen."

She yawned. "Strange, I ranted and raved at you last night, cried myself to sleep and I'm sure snubbed like a child."

"You did," he agreed, "but you didn't suck your thumb, but you were saying?"

"I seem to get a couple good hours of sleep when someone holds me." She paused, "And you don't seem angry."

"Oh?" His eyes turned serious, "I'm hung up on the first part, does that happen often, someone holds you?"

She swat at him. "You are the only one; I'm embarrassed I even said that." Pursing her mouth just so, she continued, "but it's true. Why is that? And why is it, we can lie here in a completely unorthodox manner in our strange clothing conversing and I feel so at ease with you? I feel you know my innermost secrets and I don't mind."

"You don't? Come over here, closer. I want to touch you," he saw the raised eyebrow, "not intimately," he said grinning, "Don't worry. I'm too tired for that. You slept but I had a headache." He motioned, "Come close."

"I'm sorry about your headache." She inched closer, facing him as he took her hand, his thumb rubbing across the top as she settled and then he reached to place the hair off her forehead, his hand upon her face softly touching and caressing her brow. "You are going to have to find a good man to hold you to help you replace those bad times with being held and loved. I want that, right here and now, Stormy Weathers." He turned her to look straight into his eyes. "I'm asking you to marry me for better or worse, for richer or poorer, to make me happy and I promise I'll do all I can to help you find that place in life."

She laughed. "You are kidding. I couldn't do that to you. Keep you up all night, using your studied skills as a," she paused. "What are you, a Psychiatrist or a Psychologist? What's the difference?"

"I was, I am a Psychiatrist. That's how I got this job, the go between patient and facility. I studied as a Medical doctor. Psychologists do not become medical doctors first; we do in order to treat or I should say understand the link between the physical and mental problems of our patient."

"You specialize in the link between the two," she was trying to find the difference, "the physical and mental? For instance, my brain waves compared to the damage the physical effects of my life have on my mentality. Right?"

"About that," he agreed.

"That's pretty deep. It would take a degree to understand about any one of us."

He nodded. "I'm learning more about that, every day."

"Being in my home should have been a great help in your quest for truth." Her eyes shined with mischief.

"We've had our moments," he grinned. "Yes, we have, from my falling and couldn't get up to your temper tantrums."

"Oh, ho, ho, ho," She rose up to tower over him. "I don't think you can get by with calling it a temper tantrum."

"For instance," he built his case, "the day you left the poor old cripple to fend for himself and get up the steps into the house."

She began to laugh. "Oh, that." She fell back onto the pillow, bringing his hand across her stomach, holding onto it. "I was unsettled. That was my first kiss, ever in my life. No big deal to you, but to me, unsettling."

"No big deal, huh?" he replied. "I was unsettled, as you call it. I'll have to remember that word. "Unsettled. Hmm." He leaned across looking into those eyes that went from mysterious to mischief in a flash of a moment or caught off guard could turn angry or upset. "Truly," he said, "the eyes are the window to the soul." He found himself longing to kiss her but what they had been through wasn't worth losing. Instead, he settled back onto his pillow. "You are truly a reflection of life, Stormy, beautiful beyond compare and yet an enigma of the unknown. I don't know what to expect from you, you whet my curiosity. I want to know more and yet you put the stops on me and I have to settle for the moment when I long to know if there's a future for us."

"You almost kissed me, didn't you?"

"How do you know?"

"I feel it." She smiled her expression both sad and expectant. "I don't mean to put the stops as you call it on you. I want to embrace all that you offer but with you here, I realize I'm pretty messed up inside except for knowing I am a sinner saved by Grace and it is He who brings me through these crazy moods. I can't believe we are lying here in bed together, no sin committed, when I thought you were the crazy stranger I brought into my home and had to be on constant guard against. So what's the bottom line on this Mr. Psychiatrist?"

They both rose up on one elbow staring hard at each other. "Are you serious?" She nodded, yes. "Here's the bottom line. I've fallen in love with you but you are a hard case. Still, the bottom line is this, Stormy, will you marry me, let me take you home to meet my mother and live happily ever after, so help us God?"

Tears immediately filled her eyes and ran down her face. She reached for his hand and pressed it to her cheek. "How I wish I could say yes. Yes, come and take me away from all this, but I have so much to shred out of my present life, things I have shared, some I can't and others that bog me down mentally and physically. Maybe if you won't give up too soon…I will but right now, no, not yet."

"Promise me one thing, if you begin to think of me on a daily basis, you will reconsider. Wherever I am, you will find me and we will go on from there. If you ever miss me, just send me one word. Yes."

She wiped the sadness away and tried to smile. "I will." Raising one corner of the sheet she dabbed at the corners of her eyes. "Where do we go from here?"

"I'm thinking this is a good day to start breakfast with Belgian waffles."

"And how do you make Belgian Waffle?"

"Oh, it is magic, a good bit of flour, sugar, an egg, bakikng powder, milk and butter. We have them all. I ordered. My mother adds yeast but we can do the same trick with the baking powder and I did see a waffle iron in the cabinet."

"So that's what I'm supposed to put in it? Hmmm. I think it has been used a total of one time and that was a flop."

"Some people like whipped crème on their waffle. I prefer plain ole maple syrup. How does that sound?"

"I'll make the bed and then join you." She was on her feet in an instant, pulling the covers.

"Let me help you and then we will go in to the kitchen together." She looked so endearing, "Stormy?" His eyes lingered on her face and she knew his thoughts. She came to him as he opened his arms to receive her.

"You want to kiss me. I see it in your eyes. So, kiss me, Peter, and let's see how I feel about your kiss."

It was a long kiss. She didn't pull away, but Peter thought it probably was not long enough to carry him through the weeks ahead. He finally had to ask as he held her, "Why would you allow this, now?"

She smiled. "Peter, if you have asked me to marry you, I need to know what there is about you that will make our marriage last."

"Based on a kiss?" He sounded amazed. "We are some kind of scientific study now?"

"Nope. I'm just an innocent to this game, but I need something for comparison should it ever happen elsewhere."

He groaned. "You are going to kill me. Just promise you will be careful and know who you are with."

"I promise," she replied.

His groaning doubled. "That does not comfort me, somehow." He started toward the kitchen, mumbling, "Unbelievable."

They were on their third cup of coffee and most of the waffle that covered the plates was gone. Whip crème mingled with the maple syrup and Stormy thought it delicious. "Have I died and gone to Heaven?" She asked.

He reached across with the tip of a finger to remove a dab of crème from the corner of her mouth. "Don't even think of it," he replied. "We have things to do. Today, the remainder of miy city tour and tomorrow we attend the church with the fantastic organ that is famous worldwide."

"We do?" She clapped her hands over her head, much as a fandango dancer might. "Today, then, we shall visit the only gypsy camp in the state of Missouri, right out there on the bank of the Black River which runs South from Northern Reynolds county through the Johnson Shut Ins with its perfectly boulder sized rocks that dam up and make it impossible to pass through those dangerous waters in a boat." She did a slight dip as her mother had taught. "But there are places where we can see the gypsy workings of the humans who lived there."

"You sound like a travel log," he quipped. "Should it ever happen that you see a pair of white tennis shoes while you are down at the bottom of those rocks, please do feel blessed to bring them to me or leave outside my room."

"First," she retorted. "Have you really been to the Shut-ins? And second, did you lose a pair of shoes? For real?"

"I did drive by on my way in. I had heard of them…" He grinned. "I did lose my shoes, by sitting them on a rock."

"You sure they weren't left at the hospital with your clothes? They've been there a week."

"No, a man remembers when he hobbles on rocks barefooted to the car. And Gloria brought my clothes."

"Oh," she drew out the word. "Gloria who has this thing for you?"

"Yeah, that one," he said smugly. "Seems she does. Does that bother you? Because if it does…then, that means you like me. If you are jealous," he put his index and thumb together, "even a little bit, you more than like me."

She gave him a hostile stare. "I felt invaded when she began to place her hands all over you. How did you feel?"

"Hmmm." He mused, his eyes closed. "You felt invaded and I wished it was you, but you don't want to hear that."

"You know what, Mr. Daniels?" Her eyes were pinpoints now. "I think you play with my mind and I don't like it."

"Well, Mrs. Weathers, that's where you are wrong." He leaned toward her. "I know what I want and you…well, you don't. So I'll be leaving day after tomorrow and you will have all the time in the world to figure it out. I won't be lodged in your brown checkered room, listening to you move about in yours while I pine away wondering what delectable foodstuff I can prepare next to entice you to sit down and spend a few minutes time with me."

"Food stuff?" She gave an incredulous snort. "You must be joking. But that's a man's way, isn't it? Food for the tummy."

"So what's a woman's way, Stormy? I've laid out plain and simple for you. I love you. What do you want?"

She suddenly felt trapped. "I honestly don't know. Are we fighting?" She sank back in the chair. "I'm honored you would ask me but I have led a sheltered life. Maybe, if you hadn't happened along I'd go right on thirty more years just existing but suddenly there's this world that has opened up and you and Devon…I'm confused," her voice trailed off.

"So it is Devon?" He whistled. "That is an answer. I would take back my proposal if I could…until you know, but I can't, so…let's just leave it this way. Let's get dressed, finish what we started…whatever that was." He glanced at the clock above the refrigerator. "We have a half day, tomorrow's church and then, as I said I'll be on my way."

"Are you angry with me?" Her eyes turned the violet hue mixed with worry and despair.

"No."

"But you are disappointed. I can tell, when you get short with me…I know you are disappointed."

"Yeah, I guess I am." He walked away, heading to his room. "I'll be ready in five, how about you?"

"Ten," she said realizing his sudden dismissal left her floundering. She created her own dilemma and then didn't know how to handle it. Something inside her ached to run after him but then what? The Weathers had engrained upon her she must accept less and if she didn't know what the future held, what could she offer him?

"Would you like for me to drive?"

"Why not?" She scoot into the passenger side seat and he took the wheel. She felt his coolness. "We are still friends, aren't we?"

"Absolutely," he tried to smile as though no words had been spoken or they had reached an impasse. "Now, which way do we go"

"Just head out of town North, and when get on the Interstate there's a large sgn on the right that says welcome to Akai?"

"What does that mean?"

She grinned. "It means you are here. They will look you over and say, he is bar valo, very rich."

"No, I'm not rich. Why would they say that?"

Her smile widened. "You look rich." She sighed. "These are my mother's people. My Daj's people, Daj's mother."

It was a place he would not have expected; the streets were narrow and all one way. "I take it if you enter the town, then you have to go the whole route in order to leave?" He glanced her way, "Am I right?"

"Yes, they planned it that way. In the early days they were accused of stealing and that didn't set well. So if anyone came looking, it was a momentary stall in the search as the person hunting one of the people had to use the only means of travel through their settlement." Her eyes met his, briefly, and then she looked away. "There," she pointed, "that may appear to be a saloon where the residents play or listen to the bosh."

"I'm sorry. I don't know what that is."

"Bosh,"she repeated, "fiddle. The people love music and most of them play. There's always a celebration."

"Are those stables and a buggy?" He was amazed, "It is as though we have gone back in time, your people still travel by buggy in today's world?"

She giggled. "No, they don't. Those are the times they are asked to entertain. Big business has found the people bring an aura of excitement and drama to their meetings and that's how many of the people make their living. Drive slow, now. Just ahead at the corner…see the house painted in different colors? Very well done, I might say. Gypsy does not settle for half best unless they have to. Now look to the back of the house there's an open front garage. What do you see?"

Peter whistled. "Wow. That cost a pretty penny. It's low slung and beautiful. A roadster like that cost somewhere around seventy grand. You mean the entertainment world pays that well?"

"Like any job you have to know where to go to pick up the work, how to apply yourself, and Jack Baxtalo knows."

"I take it the stigma of the gypsy curse has been lifted, the accusations of thievery, how'd that happn?"

"Mostly the family Baxtalo is responsible. If we are here in the right season there will be a huge tent erected where Jack teaches classes." She paused. "How can I explain this? In rope acrobatics, the person performs near the top of the tent, using ropes. It's dangerous but with practice and skill many have managed the act."

She did not tell him before being raped; she was one of Jack Baxtalo's most talented students. He was eyeing her with curiosity. "You do understand what I'm trying to explain about the performers and how they perform?"

"Yes, similar to Barnum and Bailey, under the big top?"

"Yes," she sighed, a longing had returned unbidden, making her melancholy. "If my own Daj had known there would be an opening to the art and skill of that day, perhaps they would not have left and especially not without me." Sadness crept into her voice. "Where my Daj went my Da followed." She tried to shrug it off. "That was a long time ago."

"Yes, fifteen years changes things. Maybe they will return." He had glanced her way and seen the lone tear make its way down her cheek. "And there, I suppose, is the tent but it appears closed with a sign by the door."

She read the words out loud. "Leave information and request. We will reply as soon as possible."

"The whole village seems closed."

"Oh, no," she replied. "They are there, behind closed doors and covered windows very aware we are here. There's always someone watching."

"You still have contact with these people although its been fifteen years and your parents have left?"

"Yes." She said, quietly. "These were my people though my parents traveled around. They needed a place to settle during the cold winter when nothing was happening. That winter, though, my mother had to seek additional employment and that is when I met Mrs. Weathers."

"They stay in touch with you? These people?"

For a moment the stigma of her own sadness lifted as a quaint smile dawned in her eyes. "When their gypsy ways fail and someone is ill they know me as the lady with the bujo."

"Bujo?"

"Yes, the medicine bag." She grinned. "I can get certain supplies they need. Perfectly legal, I might add."

"You are an interesting lady, Stormy." Peter peered her way. "You have the history of the town on the bluff down pat and you are recognized by the residents on the outer bank who were probably the first settler to this region."

She ignored the first part of his words. "Yes, I'm told they were among the first residents, but we all know the Indians were here first." They rode in silence until he turned on the Interstate. "I'm very sorry they were not active today. Usually the settlement is a riot of color as one person tries to outdo the other and it is very enjoyable."

"I did notice you wore color today. It is becoming. You should do that more."

"They do not like me to wear the usual black and browns and tan of my wardrobe. What a waste, they say. I try to please them, after all, they are my ancestors and possibly my only living relatives though times past."

"I love to see you in color."

"Old habits are hard to break," she replied. "Just ahead will be Markel's Diner on your left. My treat if you would like to have dinner early." Within a mile, Peter drove into the parking lot and followed her inside. "Our magical spell seems to be broken, doesn't it?" She opened the menu and studied the entrées. "It's my fault. I apologize."

"You win some, you lose some." He tried to grin but the hour of simple enjoyment had passed. It was time he folded his tent and left. Her mention of Devon Malloy had settled a question he held in his mind. If a woman was interested in you, they did not speak of another except to make you jealous and that was not Stormy's way.

They ate in silence while in the background soft music was playing and Peter caught the refrain as their eyes met. *It's a long time coming but sometimes you have to say goodbye. It's better to leave than to let her see you cry.*

"That's a sad song," she said, "Not exactly what I wanted to hear at the end of the day. It makes me weary."

"I know." It seemed they were both down in spirits, subdued to the point conversation was useless. "If it is all right with you, Stormy, we might as well return home. I will pack for leaving Monday but I'll see you in the morning for church."

The drive home was quiet, both lost in their own thoughts but as he was entering his room he paused hearing the phone ringing and waited for her to answer. "Hello, Devon." As if it were an omen, he closed the door, retrieved his battered suitcase and began packing everything except what he would wear on Sunday to church and his razor and toothbrush. For the first time, he turned on the television for noise to try to shut out the workings of his mind. "Authorities are still searching for the shop keeper on Divine, who has been missing three years and the then the college student."

Had he listened, he would have heard Stormy say, "Do you mind, Devon, if I turn down your nice invitation? I've had a full day and I'm quite weary." She listened to his questions. "No, I visited where my parents once lived, today, and it saddened me, that's all." But that was her own lame excuse; there was more to it and she knew it. Seeking solace she closed the door to her room and turned on the small television Reed installed in his last year. He could not love her but thinking to pacify her on occasion he might purchase an item she might use. She seldom used it but tonight she listened to the news commentator asking, "does evil live in Haven on the Bluff?" It always has she whispered. For a moment Bonnie Bruce flit through her mind. She had outlived those days but the stigma remained.

He heard her crying during the night, not as frightening as previously, and listening he decided for his own good he could not and should not go in to comfort her. The job or pleasure whichever one wanted to title it belonged to another.

Stormy awakened to find herself tangled in the bed covers, frightened from the dream of Bonnie and the Boyz chasing her. She was so shaken the thought occurred to her to go crawl in bed with Peter, but then she had rebuffed him that day, hadn't she? Soon, she would be only a bad taste in his mouth and all because she didn't know what to do. In her heart she thought he was the one but what if he wasn't? What if she hurt him further? Though she was undeserving, for some reason Peter cared for her. "Oh, the terrible tale we weave when first we practice to deceive," she whispered. "Did I deceive Peter or myself?" Tears fell onto her pillow. What had she done and what did she want to do?"

Their alarms sounded simultaneously, as though they had checked with each other to the hour. Neither went to the kitchen for breakfast. At fifteen minutes until ten they stepped out of their room, respectively an met in the hall. His was the first word, "Hi." A moment's pleasure registered on his face and she managed an embarrassed smile.

"Good morning." She managed, praying it was.

"You look fetching in your pink," he said. "I always heard the expression pretty in pink and now I know what it means. Do you mind if I snap a picture?"

She managed a wistful smile. "It would be better if it were both of us."

"You first," he said. "Back up by that window, yeah, that's good. I think the white lilies in that planter will make you shine."

"Now, you," she said when he finished. "I didn't know you had those duds with you."

"I actually had them sent here. But they didn't work with my troubles," He made the reference to her calling his feet in the cast trouble. He smiled as the camera flashed. "Now, step here by me. We'll take a selfie."

"I've never mastered that," she replied as his right arm pulled her close to his body. "Anyway, I like your suit." He did look handsome in the light gray suit and she was a bit smitten that the white shirt showed off his olive skin so perfectly.

"So you think the suit beats your husband's cut offs?" He was trying to keep it light. "They were fine if you had to roll me up the hill or push me down those steps but since I'm walking," he grimaced. "These are better, anyway, aren't they?"

"But your tie is not beneath your collar completely. May I?" Tucking it under, she then stepped around front to view her work. "You look like a well-scrubbed little boy," she said, searching for words and trying to ignore the strange feeling that had begun in her stomach and was working its way up into her chest. This was her last chance; she felt it, and hated she didn't know what to do, or did she? With no hesitation, she put her arms around his neck and placed her lips against his. "Forgive me, Peter," she whispered, "I don't know why I'm doing this." But he didn't seem to mind. Peter was kissing her, his mind in a whir and then he was stepping back and as matter of fact as if he said, did it rain last night, he asked, "Shall we go and are you driving or am I?"

She didn't answer. She was trying to assimilate the complete satisfaction she felt; wonderfully soothed and complete, perhaps a bit giddy, if that were possible, but how could the two mix?

"I'll drive," he said. "Don't want people thinking I'm less a man, letting a woman drive me to church." He grinned. "That was lame, wasn't it?" He wanted to tell her now, but the timing was off, the shop had called and would be delivering his car and he told them where to leave the key. Besides, his heart was denying the love he experienced when she kissed him; he suspected her kind intention to ease his loss.

He pat his shirt pocket beneath the suit coat where he had placed the cell. There, he thought, a picture of Stormy for the rainy days when I go on with life knowing she is here with her Devon…and still a small part of him had the sniggling wonder that she had kissed him? Typical Stormy, trying to figure out the years ahead while struggling with the past, what she had lost, he decided as he wondered if she would find the answer.

It was the typical Southern mix of hospitality he found in the church as the time of welcome came around. The regulars shook hands with the visitors and the pastor greeted them. "Do you know him," Peter ask her quietly. "He seems nice." He glanced up to the domed ceiling, "I could attend this church, if I lived here, I feel an atmosphere of holiness."

"I don't know him," she replied, "but I've seen him visiting the Pharmacy." Her eyes strayed to the front where the choir was opening hymnals. "Yes, I understand what you mean…I've been locked into Arnel's church and the people are good people. They've accepted me after all these years…but I have wanted to attend this church, forever. Thank you, for coming with me."

"Open your hymnal to page forty one, as we all join in a time of worship in song," the leader was saying as the organ pealed out the first chords.

Peter reached over to squeeze Stormy's hand. "This is what we came for, right?" Her smile was his reward. "Let's enjoy this time together, Stormy. It may be awhile before we can do this again."

She wanted to ask why suddenly it appeared there would be a change but she knew why. It was her fault. She tried to concentrate throughout the song service and then as the minister began his sermon.

"I know the plans I have for you," declares the Lord. "Plans to prosper you and not to harm you, plans to give you hope and a future." The pastor stared out into his congregation, "Now the New Living version of the New Testament says it like this; plans for good and not disaster. Have you thought about life being a disaster? Or have you realized the Lord wants you to prosper and live a life filled with hope where no harm comes to you. And, if by chance you or I mess up and do something foolish to harm ourselves he is there to walk beside us as we walk out of that bad place. Now, if you take nothing else home with you from today's message, please remember this, He is not the one who got you into the mess but He is the one will help you work your way out of it. Sometimes we have to take the bad with the good when we cause our own troubles." He left the podium and walked down the steps to be near the congregation. "Here is the punch line. God wants good for you and not bad. Turn to your neighbor and say, "God wants good for you and not bad.""

Stormy and Peter looked at each other and repeated the Pastor's words. Peter reached for her hand and held it. Small, soft, vulnerable, Stormy, he thought. I want to protect you to the ends of the earth, but its not what I want that matters. It is your decision.

She felt his strength. She felt comfort. And suddenly she wanted to throw herself onto the floor and sob until the emotions she was feeling drained out but all she could do was sit there in the presence of strangers while Peter held her hand and a lone tear trickled down her cheek. She had waited so long for love and now she didn't know what to do with the love she knew Peter felt for her. He deserved the best and she carried a of baggage from the past.

"I think the pastor is trying to tell us, drink from the glass half full, not half empty." He saw her puzzled expression. "You don't get it?" She shook her head. "Then let's just listen. You will."

"Jeremiah speaks to captives taken from their home in Jerusalem. The false prophets tell the people they will be back in their home country soon, but Jeremiah knows they were allowed by God to be taken into captivity because they had forgotten God and they were being punished. Maybe you feel at odds with the Lord, or perhaps you are in your own captivity. You say, I have to work this problem out all by myself. I got myself into it and I have to take responsibility and get myself out of it. You may even feel abandoned by God. Not so. God does not abandon his children. He hears your prayers and you know you have been praying…but the truth is, have you been listening."

"The children of Israel were in captivity in a foreign land. Perhaps you have been transplanted in life, things aren't going according to the original plan of your birth. Can you relate to these people? They were removed from the security of home to a pagan land where everything is different. What must they do? Through Jeremiah, his prophet, God sends his word. "Build homes, plant crops, raise your children. Take pleasure in life as though you are in your homeland, don't be thinking of escaping and cause yourself more trouble. But, you say, few of us have encountered such problems to want to escape, but I say to you in this room, someone has encountered similar problems. God has not abandoned you, nor had he abandoned his chosen people. He has set them down in a different land. True. Some were treated badly, such terrible actions laid upon them by others that we cannot mention them, but now God gives them hope."

"You have heard the song, God owns the cattle on a thousand hills? Not God owns a thousand cattle on the hill." The pastor smiled. "He owns the land we live and breathe on, just as he did theirs. His goodness and mercy follows them where ever they dwell, just as in our lives today. There may be times we are unsure of what we must do, we struggle when we should be praying the matter through. We may not know our own mind, but God certainly knows His. He can move mountains; he can move people to make his plans happen. What is the likelihood of God moving someone in to your life? Not much, you say, but God has no boundaries, there are no doors He cannot enter. That person you think you met by chance may be the orchestration of God."

"As we close today, ask the Lord to help you discern his plan for your life. If there is one here, today, who does not know our God, waste no time, receive Him as your Savior. Walk the aisle for recognition that you have made this decision first in your heart for the gift of salvation through Jesus Christ, His son and then allow His blessings to be added to your life. And the people said, May the reading of the word be magnified in your life and mine is our prayer."

Stormy and Peter listened as if on cue, the people recited those words with their pastor. "That was a pleasant experience," Peter whispered as they left the building. "I will attend this church on my rare stops here in Haven."

Stormy knew a moment's distress. "Why are you saying rare? You have taken an office here, a home."

"Life changes day to day, Stormy. What we think is solid one day is not the next." He tried to smile. He could not let her know his heart was breaking. He had to man up. Perhaps in another life he would find someone like Stormy. Grace, he corrected, he felt certain Devon would call her Grace but she would always be his Stormy. Devon would treat her with respect due a Grace and if he didn't…for a moment Peter's blood ran cold. What would he do? The pain of thinking otherwise brought sweat to his brow.

Stormy shuddered. How could he forget the words he said to her yesterday? Wasn't that what all the people in her life were about? Forgetting. Forgetting her? She thought Peter was different. She stared hard at him, or was it all her fault, again? She was sick of herself. She had been on a roller coaster ride of emotions since he landed in her home. She had to turn loose the torture and second guessing she had put herself through since the first day in the Weather's house. Fifteen years she had analyzed every thought, every action, fearful, resentful, saddened and confused. Fifteen years. She realized he was saying something, she caught the name, had she said something…

"Angeline?" She was puzzled. How could he know Angeline? "Did I mention her to you, Peter?"

He caught himself just in time. "Evidently. Didn't you tell me she was the only woman ever to sit with Joshua when he was a baby and that you usually sit with her in church? I was wondering about her." She was questioning him, her heart in her eyes at mention of Joshua. "Your son, Stormy?"

"Yes." She actually trembled. "Yes, Angeline was his sitter and still my friend. She probably went to our regular church and wonders what happened to me. I should have text her."

"I take it Angeline doesn't know about me being in your home?"

"No."

"Is it that you are ashamed of me or, no, you are afraid she will think the worst?"

"Angeline would never judge harshly. She pretty well makes her own impression of people and things. There was a time she might have judged your being there but Angeline is firm in her belief…" As usual when trying to make a decision, Stormy's words trailed off… "Would you like to meet Angeline? She's probably out of church by now."

"I would love to meet Angeline." He replied as she took the cell from her purse. "We could all have lunch together."

"Normally, we meet at Rochester's on Sunday. I'll give her a call." She selected the number and waited. "Angeline, are you at our regular place? Yeah, I know and I'm sorry I didn't call but I'll be there in a few and Angeline, there's someone with me." She smiled as she dropped the cell back in her purse. "She said she would be on her best manners also apply new lipstick."

Peter grinned. "I like her, already." For the first time that day, Stormy laughed.

Things picked up when they joined Angeline. It was immediately clear Angelina was smitten by Peter's good looks. He, on the other hand found her charming and definitely Stormy's friend. "Where have you been all my life, Gorgeous?" He asked Angeline.

Completely flattered, Angeline fluffed her new hairdo that not even Story had seen or been told about.

"You've been keeping things from me," Stormy accused. "I love it. You look ten years younger."

"And you are a great one to say someone has been keeping things to their self. Where did you get him?"

Peter laughed, enjoying the banter. "Let's order, Ladies, and we'll all get to know each other. She's quite a gal, isn't she, Angeline?"

As though Stormy was her own little girl, Angeline leaned over to kiss her on the cheek. "You have no idea. We've been through thick and thin, but this one, I went to church with her and after that first time my life has never been the same." Angeline began to laugh. "Remember how I looked, Grace?" Her laughter increased. "No one ever told me I needed to work on my appearance and then I go to church and there's this lady, Arnel's friend who must have thought I was the bag lady. Now, had Arnel not have told me about her…" Angeline paused, remembering. "Long story short, Arnel told me years ago the woman loved to take interest in certain types of women and apparently I was one of them, though when she approached me first I felt insulted and then I remembered Arnel saying, there wouldn't be much she could do for you, Angeline, but me I'd die for an offer of hers to go shopping together."

Stormy's smile widened as Angeline warmed to the story. "So, here I sit by Stormy and the woman must have remembered meeting me as Arnel's friend or maybe because of Grace. I don't know. But she calls me the next day after I was at church." Angeline gave a snort of laughter and reached across to clutch Peter's arm.

"She says, Angeline, I want to take you shopping. I notice about all I've ever seen you in are those uniforms, so let me help you." Angeline was fair rubbing her hands together. "I was shocked and embarrassed but I remembered Arnel and I thought if she wanted that honor then I better snap it up."

"So she takes me shopping, what a trip. Took me places that was actually nice to me because of Miss Rose and they showed me how to dress, not that I'm great at it, but I am better than I was and Grace don't have to be ashamed of being seen with me, do you honey?"

"I was never ashamed to be with you, Angeline," Stormy protested. "You stood with me through everything that happened and I love you. I'm happy to call you my friend."

"I know, honey, but you got to admit, Miss Rose taking me under her wing was a wonderful blessing."

Peter was taking it all in, watching the interactions of the two. "And that is what made church work for you, Angeline?"

"Oh, my heavens, no, it was learning about Jesus in a new way. Those folks reach out to me, a poor woman, honey. They didn't have to, but they did and our pastor came to visit me with Miss Rose and they prayed with me and next thing you know I've asked Jesus to come into my heart and life has been different ever since." She latched those snappy brown eyes on Peter and he saw she could look straight in to your soul and there would no lying. "Do you know Him?" She questioned. "Because if you don't there's nothing to stop us discussing it right now and we'll have you saved by the blood Jesus shed on the cross for our sins in just a matter of minutes. I know the scripture, don't I, Grace?" She looked to Stormy for backup and Stormy nodded.

Peter put his hands up as if to protect himself. "I am a believer, Angeline. My parents took me to church and saw to it that I met the Lord from the time I was a lad."

"How come you're not married?" Angeline asked next. "I'm assuming you would be wearing a wedding band otherwise and besides that, I see you look at our girl, here. There's none like our Grace. You will have to be a tall drink of water to meet my expectations for her, won't he, Honey?"

Embarrassed, Grace smiled and cast her eyes on something or someone across the room. "She loves me, what can I say?" Grace said, shrugging.

"Yes," Peter replied. I can see that and I understand why, you are both honest as day. You're a good fit."

"Why wouldn't I? It was Grace's influence that brought me to church in the first place. She's a loyal one." Tears rimmed Angeline's eyes. "If you pan out, young man, and my first impression is that you will, I expect nothing but the best for our girl."

"Angeline," Grace's voice was almost pleading. "Let's just have lunch while you access this poor man."

Peter found Angeline's loyalty admirable and Stormy's embarrassment disconcerting. He couldn't decide how she really felt. He thought he'd made up his mind that she was passing him over for the Policeman, but now, what he needed was time to figure it out. Stormy had pulled away as much as he was trying to. They were each building a wall to protect themselves against disappointment.

It was three o'clock when they arrived back at Stormy's home. The shop had delivered his car as promised and left the key inside the mailbox by the door. Reticient, she said, "I suppose I'll just take a nap and let you rest, Peter."

"Stormy, I see no reason to bother you further. My bags are packed. I believe I'll just head on down the road." He glanced toward the house phone. He'd seen the pad there to take notes, he supposed and going to it he jotted down an address. "My parent's address if you should have reason or need for it."

Caught off guard, Stormy felt herself pale. It was hard to swallow for a moment. "You are leaving?"

"Yes, I can be at my first appointment in the morning if I leave now, instead of driving all day tomorrow and meeting the company's people at end of day when we are all tired. I've found it better this way."

"Ah…I," she groped for words to cover her dismay. "I hope I haven't caused all this, Peter. I truly never meant to say anything to upset you."

"No, no, no," he tried to comfort her with an expression that portrayed a real need to leave. "It's business. Tomorrow's business in another town, further down the road," he said, matter of factly. He found his throat dry. It was hard leaving her. "I want to thank you again and reimburse you for all the trouble I've caused." She started to protest. "Stormy, I've enjoyed my time with you. Do you mind if I put my arms around you and hold you before I collect my suitcase?" He saw the slump of her shoulders, not certain if it meant defeat or mere submission to his request.

She walked into his arms. He pulled her close, burying his face in her hair, smelling the fragrance he hoped stayed in his memory forever. With her body pressed close he realized he'd never felt such an honest holistic need to hold a woman. She was the one, just as his mother promised, except she didn't know it and that made it unclear to him if she'd ever choose him. For a minute he rocked her gently; relieved when her arms went around his neck and he felt the moisture of her tears on his cheek.

She was crying softly. "Be safe, Stormy," he said, for lack of what he really wanted to say but hadn't he said it all ready? "Never love anyone with all your heart, that doesn't love you, Stormy. If you ever need me, call," his voice broke, "If you ever want to come to me, I'll be waiting." Tears stung his eyes. It was hard leaving her. "Stormy, if you change your mind and decide you would marry me," He hesitated, then said in a near whisper, "Just text me or email me one word…..yes."

She lift her face to peer into his eyes. Standing on tip toe she placed her lips against his. She was giving him all she could at this time. He knew and drank in the gift she offered while his heart swelled with love and his mind knew a thousand disappointments. It was he that finally drew back to place one chaste kiss on her lips, he would collect his suitcase and be gone quickly before he came unglued and shouted his undying love further humiliating himself knowing he could not face rejection again.

She heard the car drive away and with its fading sound a sadness crept into her heart. She was sick of herself. Perhaps he had offered her the moon and she settled for the black of night. A thousand stars could not dispel the shroud of darkness she felt in her soul. What had she done? Yes, she was sick of herself. Peter Daniels entry into her mundane life had been the most exciting days she had experienced and she let him slip away. He offered her a new world and she was so caught up in the past of fear and betrayal she couldn't see beyond the depth of despair she had lived through. What was wrong with her? She lay on the bed in a fetal position, no hope of seeing him again because she had failed him and herself. No man wanted a woman that didn't know her own heart nor admit to dreams of being normal like other people. She wasn't normal. She lived to herself because she didn't know how to live with another…but Peter had made her face the void…the void she was feeling now upon his leaving. She was too tired to cry, too upset to pray and too distressed to hope. God in heaven…she tried, but words wouldn't come.

The room grew dim, outside the streetlights came on and in her pew at the church where she normally sit on Sunday nights by Angeline, the seat was empty. Angeline glanced toward the door. Stormy wasn't coming. She thought of the dinner the three had enjoyed together, her, Stormy and Peter and vaguely remembered his slipping a piece of paper into her hand when Stormy was speaking with one of her employees from the Pharmacy. Glancing down, she searched her purse and found it, a phone number was printed in small perfect letters and beneath it his name. Why would he give his number to her?

Two weeks, three, Stormy did not hear from Peter. She had driven by the rented office space. There were never lights on, nor car parked in the drive. She supposed he would not be returning; he had changed his mind. She was at her lowest, sitting at her desk upstairs staring down at the employees busy with their own assigned tasks when Anna Jane knocked on the door. Anna was probably the one, after Billy, she relied on most, but Billy was withdrawn almost reserved with her these days.

"Miss Grace?" Anna seemed hesitant to enter though she had bid her to do so. "Miss Grace, may I speak with you a minute?" She twisted her hands together, obviously nervous.

"Have a seat, Anna." She leaned forward. The newspaper on the desk carried the day's story in blaring headlines. "Yes" Grace sighed, "Sadly another girl is missing. Are you upset about something, Anna?"

"That's awful." She pointed to the article. Her attention returned to why she had come up those stairs. Taking a deep breath she said, "Miss Grace, the employees are worried about you."

"Why's that, Anna?"

"Well, are you sick They, I mean we, well we all notice you've been really quiet the last two weeks. It started before that but now you stay up here in your office where you used to seem to like to mingle with us as we stocked the shelves…and well, Billy thinks you got problems since your cousin left. He didn't die, did he?" She was seriously concerned over her boss. "He says we didn't none of us think to ask you and what if he was buried and we hadn't even done anything…." Her words trailed off, "Billy's got problems, too, Miss Grace but he never talked to anyone except you. It's like he's above the rest of us. And Miss Grace why aren't you answering your home phone? Several have tried to call you."

Alarmed, Grace glanced down trying to see if Billy was on the floor.

"He's rearranging things in the backroom today, kind of like he doesn't want to face us."

"What's his problem, Anna?"

"I probably shouldn't say, but I'd guess it's a girl he fell for. He always liked her but then," Anna stopped the flow of words as if considering something. "It's not mine to say, Miss Grace. I know her and she was going steady, engaged even with this guy from college…but well, the grapevine gossip says he stepped out on her with her best friend, so she retaliated and took up with Billy. She didn't care for Billy but she was trying to make Dean, her fiancee' jealous and it worked, they got back together and she ditched Billy."

"This happened in three weeks time?" Grace was amazed she hadn't noticed the shop drift, normally they all knew what was happening with each other, but then she hadn't explained Peter Daniels, either. "Surely Billy wouldn't be that quickly attached to a girl, if that's what you are implying."

"Holly's beautiful and as I said she wanted to make Dean jealous. Ummm," she was reluctant to continue.

"You are thinking things got out of hand and Billy is the one to suffer?"

"Yes. Holly wouldn't give him another thought once her plan worked."

Grace sit back and studied Anna. "How old are you, Anna?"

"I will be twenty seven, this August."

"As I remember, you were engaged to be married…what, three years ago, and your fiancee' was killed while in training in North Carolina? You came into employment here just before everything went wrong."

"Yes, I did." Anna stared at the floor to keep Grace from seeing the tears in her eyes. "You were very kind to me, Miss Grace. I never knew why you seemed to care so much. I returned the beautiful gift you gave me because I hoped you would use it. It was so you, Miss Grace and after my loss I didn't feel deserving of it. Do you remember what it was?" Grace nodded.

"I remember it all clearly, your plans for the future were gone; you had already left to be with him and your wedding was to be the weekend he was killed. I know about destroyed dreams, Anna." Grace sighed. "You have heard the story. I married a man much older than me whose wife had died; he was floundering and when he asked me, I had nothing to lose. In my foolish youth I thought I could help him but Reed Weather's loved his dead wife to his own grave and he never loved me, though he loved my son."

"Did nothing good come from your sacrifice?" Anna asked, raising her head.

Grace gave her a weary smile. "He left this business to me, though that surprised me, maybe it was his way of atoning for the fact we had nothing together. I don't know."

"You loved him?"

"It was a strange love, Anna. More resembling the love one has for a grandfather, perhaps, though I wouldn't know that either, or perhaps respect and gratefulness to one who offers you a home." Her eyes held with Anna's. "What about you, have you found someone to love again?"

"No, it has taken this long to get over James Michael. I thought I never would but just lately I can remember him joking and smile, where I used to cry at any memory, maybe that's why I kind of understand what Billy's going through. Its disappointment and hurt, sadness and grief rolled into one and you have to learn to smile all over again and forgive people for thinking you are stronger than you are." She paused, remembering. "Miss Grace, did you ever use that beautiful gift you gave me?"

"No, it's still hanging on the door to my closet, too beautiful to discard but there's no promise of use."

"You are a very strong lady, Miss Grace. You've suffered loss and yet you kept a business going and," she smiled, "you keep us all going. Since losing James Michael, I've learned to handle the grief but I'm not sure I know yet how to handle life. I pray for strength to go forward...do you think I'll make it?"

"I believe you are strong, Anna." Grace sighed again as they sat there in their melancholy considering Billy. "But we got lost. Billy. How can we help him?"

"Everything takes time, Miss Grace. Maybe it will for Billy, too. You know that, but he's the one sent me up here to talk to you, not about him, of course. He'd die if he thought I told you, please," her eyes darkened with caring. "Don't let him know I told you."

"So you all are concerned for me?" Grace smiled. "That's very nice. I never would have thought it."

"Why, we love you, Miss Grace."

Grace considered Anna's words. "I believe you do, dear. I'll tell you something, you probably already know. Love has many faces." Anna nodded and returned the smile. "I tell you what, I'll see if I can get a feel of just how badly Billy was hurt." Anna rose to leave, her shoulders a bit more lifted. She did pause one last time before leaving to study the picture of the missing girl.

"Where do they go, Miss Grace?" There was a sadness claimed her expression. "There was another one, too. She worked at a shop near here." Then Anna Jane closed the door quietly and Grace listened to her footsteps going down the stairs. It was speculated through the years frustrated young girls left Haven on the Bluff in search of a better life to return years later having made their way back to the home of their youth which was not as stifling as thought. But there were also rumors that some were never found.

Coming back to the realities of her own life she questioned why she was failing in more areas of her life than she was aware of; Anna's genuine attempt on behalf of a friend was the best thing she had encountered that day. She made a silent vow to do better. Now, what about Billy? The question answered its self a short time later when her phone rang. She glanced down and saw Billy standing before his usual information station. They sometimes called it that because he felt it his duty to inform the public, especially those senior citizens who, as he said often, forgot to read the instructions. "Miss Grace, can you come down here?" It was Billy.

"I'll be right there." She hurried down the stairs as he turned to face her. She almost drew back in surprise. Billy's beautiful coifed hair had been spiked and he was wearing huge buttons that stretched each ear lobe beyond imagination and all she could think to say was, "Billy, you've changed."

"Are you just now noticing?" Insult or injury gleamed in his eyes and she wasn't certain which.

"I, ah, yes, as a matter of fact I am." She was sure he mumbled, "your loss my game," and then added…"Not that I expected you to." He turned to the case he was arranging. "Do you see this mess? Someone has put the eye drops in with the ear drops. Can't they read? We have a system unless someone changed it and the two don't go together." He glanced her way quickly, "I don't know what would happen if they put eye drops in their ears but ear drops in the eyes, that's a different story. Isn't it?"

"Yes, it is." She was hearing a clip in his voice, she had never heard before. "Billy, are you angry with me?"

"Not angry. Disappointed."

"Did I change my hair or something and you don't like it?" She spoke decently enough but she felt blustery. The old Stormy was rising up these days when she least expected her, and Grace seemed incapable of heading her off. "I mean," she paused. "Look, Billy, we are friends, come upstairs. Let's talk."

"I've been here every day and you didn't want to talk. Why now?"

She had already turned on her heel. Now, pulling rank, she stepped back, looked him in the face with a glint in her own eye and said, "Follow me, Billy." His footsteps echoed hers up the stairs. "Take a seat," she said closing the door after he passed through. "Let's get to the bottom of this. It's not the drops in the wrong place…what is it?" He sat there for what seemed an eternity, the tick of the clock the only noise. "All right," she finally said. "I can last just as long as you, even after the others go home."

"I've got a problem," he said. "And I can't talk to anyone about it… and maybe not even you, but we've always kind of touched on about any subject, although none's ever been as serious as this or maybe as embarrassing and I don't know what to do about it." She nodded. They sit another ten minutes in silence before he said, "I think I've got a girl pregnant. At least she says I have and my Mom is going to have a fit. She doesn't like the girl and I'm pretty sure the girl won't like her because my Mom's pretty straight laced and this girl isn't. Do you know what I mean?"

"Considering I've only been out of pocket some three weeks and that's about when we had our last talk that you didn't mention a thing about a girl in your life, yes, I think I know what you mean. She lives a different lifestyle than you've been brought up in. Does she have a name?"

Billy squirmed. "Not yet. Can you tell me what to do to be sure this girl's baby is mine, before my Mom finds out? If it is, there goes the rest of my college, my living at home and even my dreams for the future." He read something in her expression. Holding his hands up, he said, "Don't jump to conclusions and don't read the riot act to me; that will come later if my Mom finds out. The problem is, she's gone back to her old boyfriend. I was just a side trip to make him jealous…I don't think anyone knows, if they do…" He sighed, deeply. "If they do, I don't know what to say…" his voice trailed off. "I don't know anything it seems."

"Did you use protection?"

Billy's embarrassment was obvious; his face went three shades red. "Yes, but she says it must have been defective and maybe it was…how would I know?"

"Well," Grace sighed. "If she's pregnant and the test shows it's yours, I think you will know." She studied Billy as her mind made plans. "Bring her in to see me and we will set up an appointment to find out…but I question she could be sure of this in three-weeks-time; is it possible she was already pregnant when you two began seeing each other?"

"She says definitely not. But she won't come in here, Miss Grace. Never in a million years."

"Why did she return to the old boyfriend, Billy?" She watched as he slumped in the chair.

"She said we can't help who we love but that I'm still responsible for the baby in our lives."

"Do you love this girl, Billy?"

"I don't know, Miss Grace. Maybe I do, or if I can be completely honest with you," Billy seemed at a loss for words, until he finally said, "maybe I just liked making love with her." He stared hard at the floor. "I may have ruined a lot of lives. It makes me angry." He gave another sigh that sounded almost like a groan. "Mostly, I'm mad at myself for being a fool if she was just using me to make him mad."

Grace drove home with her mind in a spin. The concern she carried was not only for Billy but the girl who didn't have a name, other than the fact Anna called her Holly. She wondered how she was the one privy to such hallowed information. Wasn't there only one way to determine if the child was Billy's? If she wasn't mistaken that came after the baby was born through DNA testing. No one cared when she was raped, it was an age when things were hushed and covered up. Whether this young lady truly was pregnant was a more simple matter. But was this young lady as cold and calculating as Anna thought? Possibly she was as insecure and ignorant of the facts of life as Grace had been, yet Anna said not.

Checking her phone for messages she hoped to see Peter's name on the list but three weeks had passed. Sadly she realized she was now only a name he would associate with the time he wore casts. She had created a great void in her own life and if possible it was time to move on. She was supposed to be smarter and wiser than Billy and yet something was screaming through her conscience she was not.

Everything reminded her of Peter. She glanced at the kitchen table where he had created beautiful dishes of food they enjoyed together. He had invited her to meet his mother and she had declined. As early as the day remained, Grace wished to go to bed, go to sleep and forget everything. Depression wore a strange face and she recognized it. Why hadn't she known while he was in her home how much she would miss him and how easily she had come to rely on him all the while thinking she was fighting for her independence? She lay on the bed, thinking of Peter and Billy and what a mess life could become. She was so tired, she wasn't aware when she slipped into sleep. The ringing of the cell phone brought her from a troubled nap. Had she slept through one night in peace since Peter left? It was then Grace realized the house phone had no sound, the line was dead, no one could have called.

"Grace. Hi, it's Devon. I've just returned from a training gig in North Carolina. How are you?"

"Devon, I'm fine. It's good to hear from you."

"Have you eaten, Grace?" Devon's voice was filled with a satisfying reassurance that he was thinking of her. "If you haven't, why don't I drop by, pick you up and we could have a burger together, or something else, if you like."

"That would be great, Devon. I can be ready in twenty. I need to change into something casual and don't let me forget to take my phone. It's business. I'll explain why later. Tomorrow she would call about the house phone issue.

They were seated in the last quick stop new to Haven on the Bluff. "This is not bad," he said, "if you like hamburgers. I had about all the training camps cooks I could handle. A new guy every night tried their hand and I'm telling you, I don't believe any of them had experience, at least my name wasn't chosen."

"So you didn't have to cook?" She moved her glass as the waiter brought their order and placed it on red checkered mats before them. Devon was already diving in. She followed.

"Umm, umm. Umm." The smile on Devon's face shined with approval. "Either I'm starving are this is really good." He pushed an oversized plate of fries towards her. "They must have thought I wouldn't feed you. There's enough here for three people. Come on, you don't know what you are missing."

She had ordered a plain burger with lettuce and tomato, while Devon's was stacked high with everything one could add. "All right. I will." She tried one. "Oh, that is delicious. You'll be sorry you offered."

"I've missed you, Grace. I tried to call before I left to tell you I'd be out of town a couple weeks but I got that guy, your cousin. Did he tell you?"

Grace thought a minute. "He said some fellow called but he didn't get the name. I guess Peter didn't care who it was. He's gone, you know."

"How do you feel about that?" His voice carried concern as he stopped eating and waited for her reply.

She shrugged. "I have my home back to myself, about the only thing changed is I don't eat as regular."

They laughed together. "I'll see if we can remedy that," Devon replied. "How about we start Friday night?" She nodded approval. "I've thought many times about how well you fit in my arms when we danced."

She was a bit embarrassed. "I wasn't that great, Devon. You are a wonderful dancer and all I did was follow your lead."

"You made me very happy, Grace." He took a drink, placed the glass back on the table carefully and continued. "I'm glad he's gone, Grace. He may have been your cousin but I think Peter Davis or whatever his name was, had designs on you. I don't think he particularly liked me."

"Daniels," she corrected. "He didn't know you, Devon. Actually Peter Daniel's is not my cousin and I did find him to be a very nice man, but other than that he was an exceptional cook. It seems his parents own a posh restaurant in Springfield."

"Really, I could have chosen training in Springfield or North Carolina and I went where I thought the temperature would be warmest."

"And was it?"

He laughed. "No, they had a cold spell and rain. We trained in the rain."

"Any particular training, Devon?"

"Just catching up on the latest available and in the event of natural disasters how we could best serve." He folded the cloth napkin and pushed the basket the food was brought in to one side. "What do you think, let's take a drive down by the river and then home, I know we both have to work tomorrow."

"You are a very nice man, Devon, to think of me on your return home."

"I think of you all the time, Grace. Let me know if you ever return that favor." He was smiling but Grace heard the sincerity in his voice. Devon Malloy liked her and she didn't know if that was a good thing or not.

She liked the fact that Devon was not pushing her toward romance and she wondered that he had learned the art of not going too fast to soon, it must be his training, perhaps there was a bit of psychiatry to any career and with that thought Peter Daniel's came to mind. She had been listening to Devon but now her attention strayed. "Grace." He had parked the car facing the embankment and was waiting for an answer.

"I lost you for a moment." He opened the car door to get out and came around to open hers. "I used to fish here, until I was about sixteen but once I started driving and then got into training I didn't return. It looks like the spot has remained the same." He reached for her hand. "I'm glad you are wearing denims. Is it okay with you if we walk a little ways? I want to show you something…if it's still there." He took her hand to lead the way.

"Yeah, there it is, see that big old tree, it's huge now. I didn't know if it had lasted. Come on around to the back side. What do you see?" She peered intently at the tree, not knowing exactly what to look for? He laughed. "You can barely see it, step closer, now close your eyes and trust me, I'm going to give you one guess. Here, take one finger and let me help you. See? We are tracing an object. What is it?"

With her eyes closed, Grace let him lead her in tracing a shape, engrained in the tree but with a raised surface. Of course she wouldn't have seen it right off, but feeling it at the tip of her finger, skin against bark, and yet smooth on top with a curve that led to a point and back up. "It's a heart," she said, opening her eyes. "It is a heart." She leaned in closer. "Are those your initials? But there's none below." Remorse made her heart ache. "You lost your sweetheart?" He shook his head, no. "She didn't die? I feel so sad."

"No, Grace. I was young. I didn't have a girlfriend. I think I was kind of scared of that kind of commitment. All the other guys were doing silly things, carving their names on these old river bottom trees and they said, "Hey, Malloy, we don't see yours or your girls. What's going on. We heard the rumors." Devon glanced away. "One day they said, "Oh, Malloy, you don't know how to carve on a tree, do you? I was kind of disgusted with them and myself; so I come down here and…well…you can see…I managed the carving of the heart but the truth is I didn't have a girlfriend." He felt a sudden need to either shut up or come clean and he chose the first. "That's about it, Grace, I'm not that experienced in the ways of dating a girl, much less an elegant woman like yourself. I've never shown this to anyone before and right now for the life of me, I don't know why I'm showing you." He reached for her hand. "Come on, it's going to get dark and I know those old water snakes do crawl at night, so let's go back to higher ground."

"Wait. Devon, wait." She held steady to his hand but didn't advance, and forced him to meet her gaze. "I'm not elegant, Devon and our youth… mine anyway was a mixed up time, for some of us even tragic, but we lived through it and I think it gave us an understanding that time of life is crucial to how we are formed within our person to continue on this journey we call our life. I don't know how to say it, but a teenager's world is stepping from one world into another and it seemed to me it was an uneasy tethering time. So, if you experienced something along that line, I understand. We don't have to put it in words, we just know."

Devon pulled her in and hugged her. "Thank you, Grace. Well said. Most women would expect me to explain and sometimes explaining is almost impossible to do." She reached up to pat his cheek and pulled away to begin the climb up and then the descent down the embankment. Devon stood for a moment watching her. He wished he could tell her but the words never come at the right time and what would she think if he told her?

"It was nice, Devon. Thanks for the hamburger."

"Grace?" She turned to face him, her hand on the door knob. "Did you forget? I ask you out for Friday night."

"I almost feel I'm imposing, Devon, would you let me pay for dinner Friday night?"

"Grace, I like you. I'm asking as a man interested in a woman. Am I doing this all wrong?"

She smiled. "No, you are doing fine, Devon. Sometimes I'm unsure of what I should do. You know my husband was an older man. We did everything his way, or not at all."

"But we aren't…that situation, Grace. This is you and me. If we make mistakes along the way, we can correct them and keep going. Nothing is written in stone. Is it?" He gave her that endearing smile.

"Yes, we can go dancing Friday night, Devon, after I buy your dinner, how's that?" She opened the door as Devon smiled and turned toward his car. "Goodnight. Six thirty, Friday, Okay? Pick me up." She heard him whistling as he got in the vehicle. "What was he trying to tell me earlier," she wondered out loud. "Nothing could ever be as surprising as my story. Poor Devon, I don't think I can share that with him." Trust me, he had said, and she did. He was sweet to show her the tree with the heart. As good looking as Devon Malloy was, it was hard to believe he never had a girlfriend. What rumors was he remembering?

Standing in the shadow, too far away to recognize the couple, Bonnie heard only a low mumble of words. Maybe it was the weather, he wasn't certain, but he couldn't sleep and came here to pace and to unwind the nervousness brewing inside his head. He never knew what would bring it on…he only knew the one act he was capable of doing that eased the pain in his head though he went through stages of resistance. He could follow them, see where she lived. Did he want to do this?

She slept fitfully that night. At eleven she was up pacing the floor, at twelve trying to drown out all the day's thoughts and concentrate on something good and at one o'clock she took a Benadryl. Two thirty arrived and she gave up. She would clean house and tire herself out. The way she felt she wouldn't last an hour. By the time the clock struck four she had dust, run the vacumn; washed two loads of clothes and was still going strong. She should clean the guest room but her heart wasn't in it. She opened the door and saw the room was spotless, but there was a small note on the edge of the mirror. Area Code four one seven it read and an address. To whom would that number belong, perhaps his parents? She was tired. She shuffled back to the living room, sinking onto the sofa where she had slept well for the first time in months, to find it was because she had rested in his arms that night. She remembered him saying, "I'd have held you forever, Stormy, but my feet went to sleep and began to tingle." She longed to hear his voice. What had he said, "Call me, if you ever need me, Stormy. I'll be waiting." There was a house phone near her finger tips but it didn't work. Were they empty words or did he mean them? She wandered down the hall to her room, picking up her purse and placing it on the table by the door. This was her night to answer the emergency number the pharmacy allowed used after hours. Now she remembered telling Devon she would explain needing the phone with her but she hadn't. Maybe, he forgot, too.

She tried hard to put him out of her mind but phrases he said in their short length of time together battered her mind, made her smile until finally she felt her own tears sliding onto her chest where she had tucked her chin trying to black out the world and especially memories of Peter Daniels. Why did she miss him so much, she had enjoyed a nice dinner with Devon Malloy…but it wasn't the same. Not once had there been butterflies in her stomach or that feeling in her chest that she might explode if he didn't touch her.

"How am I ever going to leave you, Stormy?" His voice soft and gentle, from the past, whispered in her ear; but what if he didn't want to hear from her? He would have called if he did. How could she save face? Her eyes were in direct contact with the purse she dropped on the table by the door. He would not recognize that number. She dialed the area code from the note on the mirror and then the strange three two one and added one-two-three-four. Was she so far out in needing to hear Peter her common sense was failing? She waited.

"Peter Daniels," voice mail picked up. "I do want to hear from you, I am either busy or with a patient. Please give me fifteen minutes and if I haven't called you back, please call me again. Don't forget to leave your name and number. Thank you and let's make contact." Tears sprang to her eyes upon hearing his voice…but she didn't reply to the message. She pressed the cells button to disconnect.

The work days rolled from Monday until Friday and where she normally left the store in the young people's care with her trusty Pharmacist Gerald in charge, she now found herself joining them on Saturdays; Anything to escape the empty hours alone at home where everything reminded her of Peter. Devon was becoming accustomed to her joining him during the weekend for dinner and sometimes dancing. She knew he was using restraint sensing her need for time, although he seemed puzzled that she remained aloof and feigned off personal advance on his part.

It was a rainy Saturday, the day filled with customers seeking shelter, coming in to browse through Billy's section. She happened to be standing with him when a beautiful blonde blew in, her hair mused by the wind as she left closing of the door to the customer that was leaving.. Grace noticed her eyes were on Billy as she walked straight toward them. Long legs in tight fitting ankle pants, a shirt pulled to one side exposing her tanned stomach, Grace realized the girl knew every eye was on her and she enjoyed the attention.

"Billy, Hon," she stood on tip-toe planting a kiss on his cheek. "I haven't heard from you, and now that our little experiment has tested positive I thought perhaps you and I should meet up and make plans."

Embarrassed, Billy mumbled, "Miss Grace, this is Holly. Holly, my boss, Miss Grace Weathers."

Grace extended her hand but Holly ignored it, going for the kill Grace suspected, as she wrapped her arms around Billy's neck, leaning in for full body touch. "Really, darling, you don't have to be restrained with us getting married soon."

People around the couple were leaning in, interested in Billy's news and in the group of people was his mother's friend, Brenda, who stepped forward, patting Billy's arm. "Billy, dear, your mother did not tell me the news and we spoke on the phone yesterday." She smiled. "I'm happy for you."

Billy gave Grace a begging glance, as if to say, get me out of this, but Grace was at a loss for words. Instead she took Brenda's hand and led her away from the two. "Oh, Miss Brenda," she whispered. "I don't think you got the proposal. I didn't. I think maybe Billy hasn't told his parents, yet. Perhaps you and I could keep the secret until he does, what do you think?"

"What?" Surprised, Miss Brenda turned to peer at the two, by now the girl was wound around Billy. "He looks almost helpless so wrapped up in that girl. She is a beauty and our Billy, is well, he's just Billy."

Grace thought on that, later. Billy was just Billy, but she had grown to feel affection toward him. He had such expectations of graduating again, leaving college behind to find his place in the world. "It sure isn't here," he often said. "I want to get out of this one horse town. Why do you stay Miss Grace?"

She hadn't thought about leaving until now. In her secret world she had accepted so many things merely because life had happened that way, beat down at an early age and forced to accept what she must, first to exist with her baby by her side and then a loveless marriage to provide security for her son, why had she stayed? She stayed; assured they had a roof over their head if nothing more and the days turned into years of acceptance and a routine that filled the hours of those days but now where could she go?

Would she always be found doing what others expected of her, rather than what she desired and what did she want? Tonight would be the usual dinner with Devon and then what? She held him at arms bay, fearful she would bow to his wishes and not her own. Why?

Why, why, why? The word beat in her mind the remaining hours until closing. She must discipline herself not to fall to Devon's charm, for his sake as well as her own, by now she knew she did not love him. Her heart belonged to Peter and she had caged herself in, keyed the lock and didn't know how to get out. Peter. Her heart ached. I know now what I was afraid to face. Love hurts. People abandon you. They never look back but you are always searching for them. Peter, her mind whispered silently.

"Miss Grace, you need me to walk you to the car? Carry packages." Billy was peering intently at her. "Miss Grace?" She had been standing staring out the window a long time. "Miss Grace, are you worried about me?" She turned. It was time to come clean about what was bothering him. "Miss Grace?" He was hesitant. "It's hard to say this but I guess I'll marry Holly. Even if she's living with that other guy, now, she says she will move in with me."

"Why, Billy?" Grace felt her heart doing its usual thump toward sadness for another person caught in the same net she had suffered of doing right at the hands of others.

"She's carrying my baby and I have to do. Maybe she'll even come to love me. I know we will both love our baby." Swallowing hard, Billy continued, "And Miss Brenda is bound to call my mother."

"Yes, Billy, she is pregnant and no doubt your mother's friend will want confirmation but you do not have to tie yourself down to a woman that loves another man. Loving another man means she will take the baby which we truly have no proof yet that it is yours, and she will live with that man and raise the child. Holly has already established the fact she intends to turn each situation to her best interest."

Billy's face reddened. "It may be true, what you're saying, but I have decided we will give it a try."

"I hope it doesn't kill you, Billy. You're a good person and you care about others. I wish you well."

"You are really cautioning me to go slow, aren't you? Do you really care about me, Miss Grace?"

Grace raised up on tip-toe and kissed Billy's cheek. "Maybe like a second mother, Billy."

Billy ducked his head and mumbled, "Son's don't always please their mothers, do they, Miss Grace?"

The car parked down the street from her drive didn't remind Grace of any one on the block. She gave no further thought to it.

Inside the black sedan with dark windows, the man sat watching her enter her home by way of a key retrieved from beneath the flower pot to the right of the step. He was glad she had not lowered the garage door; it was hard enough watching her actions in the shadows. He could tell his presence had not alarmed her. Last week he had intended action. Did she realize the wire to her telephone had been cut?

So here was the woman his Holly felt would put stoppers on the fellow Holly claimed got her pregnant. The boy, Holly said was fair game and wanted to marry her with baby or without, didn't matter. He sighed; it was tough being a dad. Holly was hard to handle and now she'd got herself knocked up. At least the docile kid with aspirations to become a doctor would make a difference in his daughter's life. Holly was the only good thing to come from a marriage to that cheating whore that mothered her.

This one that he was watching seemed to be a lady. Grace Weathers. He let the name roll off the tip of his tongue. It seemed familiar, though for the life of him he couldn't imagine why, but then if she was causing Holly problems, whether imagined or real, he would deal with this Grace Weathers. He had come a ways from the tumultuous times of his youth but old habits remained and no one would take advantage of his daughter. Worse than bad habits was what happened to him as a youth. So he had made a mistake, the one who kicked him and knocked out his teeth made one too, but the other problem he held her to blame…that one took away his manhood. If he hadn't fathered Holly previous to that incident he would never have become daddy to any child. He blamed that one for it, the one what got away. Few knew his shame. Those who did never spoke it. He'd got that straight.

Bonnie owned a certain degree of fame. Truth was, it was not published with his name. He was the mystery they whispered, the one they hurried on the streets about. Because of him, in a small town, no one lingered near the dark corners. He did the community a service. They just didn't know it. Newspapers mentioned the unfortunate. He could handle their not using his name. But this issue was personal, whereas the others were society's blight, this one hit home. It was his child. Holly.

This Billy kid was a better choice for a husband than the other. Bonnie had checked them out. This one had a future because he had doting parents that wanted to see him get ahead, just as he had for Holly. The other one was a dope head always needing money for his habit and Holly needed to get as far away from him as possible. Maybe she had already been experimenting and if she had, now with a bun in the oven she'd have to overcome the need, he'd see to that and the other one, that boy he'd heard her talking with on the phone, he could hit the road and not look back.

He sat there watching the woman's house. Why did it all seem familiar? A police car pulled up in front; one of the locals went to the door and the woman came out. His heart did flip, adrenalin raced through his veins, memory slapped him in the face. Grace. Weathers didn't seem right. Grace Hendersen?

When he could breathe slow and easy again it all came back. They were the ones. Hidden in the fold of his best suit were pictures of the two from years past. How could they have found each other? Did they realize they had a connection? Why had he kept the pictures? Now the threat came back and suddenly his emotions changed to anger and resentment. Hadn't he told her life could never be so long but what he'd get even with her? She would pay. He hadn't meant to take her son down but the kid got in the way. Good thing he was in a rented car. Twice he had affected her life, what was one more?

That one that mothered Holly said he had a twisted mind. She had no idea. Good thing she wasn't around when him and the Boyz ran their experiments. Yeah, that's what they called them; you couldn't talk such things in public without a name to cover their acts. They'd chosen the policeman's son, to get even with him for always being on their tails, radar, they'd called that, too. Mr. Goody good policeman had raided their own homes enough, harassed their parents, "your boy is doing drugs, don't you care?" Yeah, he'd face up the old man and woman and no, they didn't care boozed out as they were on their own they didn't even know they had a boy. He was left to the streets days he chose not to go to school and a bed with dirty sheets of the night when he finally made it home. No, they didn't care.

This dame had everything. So she married the old man. They laughed about that, him and the Boyz. He was the only one left in this one horse town, now. They'd escaped while he stayed to take care of the old man and woman barely able to take care of themselves. The old man's lungs were rotten, according to the doctor and the old woman's kidneys were gone not to speak of her liver. She'd be gone soon. How'd he feel about that? They were just so much baggage but when they were gone he had nothing.

Except Holly. And that was what this was about. This one, this Grace needed to back off and leave the kids to themselves. Holly could straighten up, for all that wildness she'd put him through, one boy after another following her because she was a beauty. How did she get so messed up? Her mother said the apple didn't fall far from the tree. He glanced into the mirror. Yeah, he was still a handsome man. He turned heads as long as he kept his mouth shut. Holly's mother wasn't no beauty queen anymore but she was when he met her. Meth made a mess of a woman's skin, sores and stringiness not to mention those bugs she said she kept seeing when to the rest of the world there were no bugs, not his anyway.

This Grace; he needed to follow her a few days and see what she was about, but he'd have to avoid the policeman, maybe he'd learned a thing or two since his younger days when they'd slammed him in that motel room and told him do his thing if he ever wanted out. Her, she'd been easy prey, walking down the street like she owned it, screaming her head off when they hauled her into the car and the best part when old Sammy stuck the needle in her smooth skin. "It'll calm her down," he'd told Sammy, watching them scramble in the back seat, her trying to get out, Sammy trying to hold on to her. What a waste, all that fair skin and red hair. Hair the color of an autumn sky at sunset. Now wasn't he poetic?

Enticed, having run on to something he wasn't aware existed in his midst, something he began years ago, Bonnie showed up every morning that week, checking her daily habits, what was her routine, was she regular, could he make a plan with the boyz and know she would be there. He watched her go to work every day. This was his work. Watching her became the most tantalizing part of his life, as he began to see the evidence of a power greater than himself revealing her, when he'd thought she had moved on, left this one horse town for better things. Satisfaction coursed through his veins, the cards were in his favor. He was wrong thinking life had turned stale. He could thank Holly for this one.

If he wanted to pick her up after all these years, a reunion of sorts one might say, then he had to know exactly how to begin the process. Friday nights were out. On Friday's she spent time with the Policeman. He supposed they were a couple, but from what he'd witnessed from afar that wasn't really the case. She was a cool one, for all that red hair. He'd heard red heads were hot natured, quick tempered, but this one was made of stone as far as he could see.

"How's it going with lover boy?" He'd asked Holly thinking she'd say fine, instead she'd replied, "It's his boss. He shouldn't listen to her. We got this kid growing in my stomach and time is wasting. We need to be married and settled in when it gets here."

"I thought it was a little girl. Shouldn't you be calling her Angel or my little sweetheart, something a bit more personal than it?" he'd asked.

Holly watched him leave the house, and wondered where he was going; it was almost as though he had a job these days. She couldn't tell him the real man in her life forbade her to even speak of his own child since he felt he was giving her up to a no account college student that worked in a pharmacy for spending money. "Babe," he reminded her, "Daily I pick up more loose change from the vendor machines on the street than he makes in a week." It was true, he gave protection to the dealers and they gave him what he needed. If she wasn't so crazy head over heels in love with him, she'd run from this hick town, leave him and Billy behind…but she did have this kid to consider and it sure wasn't Billy's kid. The stories he told her about his mother made her want to throw up. Her own old lady left when she was ten, saying "I can't stand your father. I'll find myself another old man to take care my needs and you do the same."

"I'm ten, Ma," she'd replied. "Not much I can do at this age."

"But you're smart," her mother replied. "You've watched me and when it's time, you will know what to do. First things first, though, finish school and go to college if you can, learn all those little niceties we don't know about and then use them to make yourself a good life. If I don't see you again, remember I gave you good advice."

She was stuck between two worlds, the one she longed for and the other she lived in. For years she lived with her grandparents. It was Bonnie's mother took care of her, frail and sickly looking in her own way she was good to Holly. It hadn't been long after her dad returned her grandmother disappeared. Gone.

"Where is she?" She'd asked her dad. "People don't just leave without telling you."

"I wouldn't know about that," he replied. "Her and the old man left me a lot when I was a kid. You got the better end of the deal, the doctor told her she had to slow up on the drinking."

"Did you take her away?" Holly demanded. He'd given her that funny look and settled into his mother's chair like he owned it.

As for her mother, she had come back. They didn't count the years between. If Bonnie wanted to take care of her that was his business. Holly decided she was getting off this crazy band wagon.

Easing the car into motion Bonnie followed Grace to work. She parked across the street this morning. Out of the way for customers, he supposed, the employees didn't take up parking spots around the business. She was an attractive dame. How could she remain alone? Didn't she need companionship? He'd seen her with that old bag that wore the scrubs all the time and then that one was replaced with her sister he guessed, same framework but different haircut. Nah, couldn't be the same woman, no one changed that much. Maybe if his plan became active soon it would help Holly in some strange way.

Friday rolled around and Grace accepted the fact Devon would check in by mid evening to be sure they were having dinner together. Devon took nothing for granted where she was concerned. He was patient, kind and devoted; though she tried repeatedly to persuade him to date other women, he refused. Glancing out the upstairs window, from her office, she saw the car parked across the street. It resembled the one she saw each morning as she left for work and sometimes there when she arrived home. She wondered if the person lived in the neighborhood why were they parking on the street?

One thing the Weathers had done was choose a neighborhood that had not only held its own as the years progressed but their home had set the tone for others built through the years. Maintenance was a roof repair after wind damage and landscaping but the homes on the street held their own in value. She sighed; thankful she had not had to deal with many issues. She saw other neighborhoods failing, no one seeming to care about maintenance; one by one going down until the houses were removed and a new division begun.

As she observed the car, another pulled alongside the pharmacy curb; Billy's fiancée crossed the street to talk with the driver, leaning in to hug the man before she entered the building. Now Grace turned to the glassed wall that made the downstairs part of the building visible. She saw Holly make the usual dramatic entrance, wind herself around Billy and enjoy the attention of the customers due to the spectacle of devotion she showered on him. Suddenly it was as if Holly knew she was watching, an eye on the upper office, Holly gave Grace a strange smile and pulled Billy in for a second embrace.

Turning back to the window that looked onto the street Grace felt a shiver run through her body. Who was the man on the street and why would Holly find her an adversary? Had Billy told her that she encouraged him to have proper test to be certain the baby Holly carried was his and not the man's she lived with? Could ordinary people create such distrust when you didn't even know them? A Police car pulled up. The man shook his head violently, opening the door to crawl out and speak with the driver. Grace watched, mesmerized by the size of the man; there was something oddly familiar about him and yet she knew she had never encountered him in her life. Her cell rang and she answered. It was Devon. "I thought you might have gone home early so I you tried your house phone," he said. "I didn't hear it ring, you should check to see if it's working."

The feeling stayed with Grace as she drove home from work thankful no car was present on the street. Entering the garage she quickly pressed the button to lower the door and hurried inside. With an hour until Devon arrived she showered and dressed in a favorite turquoise dress trying to raise her own spirits and dispel the darkness the day's events had brought. Sitting in a wing back near the window she watched traffic move past, but was once more disturbed when the same car slowed as if studying her house. When it was well down the street she went to the front door, leaning out to be certain the sign conveying she was part of the neighborhood watch was still there and on second thought that the small logo saying she was member to the communities alarm system connected to the Police station was also in view. Both were small comfort when you realized you had no reason to feel your safety was compromised and no earthly way to prove it and yet the feeling thundered through your very being. On second thought she checked the house phone. Dead again. That meant with the phone out, the alarm system was compromised. She would call about repairs in the morning.

A mist of rain accompanied Devon to the door. Grace hurried to the car, an umbrella in her hand. "Let's take it inside," Devon suggested as they arrived at the restaurant. "You may need it." He glanced at the sky. "It's hard to say, whether this rain will leave or stay." Once seated, "Penny for your thoughts?" Devon reached across to take her hand. "You are really quiet tonight. Why?"

She glanced up, meeting his caring gaze. "I seem to have things on my mind. It's silly, I'm sure, but there's a car on the street and it slowed today as if studying my home. That's trivial isn't it, in your business?"

"Not really." He let his thumb slip across the smoothness of her hand. "Just this afternoon, there was a call came in about someone loitering, of all things near your store. A car parked nearly all day and no one seeming to bother to leave its confines. One of our men checked it out and the man was waiting for his daughter to come in from out of town and he had nothing to do except sit and wait for her."

"I think I may have witnessed either that situation or one close to it. Do you know if the man waiting became angry…a bit of screaming going on?"

Devon laughed. "That's probably the same one. Old Martin said the man chewed him out royally."

"I hope it wasn't my people called the cops on him."

"No, it was the Nail Shop. Seems the woman is foreign and she sees a lot of CSI and such type television and was certain the man intended to do something vicious, like kill her clients or raid the place." He grinned. "We men in blue can never measure up to our television heroes."

"I don't know how you stay with it. All the creepy people you have to deal with, why do you even want to?"

Devon's expression remained serious. "There was a time I was scared to death I wouldn't get to be a Policeman." He sighed, heavily. "My dad was, his brother, my older brother…and I couldn't explain it."

"Why, Devon?" She sensed his depth of commitment. "Why would you have had that concern? You were young, weren't you?"

"I've never told anyone. I was forced to do something…that if it were on my record would have prevented me going beyond signing my name on that sheet of paper that said I wanted to be in the force." He glanced across the room, but his mind was looking back to a young man thrown into a room and told you don't come out alive until you do exactly what you're told to do and you tell after, you are dead. "I broke the law, Grace, not just man's law but God's law. I was a kid. I never would have but I was made to do what I did and it has stayed with me all these years. If atonement meant giving my life, I would do it."

Grace felt his pain. Her own past flashed through her mind. "Devon, you are a fine person. Don't dwell on it." She sighed. "My life has not been easy." She closed her eyes. "But to discuss it…no one could possibly understand the misery. I would be told to be thankful for what I received and dismissed as an ungrateful human being." She shuddered, remembering. "No one cares, Devon. We have to go on the best we can and in the end we will be better for all we've encountered but at the time the pain is enough to kill us. We are loaded down with shame we didn't cause, memory we didn't create and wouldn't wish on our worst enemy and still we can never forget it, because it is with us night and day, year after year. We are still here and we have to put it behind us."

"I think we share the same agonies, Grace. I'm sorry." By now he was holding both her hands in his, staring into her eyes, taking in the sadness that lingered behind the smile she tried to shine on him. "Where do we go from here, Grace? You know I'm in love with you but I'm not sure you love me at all."

"That hurts, Devon. I love you as a friend and nothing would make me happier than to love you as the most important person in my life.

Sometimes, I think you are the most important…but what we have is not the kind of love you need. You are willing to give your all. Now. But down the road if I happened not to measure up…you would resent me and your love would turn to despair or worse."

"Never, Grace."

Tears welled up in her eyes. "I knew we were coming to this day, Devon. For your sake, I must tell you goodbye when we leave here tonight. It is only fair that you find someone to return the love you are so deserving of, and one who will give her heart to you without restraint."

"Is it the cast boy?" Devon's words were tinged with regret and resentment, much as he'd hoped otherwise. "I mean, if you don't love me and you…" His voice caught and he took a deep breath trying to hold himself together. "It's disappointing, Grace. I've tried so hard not to push you and all the while I've hoped…God how I've hoped and prayed, and maybe I even fooled myself into believing it could happen…" Pulling his hands away, Devon stared at the table. "I didn't know you were still in contact with him."

"I'm not." She rose up, laying the white napkin on the plate where they had yet to be served. She felt sadness in his way of thinking when he had no idea the void between her and Peter. "Please, Devon, take me home."

Aware of his disappointment Grace walked chin up and shoulders squared. It was the longest walk she remembered in a while but not her first. There had been many times when she hurt and was forced to walk alone; Times of anger and pain, questioning her own goodness but this was a time only of self-recrimination. She had let this go far too long.

The light mist of the afternoon had turned into a heavier downfall. Without hesitation, Devon removed his jacket and placed it around Grace's shoulders. The umbrella at the table was forgotten.

Once they were in the car, she said, "I'm sorry I've hurt you, Devon. That was never my intention. I have enjoyed our time together but our relationship will never progress beyond friendship."

"Perhaps you will feel differently in the morning," Devon suggested.

"No, I won't." When the car stopped she hopped out. "No need seeing me to the door, Devon. Good night." A crash of lightening made her hurry and as much as he wished to follow her, Devon did not.

Down the street headlights came on the car where Bonnie waited. "Uh, oh," he muttered. "Looks like trouble in paradise. I better not let the cop find me loitering again. Once was enough." He pulled away and drove the opposite direction. "Holly," he whispered, "This one's for you. Daddy's gonna fix it."

Saturday she awakened to the patter of rain on the windows. She should get dressed and go to work but she hadn't slept well, worrying over Devon. Next to Peter, she knew he was the best man she would ever know. Why couldn't she love him? She had walked the floor, struggled in and out of bed until the covers were a strangled mess on the floor and she finally slept curled up in a knot her head under a pillow. Now as she faced the day, her thoughts were only on Peter; remembering the troubled times when he had held her and those last days when he said, "Stormy, if you ever need me, just send me one word. Yes." They had eaten Belgium waffles after that and drank coffee in the most luxurious way, just the two of them… soaking up time together and she had not known how wonderful their time together until he was gone and she couldn't find him in the room down the hall, nor hear him humming or whistling in that off kilter way he owned

The phone rang and the answering machine picked up. "Stormy, this is Angeline, I am going out of town this weekend, leaving as soon as this weather settles and I won't be back until Tuesday next week. If you need to talk, call me."

Angeline wouldn't be there to sit with her in church. She sighed. Reaching down she pulled the sheet with the blanket wound around it from the floor, and settled into the warmth of the bed. It was two o'clock when she awakened. Leaving the blinds shut she wandered into the kitchen, found a mixing bowl and began collecting ingredients.

An hour later, she had finally conquered how to turn a waffle without it sticking to the grill, but it resembled a thick mound of gravy instead of the beautiful concoction she had imagined. Still she poured maple syrup over it and sat down to eat but the taste was terrible. Dumping the remains down the drain, she loaded the dishwasher for action, pressed the button and went to the refrigerator, opening the bottom drawer to take out a half used container of ice cream, she collected a spoon and returned to the bedroom.

"If you ever need me, send me a text or a message on the answering machine, one word, Stormy. Yes." Now she was adding words to Peter's sentence. Had he meant it? She found the pharmacy phone, checked recent calls when in reality it had been weeks since she found the number on the guest room mirror and still wasn't certain she should have called. She had heard him on voice mail but he had not returned the call. Why? She could only surmise. Peter Daniels was ready to take a wife, build a home and have a family. She had blown it. She missed her chance and there wouldn't be another. Obviously Peter Daniels had met someone as eager to get on with life as he. Holding the phone in her hand she alternately stared out the window, ate the ice cream and wondered did she dare try calling him again?

It was there right in front of her eyes, under recent. All she had to do was press the button, type in three letters and press send. Yes. A million times yes, she whispered and fell back onto the bed exhausted.

The rain had left the streets shining beneath the early morning hour when she awakened. The first thought was to skip church but what would she do with the hours of the day? She had spent Saturday to herself, bemoaning the state of her life, how could she go through the turmoil again today? By nine thirty she was dressed, heading out the driveway but not the direction of the church. She drove by the house Peter had rented for his satellite office and wondered that no one seemed ever to enter its domain.

The decision to attend the church she and Peter enjoyed that last day together was not part of her original plan but as she pulled into the drive it felt right. She found herself sitting alone on the back pew, until an elderly gentleman came in and sat down beside her. "If you're not saving this seat, I'll claim it," he said. They smiled. It wasn't until the first hymn was announced he spoke again. "Is this your home church, young lady?"

"No Sir. I attend somewhere else."

"That's too bad. They have a real perchance for wonderful singing here. I'm visiting my daughter." He explained with a gentle smile. "Normally she's with me but today she has a grandchild she's caring for while the mother works. Little Aaron's mother is a nurse and as you know they sometimes work Sunday schedules." He extended a hand. "I'm Johnson Clark, from Mississippi." Grace supplied her name. "I don't get up here as much as I like, but driving alone becomes bothersome at times. Still, I love this church. If I lived here I'd make myself a member." He sighed. "They sing the old hymns. Lot of church these days have forgotten them, but an old timer like me, well, the words comfort my soul."

"Oh, Lord my God, when I in awesome wonder, consider all the works thy hands have made." The organ pealed an introduction, the song leader asked everyone to stand and Grace listened to the gentleman beside her sing in an amazing voice for one as old as he. "How great thou art, How great thou art." Her own heart lifted as he offered the hymnal to her. "I know this," he whispered. "Sing, young lady. Sing." Grace sang, her heart bursting with the emotions stirring inside her mind, her heart pumping with hope that the God who formed the universe could possibly show her a way to make things right in her life.

Johnson Clark shook her hand upon leaving. "Thank you, young lady for sharing God's love with me today. It's always a boon to one's spirit to have a person stand beside them and share. My wife died two years ago and I can't seem to move beyond those times we stood together worshiping our Lord and maybe I'm not supposed to." He gripped her hand before turning loose, "We never wasted a minute, busy-busy doing what we could to further His kingdom. I'm glad I got to meet you. Did you say your name's Grace?" He pat her shoulder. "That's a fine name, Grace, and you wear it well. Thank you for today's blessing. Now you go through life and always remember if we trust him, our Lord can make everything right."

Grace thought on Mr. Clark's words as she drove home. Were they real or another idiom to add to those she heard and hung hope on such as God works in mysterious ways His wonders to perform. Her cell rang as she was turning into the drive.

It was Billy. "Miss Grace, I just received word Gerald fell off a ladder and is in the hospital."

"Our Gerald, the Pharmicist?" Stunned, Grace tried to absorb the news. "He hasn't called me. I mean his family hasn't been in contact, Billy."

"I was told he has a broken leg and collar bone. You know what this means, Miss Grace?"

"No, I'm not following you, Billy. I'm sorry Gerald has fallen and I know we will have to bring in a pharmacist but we've been able to bring in additional help before."

"No, Ma'm," Billy was struggling to explain. "There's the conference in Springfield. Gerald was going and you will have to take his place. Are you up to the drive?" Billy swallowed, a bit nervous, "I'll be glad to go with you. I can drive."

"I'm not sure I want to go, Billy."

"You have to, Miss Grace. At our last meeting you stressed the importance of representation as it has to do with our certification and you said the session on Medicare and Senior citizens is a must. There's no one else can go that knows anything about the business. You said that yourself, Miss Grace."

Listening, Grace felt the undercurrents of Billy's diatribe, he was far too involved in the subject…which led her to believe there was more he wanted to discuss with her and it was not about the conference.

"What else, Billy? I feel there's more to this conversation for you on a personal basis."He chose not to respond. Grace was silent a moment, thinking. "Billy you will be needed at the store more than ever. No one else knows the ins and outs of keeping it running smoothly as you do, and there are your studies?"

"I quit them. Holly says with the baby I won't have time for all those classes and she wants me near."

Here was the real reason Billy had called, to hear her take on his last words. He quit his studies. The last semester. How had his mother handled the news and what about her own thoughts? She took a deep breath. "I feel I'm walking into deep water, here, Billy. First thing tomorrow morning you see to being reinstated if they have even entered them, yet. When did you do this?"

"Friday," he replied. "It was late when I found time."

"What were you doing before that, Billy?" Here was her straight arrow boy, always helpful to the inth degree.

"Holly hasn't felt well this week. I helped her with laundry, housekeeping, that kind of thing, you know." His voice faltered, comparable to a little boy lying to cover his sin over a broken item. "I mean, well, you know how it is, Miss Grace. After all, I'm responsible for her not feeling well, aren't I?"

Grace was at a loss for words. "Billy, I'm going to talk to you as though I'm your Dutch uncle, you hear?" She heard him mumble. "We don't know if you are the reason Holly doesn't feel well. The testing is not complete and while I understand your concerns for the new love in your life what about your mother's view of the subject. Your parents have been with you every step of the way, through your achievement and quite honestly on those days you questioned your own abilities they were your encouragers."

"But, Miss Grace, I have to leave them behind. Holly says we don't need them, just each other."

Grace could have screamed. "Billy. Think. Would you leave behind the ones who have always been there for you?"

"Holly says I must if we are to marry."

"The place you helped Holly with housekeeping and laundry, Billy, has she moved away from the old boyfriend and now lives with her father?" There was complete silence on the other line. "Considering if Holly stays in touch with him, are you still willing to ignore the presence of your parents?"

"I have to."

Completely perplexed, Grace pulled into the garage, let down the door, got out of her car and literally slammed the door in frustration. "Billy?" She swallowed hard, keying the lock to the back door to let herself inside. "Billy, I am beyond confused. You are a stronger person than what I'm listening to and I realize you have made up your mind. Now, what exactly do I need to know about this conference since you are the one Gerald has notified about his broken leg and collarbone?"

"It is a six hour drive. The Conference material is in Gerald's desk at the store. The conference begins seven o'clock sharp with coffee hour for guest and instructors to become acquainted." Billy paused to breathe. "My suitcase is packed. If we take the company car it is full of gas, if we go in yours we can stop at the nearest station. There's reservations for two rooms and I'll pick you up in an hour."

Grace's head was in a spin. Pack and leave within an hour? But there were other things at play, here. "Billy, why are you so dead set on getting away?"

"My nerves are shot, Miss Grace. I helped Holly do all those things with her old boyfriend sitting watching me. He didn't lift a finger to help and he made lude remarks and belittled my capabilities. Even when I pleaded, Holly would not ask him to leave."

Billy's revelation needed no reply. "Are you certain you are capable of driving?"

"Yes, Ma'm. It's a different kind of nerve situation. I am full to the brim and don't know what I'm going to do but I need time to think." He sighed. "Do you want me to call the others?"

"No," she replied, "I need to call Gerald, maybe someone in his family will answer. Then there's Anna Jane will need filling in on the fact we both will be gone." Something moment of memory flashed across her mind. She had left her umbrella at the restaurant and in so doing was now responsible to return Devon's jacket. "I'll be ready, but we may need to run by the store." In haste she searched the phone pad for Anna Jane's number, running across the address of Peter's parents. For no reason, she tore it from the pad and for lack of why stuck it into the side panel of the purse she would be carrying.

We are individuals with problems we must solve ourselves, Grace thought as she packed for the trip. She had been to several of the conference that included the largest pharmaceutical suppliers. Not only was it a work conference but the companies provided entertainment and at least two party atmospheres for the attenders. For those she needed two garments with a little more flare than for the business sessions. She knew exactly which two she would wear. Closing the suitcase she felt satisfied that at least this part of preparation had gone easily. If all went well they would check in before eight o'clock and have a good night's rest.

Billy arrived prompt and wearing his business cap. Placing the suitcases in the trunk, he glanced appreciatively at the small cooler she brought out last. "I don't know about you," she said, "But I haven't had breakfast or lunch and that terrible waffle I tried to create yesterday has long since left me." Billy grinned. "Ah, ha," she concluded. "You would try my ham and cheese sandwich. Right?" She handed over the cooler. "And there's drinks, help yourself."

"Once we are on the road," he replied, his grin spreading even further across his face. "I was hoping you wouldn't mind if we made a quick stop but this is even better. We won't have to, now." He was making an effort to be his old self but responsibility was weighing heavily on his shoulders. "You need to drop by the store, Miss Grace?" She nodded, holding up a paper bag with Anna Jane's name tag on it. Anna agreed to see that Devon's jacket was returned.

"You won't believe this, Billy, Gerald answered the phone and said he would be at work as usual."

They rode in comfortable silence. "Miss Grace," Billy said somewhere into the third hour of travel, "I was wondering, if by chance that gentleman, who stayed at your house, well, if he is there, will you be spending time with him?"

"I don't think so, Billy. Remember he is a patient advocate that goes between hospitals and patients. I really can't see any reason he would be at this conference." The thought had not occurred to her, or had it, subconsciously when packing the two garments for the social hour hadn't she briefly wished to see Peter? In all fairness to self, she had not imagined him present for the conference, but they would be near his town wouldn't they?

With that Grace slid down into the seat thinking that topic fell under Mr. Clark's reasoning that God works in mysterious ways, his wonders to perform. Sighing she closed her eyes. Peter Daniels danced across the darkness of her mind, smiling, inviting her near. "Say yes, Stormy. Send me one three lettered word. Yes." And she had, but there had been no reply. Smiling as she remembered Mr. Clark's parting words, she could only wish it were true. In the secret confines of her purse resided Peter Daniel's parents address.

Oh, that it were true, that God would allow her that one moment of His wonderous love and allow her to meet Daniel's parents, to know if their son was well….somewhere, lulled by the goodness of God's love, Stormy slipped into Grace's place to rest upon her faith. Whether she ever saw Peter again or not, she must go on and in God's grace she would. It had been a long time coming, this peace that flooded her body and soul. She had tried to handle it all by herself and failed miserably; perhaps the timing was now for her to remember He had been there all these years taking care of her, he would again.

Stormy awakened the next morning to lay there studying the gray walls of the hotel. Without a hitch they had arrived, checked in, deposited their luggage to the rooms and ordered dinner from the adjoining restaurant just a hall's walk away.

As she dressed, she scanned the first day's schedule. Billy, ever efficient, had known where Gerald kept the conference materials. He had retrieved them when they dropped by the store to leave the package for Anna Jane. As agreed, the two would split up in order to cover the various classes. She had to admit there was no one from the store more compatible than Billy for this trip. She only hoped as Billy became absorbed in the conference offerings that he would also come to a worthy conclusion concerning his own situation.

For that matter she was pleasantly surprised the peace that had flooded her soul the previous evening remained. What had she done differently? All the weeks flowing into months she had battled within herself the parting with Peter, the endless dates with Devon where she enjoyed his company but had known she could never love him as he loved her and Devon deserved the best. There had always been a time in his life he wanted to discuss with her, but he held back as though there was shame attached to that time and she was not one to pry. Perhaps she would have n turn shared her own years of trial, when she was left with the Weathers and why, when all was not as well as it appeared to the world around them. But now it was a thing of the past and she felt freedom in the decision she had made to move on. It was her prayer Devon would go forward.

The smile that appeared on the face in the mirror questioned if Mr. Clark had been a real person or perhaps an angel God sent to sit beside her in church yesterday, because the peace in her soul had come after hearing his wonderful voice sing hymns of rejoicing and his parting words of wisdom, otherwise she might have continued on through life bogged down drinking from the cup of half empty instead of half full. And suddenly she remembered Peter saying those words to her the first time she visited the very church she attended yesterday. "You don't get it? Drink from the cup half full, not half empty?"

End of day arrived with Billy and Stormy meeting as planned in the lobby by the great fountain in center of the room. "How was your day, Miss Grace?"

"Wonderful," she replied. She was scanning the brochure each participant received concerning the evening meals the Conference was adding to their bill. "We can dine in the great ballroom following cocktail hour, here, or we can navigate on our own to the Blue Willow on the outskirts of town. It says there are no shuttles."

"I heard several speaking about the Blue Willow," Billy replied. "They said the food was excellent. I'm game, if you are. How hard could it be to find?" He studied her for a moment. "I'd say you are dressed for the Blue Willow. You look amazing, Miss Grace." She was wearing the off shoulder turquoise dress.

"You don't look so bad, yourself, Sir." The tease brought a smile to his face as a young lady bumped into him as she tried to avoid a waiter with his arm overhead balancing a tray filled with drinks and Billy helped her regain balance.

"So sorry," she apologized. "Oh, it's you. Billy?"

"Yeah," Billy shuffled forward, allowing her grip on his arm. "You have to watch those people carrying trays." His eyes shifted to Grace. "We were in the same classes, Karen, I believe?"

"Yes," she smiled. "That's right. You remembered. And this is your boss, I bet." Karen extended her hand. "This man loves you. I think we spent as much time talking about you and the business as anything else."

"Nice to meet you," Grace replied, as Karen obviously outgoing and approving of Billy gripped her hand.

"Where are you headed?" Billy asked.

"I was with a group taking a taxi to the place everyone was raving about…Blue something, but," she stood on tip toe, peering around the room. "I think I lost them, due to avoiding drinks being spilled on my head."

Billy glanced quickly to Grace, eyebrows raised as if to acquire her permission to ask Karen to join them.

"We are headed that way ourselves," Grace supplied. "Join us?" Karen giggled nervously as she looked back to Billy.

"It's fine." He said, "We can explore the way, together. I don't know about you two, but I'm starving."

"Thank you. I had no intention of butting in." a moment of embarrassment claimed her.

"Of course not," Grace comforted the girl's nervousness. "You had no way of knowing. We're glad to have you." Companionly, Grace reached for Karen's hand. "Come along, we'll find the car."

"This is a new place, according to the Conference Review. So we are a bit adventurous," Billy tried making small talk as he drove. "A little off the beaten path but if it is as good as those in our group today said, we can expect the best." He glanced in the mirror to the back seat. "Do you dance, Karen? Remember that red headed guy exclaiming over their music and the dance floor?"

Karen giggled again, "I'm sorry I seem to have the jitters, maybe it's being left behind by my group."

"If Billy wasn't here, I'm sure I'd feel the same way," Grace replied. "And Billy coming was an act of Providence, wouldn't you say, Billy?" She sighed. "I hope you two will dance and enjoy each other's company because the next two days will go quickly and you are going to be worn out by the time this conference ends." She yawned. "According to his mother, our Billy is a great dancer."

Billy grimaced. "Is there anything my mother hasn't told you, Miss Grace?"

"Well, I hope there is, but she does dote on you and she expects me to help keep you in line."

"I'm surprised she didn't call you when she learned I was attending Conference with you."

"Oh, she did." Grace replied. "So just settle down and drive." Turning to see Karen in the back seat, Grace asked, "Do you dance?" Karen smiled and nodded.

"Yes, after twelve years of dance lessons I had better, don't you agree?"

⬥

"The food was delicious," Grace said, folding her napkin and laying it aside. "Are you having desert, Billy?"

"I've been eyeing what's on that fellow's plate," he said in a low voice. "Just to my right, look; is that cheese cake? Something seems a little different but mostly it just looks delicious. I think I'll have that."

"That's Chocolate Crème Brulee'," Karen said. "I know because my mother makes it holidays. She adds a little cinnamon and espresso powder to give it a little twist because with that heavy crème it really does seem sweet regardless of the chocolate."

"So you are not only a dancer but a cook, too?" Grace listened as Karen explained. She liked this girl.

"Heavens, no. My mother is. I can do the basics and get by but I'm not too good with fancy desserts."

"How are you with plain ole bacon and eggs?" Billy asked.

"Why, I ace them." Karen smiled. "Thank you both for taking me in. At first I felt really embarrassed until my group called and said they were at another restaurant…but you all didn't seem to mind. I really do appreciate your kindness."

"We are glad to have you join us," Grace smiled as she reached across to pat Karen's hand. "Why don't you two go dance. I'll order your dessert Billy, and something for Karen and I to share, then we can return to the hotel sated in bliss by their lovely concoctions. How does that sound?"

"Lovely lady," the chef was a beautiful Asian woman coming now with the one who had seated them, bringing three dessert dishes. "We desire to know your thoughts on our special Crème Brulee. We have brought for you, also, our Apricot Crisp and our Mandarin Orange cake." The lady's smile widened as she saw Grace's expression. "You enjoy, my lady. Then you dance away the calories. Okay?"

Grace's smile was beyond brilliant. "You are too kind, but we only ordered one dessert, the Brulee."

"I know, my lady but we saw the three of you, your brother and sister. My place of business and we want to bless you." She turned to find Karen and Billy on the floor. "Then, you also must dance."

"I wish," Grace's voice did sound wishful. "I'm afraid I don't have a partner."

"I fix that," the lady chef replied. "Okay?" She waited for Grace to reply. "I send my own to dance with you." She hurried away, before Grace could resist or say no. "Stay, lady. Stay," she called back. "I fix. My place. I do this for you."

Grace hid her face behind her hands. Now she was into it. No doubt the lady Chef would send out her husband or perhaps one of the waiters, and she could not say no when the intention was from a good heart. What had she gotten herself in to? She sat there, staring at the floor, hoping the woman would forget as a large crowd of newcomers arrived. The three desserts sat in the middle of the table. Grace closed her eyes. If she had a menu she would hide behind it. What could she do? She placed her hands over her forehead, as though studying something on the tablecloth. Perhaps they would think she was praying and go away."

"Madam?" She must raise her head. "Madam?" An American gentleman she supposed sixtyish in age stood before her speaking in perfect English. She supposed she had expected the man to be Asian, also. "As my wife has requested, our son who has just arrived has come to welcome you to Blue Willow Dance floor, we pray for a time of dancing enjoyment you will hold in memory as a lasting blessing." A twinkle entered his eyes, "Had our son not arrived, it would have been me." With a beautiful smile he bowed and stepped aside, behind his tall frame, smiling and reaching for her hand was his son.

"Peter?"

"Stormy?"

"What? You two know each other?" The father asked, peering at Stormy and then his son. He left shaking his head. "Wait until I tell your mother."

Peter was laughing. Grace was stunned. "I thought your mother's place of business was called LaLa."

"It is. This is their new adventure but Lala is running smoothly, alive and well, as it appears are we." He offered his hand. "How are you, Stormy?" He squeezed her hand. "I'm so happy to see you." He was moving her toward the dance floor, a tropical paradise of huge spreading plants, beautiful twinkling lights overhead and an ambience of calming enticement that claimed the dancers.

"This" he said, "Is Mother's ball room. Don't look so shocked, Stormy."

"But I am," she was having difficulty believing this was real. "Am I asleep?"

He was laughing, joyously. "I figured I was being asked to dance with some elderly lady who wanted to resurrect a memory of her dead husband." He leaned down to kiss the top of her head. "I don't mean that disrespectful but my mother has a penchant for trying to make everyone happy. How did she hook you?"

"She said I must dance and I replied I had no partner and she said, I fix. I guess you're the fix."

"Are you at the convention?"

"Yes."

"Wonderful. Three full days. Right?"

"Only two remain."

"Spend them with me, Stormy." He touched her chin, "Look at me. I'm serious. I've missed you. If you have anyone with you, let them do the work, come with me tomorrow. On my turf. Meet my parents." He laughed, "Well you've met them, but not as my mom and dad. They're a bit intimidating at work."

"I don't think I can, Peter. Gerald, the Pharmicist, couldn't attend and I'm here for the information we need."

"Buy the videos of each session, that way you can take it home and use it in groups as needed to explain to your employees." His eyes held hers, a serious expression in them. "There are handouts, Stormy."

"How do you know this?" She was perplexed. "You said you just arrived, meaning you weren't there."

"No, but I will be tomorrow. I've been ask to speak at the eight o'clock session on advocates and I have the last spot on the agenda the next day." He sighed. "More and more the medical world is finding what I do, between their practice and their client, may be the most insuring protection they can have. It saves hours of mediation and countless dollars in law suits."

Still unsettled in finding Peter a son to the Chef at Blue Willow, Stormy listened to Peter explaining the success of his business, but more important than his words she was trying to make sense of his asking her to jump classes the next day and spend time with him. If he remembered her work ethics at all, he would know the suggestion was not one she could accept easily and perhaps not at all.

"Please, Stormy." His expression pleaded along with the sincerity in his voice. "We've not had this opportunity, Stormy. I beg of you, spend time with me."

"I can't."

"Can't or won't." There was hurt in his voice. "What if this is our last opportunity, Stormy?"

She was thinking of Billy expecting her to finish the conference. Was it really that important? Her work ethics had never been questioned. Why was she being stubborn? Why didn't she face him with the question burning behind her lips? "Why didn't you reply when I sent you the one word you requested?" She couldn't stand the thought that he had received her text and discarded it. She had longed for him until it affected her health. Here and now the fact he wants to spend time together today cannot diminish his lack of reply.

"Stormy, let's dance. If we talk we will only get in deeper. I can't bear your being upset with me." Arms spread wide, he waited for her. She walked into them, drawn into the comfort she had longed for; wondering if they could get through these moments of unrest but knowing until her question was answered she could not and would not give her all.

Billy arrived as the lights were dimming, an encouragement to leave graciously as the Blue Willow was closing. "We've been out on the streets." His voice carried an energy she remembered before he met Holly. "They have different groups staged here and there, playing wonderful music." He smiled at Karen. "We danced." Patting himself on the back, he continued, "We dance marvelously together."

Good natured, Karen stepped over to Grace and gave her a hug. "He's a good dancer." She was nodding approval. "Are you ready to leave?"

Peter returned from telling his parents goodnight as Billy reached for Grace's purse. "There's those wonderful desserts, Miss Grace. Shall we take them with us? After the dancing, a midnight snack woul…."

"Yes, great idea." She was saying when Billy stopped speaking. Peter Daniel's had arrived and was standing behind her. "What were the chances,

Billy of driving this far to convention and meeting my former house guest? You remember Peter? Meeting him here was quite unexpected but here we are."

There was an amount of small talk while Grace was aware Billy was sizing up the last one to join their group. In the past, Billy's remarks had bordered on dislike, now she wondered what he was thinking.

Peter had extended his hand and clasp Billy's hesitant return. "I would like for Grace to ride with me back to the hotel, if it meets your approval, Billy. I promise I'll take good care of her."

Billy was looking askance when Grace nodded. "You and Karen have a nice drive back," she said.

Always the perfect gentleman, Peter held the door for her to get into the car. "I see it's holding up," she said. "I don't suppose any wheels have rolled off lately?"

"No," he smiled. "Your town's people did a good job. How are they all doing, the one's at the Pharmacy?"

"Well," she replied. "We thought you were coming back through on occasion." He peered at her a somber expression. "I've driven by your office but there's never anyone there."

He rubbed his chin for a moment. "Yeah, well, things took a turn about the time I was leaving as you recall and there seemed to be no need…my return and then my work load was all in the other direction." He smiled suddenly. "I just remembered. I have a surprise for you, but that waits until tomorrow." Reaching over he pressed a button. "I bought this CD in hopes you and I would one day listen to this song together. Listen to the words, Stormy. Maybe you saw this woman on television." She was shaking her head, no. "I forgot you don't watch television much. Listen… right here. " Peter sang along, I dreamed that she will come to me and we will live the years together."

"Aww, you are crying." He reached across to pull her close but there was the barrier between them. Still he took her hand and kissed her finger tips. "Stormy, I've missed you. It was my hope you missed me, too." Driving with one hand, holding her hand with the other, he sang the last lines, "If there are storms we cannot weather still I dream you will come to me to take me from this hell I'm living and let me live the dream that I keep dreaming." His smile was tender as he kissed her finger tips once more. "Those are not the actual words, my darling…I ad lib when I don't know…but my heart is in each word."

That was her moment and she let it slip by, lest she become a blubbering idiot, so stirred were her emotions she wanted to howl, pull her hair and demand Peter Daniel's explain why he had not answered that moment when she sent the text on the pharmacy phone and would have bowed to his every need, so desperately had she wanted him to know she had come to decision. Yes, she loved him.

He kissed he good night, not lingering, while she was weak in the knees and wondering why. "I'll see you in the morning," he said. "Eight o'clock."

He made it to the car, slammed the door and lay his head on the steering wheel, "That was the hardest thing I've done all week," he whispered out loud. "Tomorrow, if she goes with me, I will know. Tomorrow if she does not go with me…." Sadness claimed him. "I will know."

It was the second day of the Conference. Six thirty in the morning according to the bedside clock. Grace yawned and turned toward the window. What must she do? Peter had the eight o'clock session and then he asked she leave for the day with him. Billy would have to take notes and receive all handouts if she did as Peter asked. Her heart said yes but her busy mind wanted what was best for the business.

She called Billy's room. "Good morning, Miss Grace, I hope you slept well. I did." He sounded chipper. "Miss Grace, I won't be in session this morning for your friend's speech. It doesn't seem to resonate with our need at the Pharmacy at this time, so I'm going to take the morning off and spend it with Karen."

Her silence must have piqued his interest. "You know what, Miss Grace? I think I've made a decision concerning Holly. She won't let me see those strips when she tries to make a point that she is pregnant. I've decided not to fall into her way of allowing that boyfriend she lives with to scare me. If she wanted to be with me, she'd leave him wouldn't she? He does intimidate me, scares the beegee's out of me."

"How did you come to this conclusion, Billy?" Grace wasn't certain she really wanted to know but ask, anyway.

"I talked it over with Karen. This girl has a lot of common sense. You know what, Miss Grace?" He paused a moment. "We are going swimming today. We're going to walk down town and listen to music." She could almost feel Billy's grin spreading across his face. "I haven't felt this good in ages. I hope you and your friend enjoy this trip as much as I intend to, Miss Grace. I just want to thank you."

"But what about Holly, Billy? Don't you feel she's due some kind of explanation?"

"I was preparing myself to call her, Miss Grace, when you called me. I'll do it now." His voice sobered "I think its best I prepare Holly that I'm not going through with a wedding or paternity case for her child."

"I wish you the best, Billy. I wish I could do the same. Just leave the conference, but we need the info…"

"You can, Miss Grace. Just turn loose and skip the conference. I could tell Mr. Daniel's cares deeply for you. You told me once you were waiting for Mr. Right to come along, maybe he's here right now."

"You've turned Philosopher, Billy." Grace smiled in spite of herself, a chuckle reaching Billy's ears.

"Miss Grace, I've selected from the handouts what I feel most beneficial to the Pharmacy. You can skip sessions if you want to, the information is already in the car and I'll deliver it when the time comes. Now maybe we can both enjoy a nice day and worry over the rest next week. Thank you for letting me come to Conference, it may change my life, Miss Grace, for the better. I pray for yours, too."

"Billy, why now, why are you conceding in Mr. Daniel's case, when before you were against him."

"I never really listened to the two of you talk or had you near enough to observe, Miss Grace, although I made an assumption, now I know I was wrong. You just need time together and time to accept what I believe God is trying to tell you."

"Why would you say God? That's interesting."

"You're different, Miss Grace, you smile like a woman who knows you'll be taken good care of." He gave an embarrassed laugh. "I hope that makes sense. Sometimes I feel that way. There's something in you that you try to give to other people. You wanted so badly for me to believe God would take care of everything I was going through worrying over whether it was my baby Holly was carrying." He paused for a moment as if gathering words. "You just seemed so certain."

"The truth was, Miss Grace, Holly told me I was the father quicker than it was physically possible. You mentioned that when we talked. I've always been able to talk to you, Miss Grace and for that I'm very thankful. It wasn't something I wanted to tell my parents even at my age."

"Well," Grace found herself laughing. "It's not the end of the road for either of us and Billy I'm glad you approve of Peter Daniels. He is a good man and there was never more to our relationship than having breakfast or dinner and laughing over a cup of coffee."

"But I can tell he is in love with you, Miss Grace. The way he looks at you and reaches for your hand and I don't think you even realize those times because its so natural." Grace had become quiet, not knowing what to say. "I've tried to make you think he wasn't good for you, maybe in a way I was jealous but I'm trying to make up for my interference when I say now that I believe he would be good to you."

"Thank you, Billy for having my best interest at heart. All we can do is wait and see what is God's plan."

She considered her words. God's plan. She had worried and wondered, prayed and pleaded, cried and scolded herself these last months. Berating herself for not having the wisdom to see into the future, and for letting Peter leave without asking him to give her time to think things through; she had wasted precious time and now, though her heart begged to go to Peter her mind continued to hold her at bay. Why had he not answered when she sent the one word he asked of her. Yes. How many times had she examined his possible reason and come up with nothing of value, no way to forgive his inattention. This was her life, the future she longed for and yet she had been hurt so many times it was against her will to plunge foolishly into a relationship where there were unanswered questions.

Bonnie Bruce let the conversation roll over in his mind and then did a play back to be sure he hadn't missed anything. He'd found Holly in a strange mood last night. Angry, he could tell by the way she slammed the refrigerator door, threw herself onto the couch and drummed those long painted finger nails on the side table. "What's going on?" She'd ignored him, flouncing across the room, taking the remote for the television and flipping channels. "I was watching that, it's not every day you see a piece of equipment of that caliber."

"Who cares?" She retorted, slinging blonde hair over her shoulder. "You've been on that channel all day. Let someone else have a chance." She slid back onto the couch, eyeing programs, ignoring him, placing her feet on an old foot stool, long legs and painted toe nails in his face.

"Well, aren't you the chipper one and got the sharp tongue to prove it. I said what's going on?"

"Like you'd care?"

"I think I've proved where you are concerned, I care. Now, fill me in. What's ruffled your feathers?"

"I got this kid swimming around inside my belly like a tad pole and Billy calls me from that conference he went to with his boss and tells me he won't be back around. He knows this is not his kid and he's done."

"Is it his?"

"I told you."

"You tell me a lot of things; however they're not always true. This kid. Is it Billy boys or that good for nothing hoofer you live with?" Agitation crept into his voice. "Why'd you risk it all living with him?"

"I'm not living with him now? I'm here. I didn't like what he said. "If I value my life I better listen."

"Why is that?" Bonnie drew in his feet and leaned close, studying his daughter. She definitely had begun to show the pregnancy. "Listen to what?"

"He … He's jealous of my time with Billy, thinks I'm sleeping with him."

"So?" Bonnie rose up to loom over her. "Who cares about the good for nothing? That college kid you claim knocked you up, Billy, Right? Now you're acting like a loser ready to marry him when he's said no same as the good for nothing." Bonnie's voice boomed. "I'm not buying this. There's more. Did he really kick you out?"

She screamed back, "Yes, he kicked me out after he threatened to kill me and Billy. Did you miss that?"

Bonnie kicked the foot stool out from under her feet. "This ain't gonna work. I told you I can't take care you and a kid, it's best you find a stable place and hunker down until he's old enough you won't worry whether he's safe all time, or not, then you get out and collect child support or maybe divorce the jerk and draw a fat settlement. Who knows you might fit into the ordinary mainstream of life. But right now, being safe from that good for nothing matters." Bonnie began to pace the floor.

"What's safe? Neither one want me. I thought Billy was a sure thing, then I get a call." Holly's face contorted, a sea of emotion. "It's her fault, that Pharmacy woman. She took him with her to conference, probably to get her digs in on him, their relationship's not real. She made him call. It's her fault."

Bonnie stopped in his pacing and turned sharply. "What do you mean her fault?" He towered over her.

"It is," Holly whimpered, "She don't think I'm good enough for him."

"Who said?"

"I feel it."

"You want me…take her out? Him?" Bonnie's mind had gone into overload. "You gotta say what you want. Ain't much I can do for you but that I can."

"Where's Gramma?" The thought just popped into her mind. "That… that scares me…when you say things like that. Did you send her away? She's all I had when Momma left and you were gone."

"Gramma left. She was sickly and needed medical attention. She's probably holed up in some institution."

Holly turned away. He was gone. With the flip of the remote she shot him out of her mind. He could sit there til dooms day staring at her if he want, she had always shut out the bad parts, when he left, when momma left, there were ways to cope, you closed your mind to that and went on to the next part life handed you. She'd managed to finish high school and found a way to college. Night work wasn't ideal but it paid. She closed off that section. But there was something different to him today. More crude, even his appearance had changed. Though it niggled at her mind she shrugged it off. God must not have liked her from the beginning if she considered the parents she was given. HGTV had a new project. She wanted a home like that. She didn't stir when he left; though she'd felt his nervousness, agitated with heavy sighs that spoke of boredom, usually he took a walk around the block, until finally she would hear the sound of the car driving away. Where did he get the money to keep that old car running?

Bonnie drove the streets, ignoring her address, staying on the outer drives, considering Holly's words, 'she don't think I'm good enough.' Hadn't it always been that way; his old man, old woman, drinking til their livers rotted; adding the drugs for Euphoria, paying the price? His life shattered the day that metal gate fell from the ceiling, the blood, the pain until finally the emergency room and surgery. Holly was right…it was her fault, that one he'd been watching from the street. She hadn't learned her lesson, to stay out of sight, stay low don't make waves…all those years and then one day he saw her and she looked familiar. The stirrings began, again, hard as he'd tried to press them down. There'd been that girl, the one right after he'd come home from detention…what a lark, the school pressed charges for property loss, not the real reason what him and the boyz intended for Grace Hendersen in the boiler room, no they got him on property destruction. That gate caused him far more loss than it did them.

There'd been the woman three years later. The one from the gas station, teasing him on day after day not realizing whatever she needed he couldn't supply and then she slips into his car. He didn't invite her. She didn't go home that night. Her name was on the news next day. Missing, they said, who cared? How many? Three. The girl was unintentional. He had a daughter. But that one was rotten to the core and she'd ridiculed him after coming on to him for money. My favors your money she'd said. He couldn't stand ridicule. He'd grown up with that. Then she pulls a knife on him. Him the size he was and her with a knife she wanted to use on him? Three. He wasn't a serial, no he wasn't. He'd managed to curb that problem, going to AA when he didn't drink, listening to others stories, trying to use the advice they gave to hold down his own problem that wasn't liquor but a need to get even for all the injustice, the ugliness of prison doing things you didn't want to do, thinking about the one pure thing in your life; that little blonde haired beauty growing up without her daddy, Holly. He'd do anything for her.

His mind was made up. He turned onto her street. Holly said she was away. He'd come back for her later. Right now, he'd give them a sample of what's coming. He parked down the street, walked in the shadows to her home, found the key beneath the mat and entered. Downstairs he found a window, moved the mechanism that locked it in place, it was stuck, putting his weight into it, it moved. That's what he needed. Entrance when she least expected. What was there about dark dank places made a person shudder? He'd think on what he'd do to her. What he'd make her do.

He left there. She'd never know anyone entered her home. The store? A different question, all lit up, no doubt an alarm system connected to city hall, but he'd disabled the one at her home, again. He worked for the company, once, until he learned what was necessary to disarm a system. He was no dummy. They would feel his wrath, come morning. He smiled, knowing the question, "Who did this?"

Dressing, Grace found the battering of her mind had tired her too soon. Exhausted she took the elevator, listening to two women's discussion. "He doesn't do everything alone. There's this woman helps him. I've heard he has someone. No, I've never met her. Him, yes, he is full of charm. No one has seen her, she is a mystery woman. Yes, his office is downtown and his parents do have the new restaurant in outer county plus the one uptown. Blue Something….that's right, Blue Willow."

She was actually shaking. They hadn't mentioned his name but the name of the restaurant, Blue Willow. Another woman? That would be the reason. No further questions. It was time to move on, maybe she should move. But where? What about the business. "You try to give of yourself to others," Billy had said. That was ending, as of right now. She would keep her opinion and efforts of good will to herself from this moment on. If she couldn't handle her own life what made her think she could help others?

Entering the conference room, Grace chose the center aisle on the back row. The woman in front of her was busy, marking off the day's schedule, making notes here and there and folding brochures still being handed to the attendees. One of the Conference attendees was helping her and blocked Grace's full view of the woman. When he left she placed the stack of papers in the chair next to her. The slick surface caused the papers to slide and land in the floor in a scattered display which she quickly leaned down to retrieve. Automatically, Grace began to help collect the papers nearest her feet and gently tapped the lady on the shoulder to hand them to her. The woman turned to thank her.

"Angeline?" If Grace thought she was shocked to see Peter, seeing Angeline was more tramatic than she could explain. "Angeline?" She repeated. "What are you doing here? Did you know Peter was speaking this morning, within the hour?"

"Why didn't you tell me you were coming?" Angeline was collecting papers to come back to sit by Grace. "I tried to call you, but you never answered your phone. I left you a message. Did you get it?" Angeline searched Grace's face. "Why are you looking sad? Are you sick? You are here, to see Peter, aren't you?"

"I'm in utter shock. Evidently you have seen him. Are you working for Peter, Angeline?"

Angeline laughed. "Kind of sorta, I guess. He called me, said he was trying to reach you and couldn't and he needed help this week end, some kind of seminar or maybe he said conference. I asked what exactly he needed and he said someone to hand out papers, can you imagine? I said I'll help you. I thought he said I could come back home Tuesday, what he really said was be here Tuesday and leave Friday morning." Angeline gave a happy laugh, throwing her head back, tears in her eyes. "What a treat He made all the arrangements. Paid my way, even paid me for doing this and it's the easiest job I've ever had."

"You have been in contact with Peter?"

Angeline eyed her curiously, "haven't you?" She thought a minute, a puzzled expression on her face. "He talks about you as though you both talked yesterday." She leaned back to peer earnestly into Stormy's face. "When did you last speak with Peter?"

"The day he left our community after we had lunch together."

"You're kidding." She gave a hurried glance, just as she thought, first pain flickered in Stormy's eyes then she saw that glint of anger. "Are you mad at me girl? You should answer your phone."

"I couldn't. It hasn't been working and the repairman said the line had been clipped, I don't know what's wrong with it. Things just aren't right Angeline. I think I've made some wrong decisions."

"I know you've been seeing Devon… and he…did you make a decision concerning Devon, Stormy?"

Stormy's head dropped. "I'm sorry, honey, I didn't meant to sound so harsh but I'm confused. Peter said he couldn't wait to see you. Tell me, do you just not feel the same about Peter as he does you? The man loves you, Stormy." Angeline was trying to piece this situation together but she had very little material. "Honey, if you want this man, you better get off your reserve and years of trying to do everything right and act like you want him. I think the man has been as patient as he can afford to be, the years are rolling around and you heard him say that day, he's ready to marry, settle down and have a family."

Stormy sat there shaking her head, tears welled up in her eyes and it came to Angeline, like a flash. What if Stormy had agreed to marry that Devon fellow, the Police officer? And here she had been thinking Peter and her were ready for marriage. Why he talked as though they'd made plans and she fell for it, hook line and sinker, except now that she thought it over he hadn't said it happened, but there was such hope in his voice she believed on her own it had and now there sits Stormy saying she's made a wrong decision. Lord help them all. For a minute she wished she hadn't even come to help Peter this week end.

Angeline stood, her agitation was fair demanding she get out of that chair. She practically hissed. "Honey, I'm telling you if you want him, you better do something, today." She left Stormy sitting there and Stormy heard her muttering two rows away about stubborn people and she didn't know what anyone could do with them. Her friend disappeared through the door, no doubt going to check in with Peter.

"You have all the papers I gave you, Angeline? The ones I had my Secretary run off and a copy of the text I received while I was on the road. I need to hurry through them, just in case there's someone out in the audience has sent me a question I'll need to acknowledge." He was thumbing through. "Okay, one here. Now the text." He was flipping through when he suddenly became quiet. "Angeline, do you recognize this number? It's from your area." She shook her head, no. "How's our girl?" He asked. "Is she out there?"

"Yeah, she's out there." Angeline's voice carried the threat of dread. "I wouldn't say happy, though."

"Why?"

"Maybe because you and I failed to tell her I was coming here to help this weekend, but she didn't answer her phone. Stubborn is what she is. I've always known that. She lasts longer at it than me, too." She didn't tell him her worst suspicion, either. Some things people needed to find out for themselves. If Stormy was engaged to that Devon, then she'd have to tell Peter. "What's that you're studying?"

"A phone number I don't recognize. Therefore I can't decipher the message." He tore the paper and placed the text in his pocket. A nagging thought was tearing at his imagination. Could it be? Nah, it wasn't her number. She would have told him. Or, would she?" The number chewed at his mind. He hurriedly called his office. His secretary confirmed a one word message came through from someone, if she remembered right a Mr. Storm. "It's in your messages, Peter. Look for it."

Angeline went back to sit with Stormy. Peter walked onto the platform and waited to be introduced. He saw Angeline take her seat and next to her a stormy looking individual that made his heart do a dip, twist and slide, back into its regular rhythm, he didn't know whether to laugh or cry.

He found himself locked into giving a speech he'd given a thousand times, knowing the words and the meaning of each sentence but his mind was on other things, specifically the number In his pocket. He was half through his presentation when Stormy rose up to leave the conference room. Angeline shook her head, trying to give him a message, Stormy would not return. She was headed home.

⚬⚬⚬

Billy met her at the front desk. "Billy, I received a call saying something is wrong but I couldn't understand if it is the business or my home. Have you heard anything?"

"Yes, Ma'm," He replied, ducking his head as though bearing bad news. "We need to hurry."

She saw he already had his suitcase in hand and was calling for their vehicle. "Miss Grace, your car is parked several blocks away. They have agreed to let me go after it. Do you think you can pack by the time I walk over and drive back?"

"Are we in that big a rush, Billy?" The look in his eye told her they should have left early morning. "Of course. I'll be here. Our expense will be on the credit card I gave when we checked in, so that is of no concern."

"Hurry, Miss Grace. Time is of the essence." When she would have questioned further, he waved his hand and headed toward the door. "I'll explain when we are on our way."

Bonnie slouched down the street. What did they say? The killer always returned to the scene of the crime? But no one had been killed, yet. Maybe a few spirits ruffled, if she was home to see the damage. One thing for certain, the police had enough to keep them busy the next few days. Someone had broken into the Pharmacy, unable to breech the steel door to the back where prescription medications were kept the perpetrator had literally destroyed the over the counter section; a criminal offense. Word was on the street. Of course it was, Bonnie sighed, a criminal in the act of performing an act of justice, for the injustice done his daughter. That would teach them both, the owner and Billy boy.

He hadn't decided what would be her punishment for interfering in Holly's plans to marry Billy Boy. He hadn't acted in a while and the adrenalin pumping through his veins was a nice rush. Maybe he'd go back to prison, there he had a roof over his head, two meals a day he could count on and if his size proved worthy to bluff his way through, he'd have the niceties others provided. The problem was he would be a second time offender and the court might not take pity on him. "You are not crazy," he could imagine the Psycho ward passing him by. All their babble.

"Repressed feelings and anger perhaps, what you really are, is a mean individual and I'd like to know what made you that way." He'd heard it all.

Now he wondered if he was crazy. Go back to prison? He had enough scars on his body and soul to skip that lark all together. Maybe they'd shoot him. He'd run and they'd have no other course but to put a bullet through his head. He couldn't imagine leaving Holly. She was the only thing he lived for; strange, she didn't feel that way about him. She loved his mother. "Grama," she'd say and those were the only times he saw a glimmer of humanity in her otherwise scheming soul. "Shrewd," the old lady said. He'd seen it coming, the old ladies days were numbered, the coughing, the sprinkles of blood on the handkerchief she carried, "You take care of our Holly," she'd whisper, her runny eyes filling with tears. "There was a time she was so sweet." He didn't know; he'd been away. They told her he worked on an oil rig out in the middle of the ocean. She believed that for years. Then he came home. She was older and he wasn't what she imagined. She had no use for her mother, the one who birthed and left her to fend for herself. Now that one returned, used up and unable to help out. The bills kept coming but she couldn't work. Drugs owned her. Now she had nothing to offer for drugs. The druggies feared her.

What was he supposed to do? Life was hard. There were bills. The old ladies check covered utilities and nothing else. They scrambled for food, the mission, government hand-outs, cans behind restaurants. Life had become a hardship, all right. How was he going to keep the car running? Business had dropped off, the upright citizens who used him were tightening up afraid the officials would quit looking the other way. No one would believe how hard life was, they sit in their air conditioned homes wasting food and everything under the sun, while he struggled. It wasn't his fault.

He hoped Holly didn't ask for the old lady again. He saw himself in Dryden's plate glass window. Not a lot of those anymore, buildings were bricked front to back, awnings over windows placed high off the sidewalk to deter criminal activity he supposed. He smiled at his own image, no one would recognize him but then he didn't stir among the population. The less they saw of him, the less they remembered.

Beginning to feel sweat trickling down his back, he wished he wasn't wearing black but then that had always been his signature color. He remembered the grape dye they'd used on their lips made their teeth appear yellow, until his teeth had been kicked out and he hadn't the money to replace them. He needed a shower. He could smell himself. It was time to go home. Satisfied, the damage was done and everyone had a job to do, he turned to cross town. Yeah, the Police would be busy. He'd left the car parked a mile away. No need creating suspicion. She'd be home today, for sure, and then he'd finish the second part of his plan. Retaliation was good; it cleared a man's mind and let him forget the worries that pressed on him daily.

Devon studied the complete destruction of the Pharmacy's interior. How had the night force missed activity inside a well-lit building on Main Street in one of the most patrolled districts of the city? The building was further protected by an alarm system connected to city hall where someone was on duty at all times? City Hall had no record of anything going amiss, the alarm system showed everything properly working except it wasn't and there had been other calls answered which proved the employees were doing their job. He was told to pick up Miss Anna Jane, the one who had returned his jacket on Sunday evening. She was said to have a key to Miss Grace Weather's home. There was need to see if damage had been done there. All areas were covered as the question remained whether there was a personal vendetta toward the owner of the Pharmacy on Main Street. There was a growing suspicion as to a connection between the owner and the one perpetrating the crime.

He waited outside in the Police Car. He had been surprised when she had come to the Police Station and asked to see Officer Devon Malloy. The others had teased him unmercifully. "Why'd that pretty girl have your jacket, Officer? You been catering to a damsel in distress, Officer Malloy?" He'd finally left.

She was a pretty girl, late twenties, he guessed but with a hint of sadness in her eyes. He'd wondered about that and if anyone could read him? What would they say? Here's a guy pining over a woman that rejected him while praising him? A woman he was ready to give his life to but denied him that honor?

She came toward the car and he hurried to open the door. "Thanks," she said, a bit breathless, scooting into the seat and drawing the seat belt around her. She was wearing a dress, the folds of the skirt settling around the seat so that he had been careful the material wasn't caught as he closed the door.

"Not many women wear dresses anymore," he said, for conversation. "That's nice."

She smiled, turning to face him. "It's summer. We wear slacks all winter. It's kind of nice for a change."

"Your boss wears dresses, too. I've noticed."

"Miss Grace," the smile widened. "She's a lady. I guess the rest of us take our cue from her. You know it's a man's world." The smile disappeared. "I hate the fact she's coming home to this mess. Is that why we are going to her house? To be sure nothing's happened there?"

"It appears so." They were on Grace's street now. "She doesn't live far from work."

"No. She lives a pretty quiet life. She did have a house guest a while back but she handled that like everything else, without a hitch. There'd been an accident." She suddenly turned quiet. "I really shouldn't discuss my boss, it was Billy who had all the information and he adores her, but it bothered him that Miss Grace was being taken advantage of."

"What do you think?" Devon couldn't help asking.

"I don't think so." Anna Jane mused, "it was probably the only time I'd seen her laugh and seem to have joy. She lived a really restricted life with Mr. Weathers, him being older. No, I think her house guest made her happy."

"That's interesting." He noticed she was searching the pocket of her skirt. "You have the key."

She laughed. "Yes, somewhere in my pocket. I do."

If she didn't he was thinking, there's one beneath the mat by the front door, but he remained quiet.

He pulled into the drive. She unfastened the seat belt and in the next second produced the key from her pocket. "I have it," she said, grinning and handing it to him. "You may do the honors."

"There's a security system," he remembered. "First, I need to check whether the alarm has been tampered with as suspected." He found the entrance to the alarm system's wiring, returning to where she waited, "It has been disarmed. Whoever shut down the system knew exactly what to do."

"Isn't it just a matter of clipping a few wires?"

"Not on some of the new systems. If it were that easy there would be no need for the service."

They walked up the sidewalk; opened the door and went in. She followed. "Nothing seems disturbed," he said after a quick view of the living areas. "If you know the lay-out I'll follow you." Strangely at odds with himself he remembered his first date with Grace he brought roses. She invited him to follow her through to where she put the bouquet in a vase of water and set it on the table. He had not seen beyond the open rooms of house. But he remembered the stern pictures of two he decided were not her parents. Now he suspected Grace had out of respect left the Weather's pictures hanging.

"This way to Miss Grace's room, on down the hall there's a bath and a second bedroom." She turned left, he went right.

He noticed doors were open to both rooms and at the end of the hall a large mirror gave him a view of Anna Jane entering what he supposed was Grace's bedroom; Except, she had not entered, in fact was clutching the door frame as though mentally hanging in without putting one step forward. "What's wrong?" He hurried to her side and peered over her head into the room he had not seen before. In fact he had been no further than the living room where she often met him at the door. A sudden realization thundered through his mind that he should have taken that into account long ago, had Grace been interested in him they would have sit in the rooms together, laughing about things people who care do and probably he would have known where the bathroom was. But what he saw now was disturbing.

Still hanging from the rods, beautiful lace curtains had been torn to shreds, the bed covering, a simple white quilted material he supposed called a comforter had been slashed until the inside stuffing shown through while the matching pillows were marked with red. Lipstick he guessed, as was the writing on the walls. REMEMBER THE BOILER ROOM. DID YOU FORGET?

Anna Jane rushed to her closet now that he was beside her. Inside was as much havoc as out, cosmetics that possibly had sat on the dresser had been thrown on the clothes, the shoes were trampled and underclothing strewn across the floor. One lone garment remained untouched, hanging on the inside of the mirrored door, a beautiful peignoir and behind it a matching gown. "Oh," there was pain in Anna Jane's expression of dismay. "Miss Grace's beautiful clothes." And then she saw the matching set. A shudder began mid-section of her body, her hands began to shake as she remembered Miss Grace saying, "there's no promise of use."

"But," Devon was pointing to the garments on the door. "Why are these untouched? This makes no sense, at all." He turned to face Anna Jane. "Why are you trembling, are you nervous, does this mean something to you?" He peered down into her face trying to make sense of it all. "The room is in shambles, but what does this have to do with…" he spread his hands…"you?"

"I don't know. I mean, it doesn't have anything to do with me." A nervous half cry-half-laugh welled up in her throat. "It's silly. I guess its nerves. I mean, Miss Grace and I spoke of those…those clothes just recently. She left my name on the tag. Do you see it? It says *For Anna Jane and happiness always.*

"Why is your name in Grace Weather's closet on a piece of clothing?" He took her hand and led her to the living room. Pointing to the sofa, he said, "Sit and please try to explain whatever it is I'm not understanding."

"A little over three years ago, I was engaged to be married. It was all planned, the white gown, the formal wedding and there were bridal showers. Miss Grace gifted me with a house hold gift but also that beautiful peignoir set." Her face turned suddenly sad. "My fiancée was killed the week we were to be married; in some covert military situation I will never have the privilege of understanding." She fingered the folds of her skirt as she raised her eyes to his. "I wanted to give the set back to Miss Grace hoping one day she would use it, wear it in happiness that I was robbed of my wedding night." She sighed, wiping a tear. "It is embarrassing, perhaps, to give you the intimate details of that garment but otherwise you might not understand. I don't know why the person who destroyed Miss Grace's room didn't destroy them too, except perhaps my name was on the tag she left attached and whoever it was realized the garment was intended for someone else."

"I am trying to understand…"

"Which part, do you not understand, Officer Malloy, that a bride desires to be beautiful for her husband or that I gave the garments back to Miss Grace or that perhaps a grain of decency lies within whoever did this?" She sighed. "I am as in the dark as you. Could we leave, please?"

Devon was at a loss for words. "Miss?" She was up, moving towards the door. "Hold up, just a minute, please." She waited; her hand on the knob. "I certainly didn't mean to upset you. I don't always know how to speak with ladies and I make these terrible mistakes by asking questions."

"It's part of your job. I was upset. I over-reacted."

"No," he tried to ease the situation with a smile. "It was me. I'm sorry for your loss. I'm going through a bad time, myself, presently. Could we just put this behind us? I'll report back to the station and let them know that someone has been in the home and they will take it from there."

"Could you at least wait until Miss Grace returns from Conference? Billy has text they are on their way. Surely a couple hours won't matter. It is her home."

Taking a deep breath, Officer Devon Malloy tried one last time to right the situation. "Of course." He followed her out, closing the door firmly behind. The key was in his pocket but the home was already compromised and he realized the team arriving later would find an unintended entry.

"Miss?"

"Anna."

"Anna, do you wish to return to the Pharmacy or may I drive you home."

"I was told no need to return. Gerald picked me up this morning because I have a flat tire on my car."

"God works in mysterious ways, Anna, perhaps that was to detain your arrival at the Pharmacy. I was told you were the one supposed to open this morning and that you always went in early. I cannot bear to think if you had come unexpectedly upon the one who caused such destruction."

Anna shivered at the thought. "I live on Autumn Street," she said. "201 Autumn. Thank you."

Bonnie had not intended returning but the draw back to her house was magnetized when he saw the Police Car parked in front. He had found Holly asleep on the couch, taken a shower, dressed in better clothes and popped the bridgework in his mouth that made him appear a man of means. That act alone reminded him how his teeth were kicked from his mouth and why the gate had fallen on vital organs. In trying to escape one of his own boys had released the gate rigged to prevent entry by the boiler room's window. Evidently the gate was an after thought, poorly constructed, but then it wasn't his boyz fault. It was hers.

Parking down the street, as usual, he had walked onto the property as though he owned it and stood in the growth of ivy to listen to their parting words. 201 Autumn street, if he needed to go there, he would. Bonnie waited until they left and re-wired the alarm system. Someone would be in trouble.

"Do you have a spare?" Devon asked, examining the tire on the right hand side of the Impala. She shook her head. "Only the do-nut?" She nodded. "Then I will remove the tire, take it in and return probably within the hour if that meets your approval."

"I should have called the garage." Her voice carried the worry that she was imposing on his time. "They would have come out but once the Police report went in, someone had to be there and Gerald, well, he has a broken leg and collar bone…" She paused, "Still, since the Police also notified him he called me, when he heard I had a problem getting to work, he was here within minutes, just as he said. After I saw the store, I completely forgot about the flat."

"It's understandable." Devon had the jack scotched, and was removing bolts. "Like I said, I will return, no need to worry I'll run off with your tire."

She gave a nervous laugh. "I know you wouldn't the Calvary.

"I'll fix dinner for you," she said. It was his time to protest. "It's the least I can do," she replied. "I know there are two potatoes ready for baking…after that your guess is as good as mine."

"I like baked potato," he said. "And a glass of water, please." They laughed together. "Sometimes in my bachelor quarters there are meager pickings. I eat a bowl of cereal and go to bed."

In the kitchen she found the two potatoes and inventoried the refrigerator. One steak the size of a small plate, a head of lettuce, a tomato and a handful of strawberries. It was all or nothing and just about not enough, but she could open a can of green beans and add a few onion rings for flavor.

The table was set, the steak ready and a salad in two bowls, topped by tomat.o, strawberries and mandarin oranges from a can left over from holiday festivities. The baked potatoes were still in the oven. She had made tea, not knowing his drink of choice and the can of green beans were simmering on the stove with their topping of bacon bits and chopped chives.

She knew he had returned and was putting the tire back on the car. She heard the slam of a car trunk . He entered, his hands soiled, but smiling. "Everything's to go, on your car," he said as she pointed him the direction of the powder room situated between the kitchen and laundry.

He heard the clink of ice going in to glass as he washed his hands and eyed himself in the mirror. A hand towel lay by the lavoratory's bowl, black with leopard spots. He liked her style, a picture of a lioness and her cub was over the commode and a gold candle set atop the lid. He wondered if he would see more of her house, the fact he hadn't been farther than the front room of Grace's home had thrown him.

She settled into the chair nearest the stove and he sat on the opposite side. He was almost settled when he remembered something. "One minute," he said, "I have something to contribute."

He hurried to the Police car and returned with a foil wrapped item and a small sack containing cinnamon butter. "I couldn't resist. While I was waiting I kept smelling this heavenly fragrance, fresh bread from the oven. I checked it out and bought a loaf. Of course the lady said we needed the butter." He was unfolding the foil. "Good, it's still warm."

"Shall we say grace?" Anna asked. His nod was acceptance. "Dear Lord, thank for the day you have given. Thank you for food for our bodies and friendship for our spirit. Together in your name we ask blessing on Miss Grace as she faces this terrible ordeal. We ask your safe care on all.

In your Holy name. Amen. Sorry I was a bit long, but Miss Grace needs our prayers. Sometimes the prayers of others is all that takes us through the rough times."

"I agree," he said. She had placed a baked potato on each plate and the steak, his being the larger portion. "Are you limiting yourself because of me?" He asked as he saw the size of the steak on his plate.

"Oh, no," she smiled. "I intend to enjoy the fresh bread you brought. What a treat. And I'm really not a big meat eater," her grin widened, "unless its one of those days you just have to have a hamburger."

"Anna, I've had a few minutes to think. Whoever did the damage to Grace Weather's home has your name and it won't be hard to find your address, I wonder if before I leave would you consent to my viewing your home as to he ease an intruder might enter."

Her fork stopped mid air. "Your words scare me."

"That's not my intention. I just don't feel good about his knowing your name." He shuffled his feet beneath the table, a worried gesture she couldn't see but probably was aware of. "I am completely on my own in this concern, I haven't addressed it with my Superior, but I considered asking your permission to stay over tonight." He held up a hand, lest she would protest. "It's a gut feeling, Anna, and I don't get these often but when I do, there's usually a reason."

She was silent. "I realize we have only met this weekend and I will be happy to sit on the curb in the car." Her phone rang and she rose up to answer.

"Miss Grace." Relief was in her voice. "Come stay with me." She was silent, listening. "You've already taken a room? Do you need clothes?" Her expression changed. "Of course, I forgot you had a suitcase with necessities. I'm here if you need me. I'm so glad you are home, Miss Grace but I'm sorry you returned to such a mess." Her expression changed again as she listened. "You feel that, that strongly? I will. Goodnight."

She returned to the table. "Her last words were, Anna Jane, be careful. Everyone, all our employees are under surveillance, tonight. Did you know that? Did you forget to tell me?" She was scolding him as his cell rang.

"Yes, sir, I will sir." His was an unrecognizable expression as he listened. When the call finished he said, "No, I didn't forget to tell you, I just now received my orders to keep you under close watch. You have a double garage. Would you allow me to pull the police car inside, out of view?"

"Do you have a choice of where you will sit up surveilance?" Her troubled eyes rest upon him. "I consent."

"Are you adverse to a stranger taking residence on your living room sofa?"

"I'll get you a pillow and a blanket," she replied. "My normal habits are going to bed early. Should we observe them?" She moved around the room, closing the window blinds, her usual nightly ritual.

"Yes," he arose, "I'll take care of the car. If you have an opener, I will drive around the block to be certain no one is watching and then enter the garage." She was nodding. "In the car?" he asked. The seriousness of the situation was sinking in. Speechless, again she nodded. "Anna, we can talk and don't worry about Grace Weathers, two policemen are in the room next to hers at the hotel with an unlocked door between them."

She was an old fashioned girl, letting down her hair, removing the day's make-up and showering as usual to put on pajamas and a robe. He was a Policeman, for heaven sakes, and still she hurried to be finished by the time he made his way around the block and parked the car in her garage. She heard him settle onto the sofa, wondering had he removed the gun holster, his shoes, would he sleep?

The hall clock chimed each hour. Strange, she had never noticed it before and now, suddenly every sound was magnified. A car passed on the street driving slow, she could see the lights through the holes in the blinds. It stopped. A car door slammed. Someone was running and came into her yard. She pulled the cover tight to her chest. A man's voice said, "damn you Kitty. You're not running away from home again. No more babies for me to have to deal with. " The noise unnerved her. She listened for the car to move forward, a door slammed, a gear changed. An hour passed. She couldn't sleep. She padded down the hall, to the living room where he sat in the shadows on one end of the sofa. "Can I sit with you?" She whispered. "I'm too keyed up to sleep."

He nodded, a finger to his lips as he pat the space beside him. She crept close and sank by his side. It was then she heard the noise, someone was at the window, peering in. They could not see into the shadows where they sit. A beam of light cut through the side slit, aimed first to one side then the other. His arm came around her. "Don't move a muscle," his words were so low she wondered if she imagined them but he hadn't let go, as now he tightened his hold.

It seemed an eternity, they sat there listening as footsteps rounded the house, a tap on the window, the deep silence that followed as someone waited to see if their presence was known. Then came the turning of the back door knob. It was a heavy door with two locks, no glass panels, pure oak, in the forty year old home. He tried the windows, nothing moved. He'd been there thirty minutes or more. Tomorrow, he said. This will wait until tomorrow. They heard him walk back around the house passing the window by the sofa. There was a soft thud of a door closing down the street, the motor turned over. He was gone.

"He probably won't come back, tonight," Devon said. "I have orders to stay. I think if possible we should get some sleep. I'll have to go home early in the morning to shower and change

Anna was quiet, thinking. "Do you mind if I sleep in that chair? Once, I'm sure someone came to my window and it freaked me out. I just can't go back in that room by myself tonight."

"I'll take the chair," he said. "It is your sofa." He arose, stretched and walked over to the chair. It was overstuffed and comfortable looking but he already knew as tired as he was it wasn't going to provide a good nights rest. He yawned. "We have four or five good hours, let's try."

He wasn't sleeping and she kept tossing. Finally she cleared her throat and spoke. "It's not where I sleep, I'm thinking, but the fact I'm scared being alone. Now I'm in here worrying over you. Get up. We can't rest here, but stretching out on the bed I believe we will."

He wasn't getting the meaning.

"I have a king size bed. You are a policeman. I am a sensible woman. If you can sleep fully clothed in a chair, I'm certain you can manage on a bed that has a heavenly mattress…" She sighed. "I love my bed. We will put a pillow between and not bother each other at all. I'm sorry but I can't be alone tonight." She motioned. "Get up and follow me."

Tired as he was, Devon realized this was a first for him and it was certainly not according to protocol.

"If you are concerned I will tell this bizarre situation, take my word I won't, I value my reputation."

"I'll sleep on the sofa," he said as she rolled her eyes. He hadn't expected this out of her. She was going to the chair, her head on one arm, her knees laying side ways. "Okay, I get the picture. Lead me to your heavenly mattress."

He awakened to daylight. She hadn't moved an inch from her side of the bed. He had slept like a log. He learned it is possible to listen and sleep at the same time. Retrieving the gun and holster, and putting a hand full of nothing he'd pulled from his pant pocket back, it was time to hurry home. Turning to leave the room, he found her awake, waiting for something it seemed by her expression. She smiled.

"Good morning," glancing down, she chuckled. "I'm still wearing my housecoat. How are you? Did you rest at all?"

"Must be the magic mattress," he grinned. "I slept wonderfully, listening but sleeping. It's an art."

"Are you leaving me? What if he returns while you are gone?"

He saw her fear. "I have to go." He had orders. "I do have to. It's out of my hands." She was shaking. Inwardly he silently groaned, "but you can go with me." He sighed. "There's no other alternative."

"Ten minutes? Please, only ten minutes." He groaned out loud and settled into the old chair. She accepted so quickly he knew her fear was real. But then, this had been thrust upon her yesterday.

In ten minutes she showered, dressed and put cosmetics into a small bag and dropped them into her oversized purse. She was a bit breathless, the bed was unmade but she was ready to go with the Police Officer. "I'll have to work late tonight, this all seems so strange." She saw his puzzled expression.

"Just that life has its twists and turns but I'm happy, if that choice of words works, that you are here and that you allow me to go with you. I am scared out of my wits after seeing the mess at Miss Grace's house."

"You speak of her with such respect, how much older is she than you?"

"It's the respect she deserves," Anna replied. "Not a lot older but she's been through a lot."

————◈◈◈————

Bonnie sat in the park, intermingling with a group enjoying the late evening weather. Two young men were strumming guitars, one humming along. "We're here to do a gig at the Steak House on the outer edge of town," the hummer said, as though he asked. "We can't practice at the hotel and there's a few chords we need to correct. Do you mind?" He shook his head no and slunk deeper into the oversized sweat shirt he was wearing. He'd hotwired the old van the company put to rest. In the tray there'd be a key. He had placed it there himself and covered the tray over with used cigarette stubs.

He'd be there to see her reaction when they drove in, her and Billy Boy. He'd already told Holly, "you have nothing to worry about. It's out of your hands. Do you want him, or not? If you choose good for nothing, then you are on your own. I'm done. I'm going to mosey on down the road. You and your mother can raise the boy. I'm tired of it all and going as far away from people as I can get; those who take what I give but give nothing back in return. She'd looked at him as though she had not one single idea what he was talking about. "Where's Granma, Bonnie?" He gave the old, roll of the shoulders how should I know sign. He'd give everything he had for Holly to feel better and does she thank him? No, she asks, "Where's Granma?"

Whine. Whine. Whine. All the days he'd known her, Granma whined, demanded, whined and demanded that he tow the mark. They cleaned the house on occasion and she didn't miss telling him what a pig he was. Then she says, I'm taking your chair. You can find another. You don't deserve this one. He'd been unable to make her leave his chair. He felt belittled, He felt the burden. He had brought the one he planned to marry to meet her, that was years ago, before Holly, before the accident and she married him in spite of the old lady revealing all his hidden traumas. It hadn't helped that she wanted to talk about herself. "Because of you my life's a mess. So there's a kid, I said to my ex, "You're the daddy, I said to him but he said, the kids not mine. So, good person that I am," she says, "I found another daddy and you were both ungrateful." When I started to set the record straight she says, "Don't even go there. You were a bother then, you are a bother now." He was glad she hadn't brought the kid with her.

She wouldn't bother him again. Ever. He saw the gray sedan pull in to the park area. Billy Boy was driving. Miss Grace Weathers allowed him to open the door for her. Bonnie saw her mouth work, thank you, he thought.

She said thank you. Billy tipped his head, leaned in to whisper to her and then ran, to open the door, to make way for her to go through to the back room protected by the steel metal door.

Would the vandalism frighten her to know someone thought so little of her they destroyed her business? Would fear claim her that someone might come after her? Oh, yes, he was on his way. He watched as she examined the carnage. Would she remember his warning, when you least expect I'll come for you. He couldn't resist. He dialed her number. "Hello, Grace," he said, when she answered in that soft voice. "Did you forget I told you when you least expected, I'd come for you. You've been bad, Grace. Punishment draws nigh."

Peter was desperate. Angeline had no clue as to Grace's leaving. The conference was not over. But as of an hour later his part was. He called the one person he remembered from his time in Haven on the Bluff. "Hello, Doll," she said breathless. "You been running?" He asked. "Hon, I'm out of breath getting to the phone to talk to you," she replied. "You need more therapy, Hon?" He remembered those straying hands. "No, I was wondering how you are, how's the fair city these days?"

"You haven't heard?

"Heard what?"

"That lady you stayed with, we didn't realize she owns the Pharmacy on Main. Well, Hon, it was vandalized according to the Police report and it not only made the newspaper but went live on KZXR television. I guess you don't get our local news."

"Not hardly," he replied, trying to sound casual. "You mean Grace Weather's, her business not her home was vandalized?"

"Both, Hon, the business destroyed but the reporter didn't show her home, seems she was away at the time." She gave a deep sigh, "Word is someone with an old grievance is out to get Miss Grace Weathers. When you coming through, Hon. I'm available if you want to do the town."

"Just checking to see how you are and thank you for coming to the home for my therapy sessions."

"Oh, that's just part of the job, Hon, but you know some people you enjoy, others you don't."

Within the next thirty minutes he had filled the car tank with gas, filled the thermos with coffee and headed toward Haven on the Bluff, that seemed a million miles away. "Don't do anything you shouldn't, Grace," he whispered, remembering her stubborn streak. He prayed Billy was with her when she toured the Pharmacy, because he knew that was where she would go, first. He was an hour behind her. Driving by the Municipal Airport an idea came to him. A second call was necessary.

"I need a room next to Mrs. Grace Weathers," he said, flashing his card for the desk attendant. "I'm her doctor and I'm sure you are aware of the trauma she is going through since the vandalism to her home and business. I've been called in to help defuse the situation with the police and the perpetrator."

The desk clerk studied his credentials, and then called the assistant manager to view them. "Do the Police know you have arrived?" She was sizing him up. He was dressed in a suit and looked as she thought a head shrink should. He checked his phone, handing it over, the message available.

"Need to see you as soon as you arrive. Situation here sticky as usual and need your help. Signed by P.D.," she read. "I assume the P.D. stands for Police Department?" He nodded. "Go ahead," she told her employee, put him in the room next to her.

As in all things, Bonnie thought it is a hurry up and wait situation. He imagined his mother was in a hurry to have him and then couldn't wait to get rid of him but who would have done all the dirty work if not for him. When he reached driving age he began to find jobs and once he had his own money he quit listening. That's when he formed the Boyz and they listened to him. The only difference; he was the leader. They looked up to him. They'd have followed him through hell.

Hell it was after the accident and him blamed for the boiler room incident with no mention of the girl, just destruction to school property; sent off for punishment while the real punishment was lack of medical treatment from the prison's underground hospital and a long siege of trying to heal that took years and the mental anguish he suffered.

Under his mother's clutches Holly had little respect for him, like his mother all she wanted was the dollars he could provide and life was hard. Blame had to settle somewhere. First it was his mother, then that shop keeper, then the young woman who ridiculed him…but it was always what happened in the boiler room ruined his life and she was at the root of it all. So he waited. She didn't go home to see the damage. Surely they told her. By the time she returned with Billy he was in the old van watching. They drove by the hotel, on down the street, turned into a private drive and sat there while he passed by. He made a U-turn, came back by the private residence but the car was gone.

He drummed his fingers on the steering wheel, where would she go? He called the hotel using the company name where he last worked. "Yes, ma'm. What room was that the air conditioner isn't working in? I'm here to make repairs. Grace something, the desk said. You are the desk? Then you know what I'm talking about." He gave a light apologetic laugh. "Housekeeping called me. There's no one there tonight to handle the task. They said it's important. If you want, I'll wait until morning."

"That would be great. If you're with me no one will hesitate to let me in. Much appreciated, see you in about five minutes." He slipped on the company jacket with the logo on the upper left pocket, collected the box with his special tools and went in. The desk attendant smiled, held up a key and a tablet and motioned for him to join her. "Thanks a lot," he said, not once opening his mouth, he'd left off the bridge that made him appear decent. He wanted her to see the damage she'd done all those years past. But the real damage only the doctors at the prison were privy to. "Not a pretty sight," one said. He died while Bonnie was there; no great loss to society was Bonnie's way of thinking.

Like clockwork, she knocked on the door but no one came. "I think she and a friend went to the dining room to have dinner," the attendant said.

He nodded, "then I'll do what's necessary and be out of the way by the time she returns."

"I'll have to check that no valuables were left in the open," the attendant said. "Its policy and you will have to sign this form with your company name and initial it."

"No problem," he said, signing the form. She left and he was on his own.

Peter slipped into sweats and settled down by the side of the wall between the two rooms. He heard voices in the hall, a man and a woman, but it wasn't Grace's voice. There was a slight ding of metal on metal, a repairman? He picked up his own tool, listened for a voice and was satisfied Grace was not in the room; if he heard right it was a repairman. The settling of tools, the subdued sound of settling in, brought hesitation on Peter's part. What was going on, there was no activity, why was he staying? The phone rang. He heard the man say, "I'm almost finished." There was a brief pause, and then, "Sure, if you stall five minutes and then send her on, she'll never know I was here. It's fine, if you want to play it that way. I promise, I'll never tell. Save your job."

Peter waited. No activity, no noise came from the room next door. He heard the elevator. He couldn't risk Stormy entering the room next door. He hurried, out of his room and was down the hall as the elevator stopped, the door opened, "Peter?" Her eyes were wide in surprise or fear, he couldn't read her expression.

"Push the button, Stormy, go back…" That's when something or someone hit him from behind. The blow glanced off the bone of his head, Peter staggered and would've gone down but he was that close to the elevator door. "Shut the door, Stormy…." Someone was behind him, he felt a body brush past and someone headed down the stairs. He was struggling as his world went black and the elevator was moving in slow motion. Peter Daniels was a heap of flesh and bone on the fifth floor of the Haven on the Bluff's finest hotel.

Hotel security arrived, breathless, led by Stormy's guard. "Whose the guy on the floor?"

Night shift came up the stairs, the desk attendant's face a worried expression as she spoke. She was explaining to an armed Policeman, "That's her doctor. He's here to talk to the guy that's after her." The officer stared at her, assimilating the news. "He told me, the Police have talked with him."

"I'll check the room," the officer said. "I know there are two in there. They're not to open the door under any circumstance. Then I'll check to see if this guy's legit."

The doctor was coming around, addled but blinking his eyes and trying to nod, yes, as she said but the effort was more than he could manage. "Where's Stormy? He asked.

They were a confused group. "Who's Stormy?" The desk clerk asked. "Only persons we saw were the repairman and Miss Weather's. Is the elevator out, too? Is that why they were taking the stairs?" She might lose her job over this. "I didn't know there were two people," she said "No one mentioned anyone named Stormy."

Groggy, Peter was able to get on his feet, no thanks to anyone standing around him. "Where's the stairs and is there a way out the back instead of going through by the front desk?"

"If you hurry take a left off the stair, there's a metal door, it won't be locked until repairs are complete." Security was keeping an eye on the outside through the window at the end of the hall. "You will see the fellow from the Heat and Air Service putting his tools in the back of an old van. I don't know what happened to Miss Weathers. But if you're going somewhere follow him, he'll lead you out.

Peter made a dash for the stairs. "Where are the people supposed to be guarding Miss Weathers?"

"I was to meet her at the elevator. There are two in there, Buddy. I called their names, they responded but they're giving her a little privacy. She's in the bathroom. They're not to open that door under any circumstance. She'll be safe under their eyes."

"No, she's not. He's got her. She was in the elevator, and now she isn't."

He had never descended a staircase at such break neck speed. He was through the metal door now and cautious. The repairman had his back to the van. Peter surmised, he had to sign another form to leave the parking lot. The van was parked next to the curb and the door to the back seat of the van was open, he dove in and tried to slam the door shut once he unfolded his body enough to turn and reach the handle. But it didn't close. He heard a whimper. Maybe it was his own, he'd landed on a box with a heating cooling logo on it and a tool he couldn't identify sticking in his ribs. The whimper sounded again. He heard the parking lot attendant say, "Be careful, Mr. Bruce." Bruce? Bonnie? Bruce?

Peter's heart did a sudden jerk. Bonnie? Bruce? Where had he read that name? Read? He was jumping to conclusion. After all these years would Bonnie Bruce still live in Haven on the Bluff? His mind was cluttered knowing Stormy was in danger but the name…could it be?

"Stormy?" His intended whisper was more a hiss. "Stormy, it's Peter. I'm in between the seats. If that's you. Be quiet. Give me a chance at him, Stormy. Things don't look good with him driving, but we'll have to play this by ear." He felt the slap of a hand on the van and then the door pushed shut as the driver threw something resembling a clipboard over his shoulder that landed on Peter's head. At that moment Peter thought he felt a searching hand. Stormy's? It was his imagination. He was that desperate. How then, must Stormy feel?

"You okay back there, Gracie? If you're not, I'll see that you're just peachy in a few minutes. I'm going to take you home and treat you like you've never been treated before." Bonnie gave a laugh that bordered on weariness. "Maybe you're asleep, Gracie. I did shove sleeping pills down your pretty little throat, didn't I?"

Peter had wondered why Grace became quiet but her breathing was as regular as the ticking of a clock. Peter was searching beneath the bench seat. Any tool would be better than none. His hand was empty but there was the item sticking in his ribcage. If he turned, Bonnie would know, it was a tight space and he was a tall man with no room to spare. He had to wait until they stopped, and he had to pull this off. He thought he touched her, but he wasn't certain, his own mind was playing tricks on him.

The van rumbled down the street some fifteen minutes. Grace did not whimper. The tires turned on to the crunch of gravel and Peter guessed they were in an alley. He knew when the driver turned off the motor and went around to the back of the van was not his best time. He had no choice but to wait while Grace was removed and bodily carried inside. He listened for a door to close and then slid out of the van. Hiding was complicated, a tall man could not fold up that easily, still he flattened himself behind an old oil barrel probably used by the drug dependents during winter months the reason it was left in the alley. In the unfolding of his body he found his cell phone, he had no memory of placing it in the back pocket of the baggy sweats and in amazement opened it to send a message to the police But it was not his cell. It was Grace's. Somehow, she had been able to reach beneath the seat…God in heaven, Peter whispered. She had touched him. Scrolling down he found Devon Malloy's number and then nine one one. Grace. He pressed letters, his hand shaking. Bonnie Bruce has Grace.

Bonnie returned to the van, removed the two bags from between the seats and headed back inside. Peter's conclusion that he was to follow the man into the house wasn't easily accepted, except if he didn't go now he might never get in. The door was slightly ajar, evidently the neighborhood did not pry, or maybe not have the energy to walk the streets at night. Mostly it was a street of empty buildings; one window was lit by an insurance sign. Whoever ran it must be desperate to have an office here.

He slid around the door to find himself inside, in some kind of utility room though the utilities were not just a washer and dryer and sink but an array of saws arranged on a peg board, from small toothed blades to large, similar to those he'd see the summer he worked at the local meat shop. Bonnie's profile listed carpenter work, not slaughter house. The sound of a slap against human flesh came to his ear. If he moved just so, he could see around the silver sheets that housed what he supposed to be a furnace he doubted worked. The room was dark and he stood in the corner shadowed by a strange piece of furniture he assumed a wardrobe, by straining forward he could see. He didn't have to see to know something foul clogged his airway.

Grace was tied to a tall backed chair, the lower rungs strung with weights he supposed to keep the chair from tipping. A red streak was obvious on one cheek, visible when Bonnie grabbed a huge portion of her hair and jerked her head back. She was still asleep. Why the chair? A row of weapons lay on a six foot divider that was meant to block view from the kitchen to the dining area. But it would not hide Bonnie's intention to shame her by taking away her clothes.

"You need to open your eyes, Gracie," he taunted. "See all this beautiful skin that will be revealed. I'll show you yours and then, if we are lucky I'll show you mine. Piece by piece, we're in this together."

Standing where he was, Peter looked for a better way to reach Stormy. The stench was nearly more than he could handle; an odor so strong it took one's breathe, what could it be, a pet died? For certain something was dead and close by. He pressed back thinking no one could stand the smell therefore it made sense to move away from the spot. Trying for a better foothold he nearly lost his balance and leaned too heavily on the wall behind him. There was a swooshing sound as though air were being let out of a tire. But it was the wall took his weight; a bulge appeared as the sheetrock came loose where it joined and a gaping hole appeared. Drawing as tightly into the shadowed corner as possible, Peter wondered if the sounds were heard. Now the taste was in his mouth and nausea had taken hold.

"Is that you, Momma?" Bonnie Bruce called out. "Making your sounds and expecting me to come running as usual. Well, I'm busy, Momma." As quickly as the words left his mouth, Bonnie had risen and was standing in center of the room. He touched a switch and light flooded every corner but one. "You, back in the shadows, come out. Or I will gut her." Turning, Bonnie chose a curved sharp bladed knife and placed himself directly in front of Grace Weathers sleeping form. With his left hand he placed one finger beneath her chin and raised her face. "She's beautiful, isn't she? I've not decided what nationality flows in her veins. Spanish?" He gave a soft chuckle amused at his own thoughts. "However it will be red when her blood flows if you do not step forward." He placed the tip of the knife at her throat, a tiny drop of blood appeared. "It 's up to you."

Gagging, Peter lumbered forward. "What is that awful smell?" He would try to beg time, anyway possible. "What are you doing, man?" He found an empty stool and slouched down onto it as though they met every day. "You got any…"

"I got nothing for you. What are you doing in my house?" Bonnie was standing behind Grace. "I could have killed you and nobody know, nobody care." He sighed. "Maybe I kill you and her."

"Whatcha doin, why, man?" He leered forward, "Can I help you with that?"

"Oh, no, this one owes me. You wanna see what she done for me?" Bonnie faced him full on, opened his mouth, showed him the broken teeth, the gaps where teeth were missing. Kicked me but that ain't all."

For some reason Bonnie's free hand went to his crouch. "She hurt me there, too."

"You drunk, man?" Peter rose up, aiming to circle the room. "That ain't nothing. Lots people got no teeth. What you care? It take lots more than that to take a strong man down. That ain't nothin."

"You're in no position to know if its nothing.' I already ask you, once, what are you doing in my house."

"It looked empty. I just need a place to lay my head."He glanced at Stormy. "I'll take her bed. Looks like she's dead."

"She ain't dead." Bonnie grabbed Grace's hair roughly and pulled her head back, peering down at her.

"You sure you ain't got no drugs or something? I know that sleep."

Bonnie grabbed a knife from top of the divider. "When I finish with her, you won't need drugs."

Peter eyed a dirty overstuffed chair. "That's cool, man. I'll sit here and watch til you're done."

"Why you got that fancy hair cut? You look like one those preppy boys, all money no class."

"Really?" Peter slicked a hand over his hair. "I haven't even seen it. They said they'd spruce me up for court and if I Iooked good and acted right, maybe the judge wouldn't send me away." He gave a weird laugh, "But I sneaked out the bathroom window. This is far as I got. I'm glad your door was open."

"Cops after you?" Bonnie's eyes tightened, as Peter backed into the chair. "Don't think of sittin in my chair. Momma wanted it and then Holly, but it's my only thing I like in this house." Bonnie was rehashing the man's words. "Where you runnin court from?"

"Yonder, you know that way," Peter pointed. "Fellow picked me up, big burly guy I wouldn't cross for his money or his keys. Dropped me on the outskirts and I've been in back alleys ever since."

"You look familiar. Where have we seen each other, before?" Bonnie was up in his face, his hand on the sweat shirt bunching it up around Peter's neck. "Where do you work?"

"Come on, man. I used to work, down the street, for that Insurance Company." Bonnie's grip tightened. "Hold off, you're choking me. You know the one down there at the corner. I've seen you before, too."

"I think you're lyin'. I believe I saw you tonight."

"In the alley?"

"Somewhere." He glanced from Peter to Grace tied to the chair her head hanging down. "If I could keep her and no one ever know, that's what I'd do, she would pay every day."

"I'm curious," Peter asked, "What did she do to you?"

"I think you know." Anger flashed in Bonnie's eyes as he lunged toward Peter and Peter threw himself out of the way. Bonnie landed on a hard backed rocker packed with clothes. The chair went over on its back and Bonnie on top of the clothes.

Peter scrambled, throwing himself on top of Bonnie, swearing that he hadn't taken the moment to grab one of the knives from the higher shelf, but he was trying to make the most of the man being on the floor, the knife Bonnie held flew through the air and landed out of either of their reach.

Bonnie outweighed him a good twenty or thirty pounds but his body was not as toned and at the moment it seemed Peter's mind was functioning better. The fall had addled Bonnie, the absence of the knife in his hand frustrating him more. As he struggled to get out of the floor, Peter was on him using the pieces of clothing; wrapping Bonnies arms, a piece over his head, straddling the man, trying to subdue those arms that aimed to kill him. But Bonnie raised up, struggling to his feet, seizing Peter in his massive arms squeezing as Peter's feet came off the floor, until Peter felt his oxygen cut off, unable to breathe he couldn't fight back; he was going limp, but the scramble of feet was heard coming through the door, passing through the odorous smell and into the room when a voice commanded, "drop him or I'll put a bullet in you, Bruce." Bonnie dropped Peter to the floor. "Turn around," they were hand cuffing Bonnie. A woman, another Cop was cutting the ropes that held Grace to the chair. Grace was struggling to breathe deeper and ward off the sleepiness.

Peter was by her side, instantly. "Stormy, are you hurt?"

"Peter?" They were trying to help her stand but she buckled. Peter reached across, an arm around her waist, her arm on his. "Where…I mean what are you doing here?" Her voice was raspy.

"Can I take her home?" He asked the Police Officer? "She's had a lot of excitement for one night."

The second Officer turned, it was Devon. He took in the scene. "Grace. Daniels." He sized up the situation. "I heard your question; I believe that would be the thing to do, unless she's hurt and needs to go in to the hospital first. Otherwise, I'll clear it with our Chief and you two come in to the station tomorrow morning."

"Sir?" A young officer beckoned to Devon. "I think you need to see what's in the back room."

Peter heard but he was intent on getting Stormy outside. "Can you drive us back to the hotel?" He asked and the officer opened the door for them to get in.

"One minute," the officer said, "I'll need to tell my superior where I'm going." He was gone a minute. "Which Hotel?" He asked as their attention was drawn to the young officer bent double, heaving.

Grace was a shivering mess, her teeth chattering and her body in a form of shaking she couldn't control. "I-I-don't know what's wrong with me," she managed. "I thought he was going to kill me, when he forced me to take those pills it was almost a blessing, then I wouldn't know what happened."

In the bathroom, Peter turned the faucet on in the shower. "Where are your clothes, in the suitcase?"

"Yes," she murmured. Peter was sitting the suitcase on the bed, finding her clothes for the night, turning back the bed..

"Now, Grace, a warm shower will stop the shivering. I think the temperature is fine. I'll be in the outer room. Call me if you need me." There was a knock at the door. The lady Cop was standing there.

"May I come in? I have a few questions we need answered tonight."

"She's in the hower; if you will listen for her I'll go next door and get out of my stinky clothes."

Devon was standing outside the door. "I didn't come in, not knowing if Grace was fully dressed by now."

"I see," Peter nodded. "I'm just going to my room to take a quick shower and get out of these smelly clothes. What was that horrible smell. I thought I was going to up-chuck."

"That's information I'm not allowed to discuss until it's all recorded and then the paper will carry it. I will tell you, it's bad."

"I figured Bonnie had kept a dead animal inside, too long."

"Worse." Devon grimaced. "Don't ever say I said this, I'd have to deny it. "A person, we think his mother."

"Lord have mercy." Peter shook his head. "I don't know if Stormy can handle that tonight, she's pretty shaken, almost in shock. It's like she's dead on her feet and whatever that medicine was he gave her."

"You call Grace, Stormy?"

Peter grinned. "Yeah, believe me, she earned it." He turned to go," This won't take long. I've got to get out of these clothes, they picked up the odor and since you and Miss Cop lady are here, I know she's well protected." Still, he hurried and was back as Stormy scrubbed clean, looking like a little girl in the hotel's oversized house coat returned but she almost seemed to be wavering more in her walk.

The Officer's phone rang and he stepped out into the hall to answer. Once inside again he asked Peter, "Are you staying in this room with Grace, tonight?" Devon shrugged. "I'm asking as an officer of the law."

"No, I never had any intentions of…"he paused, "Do you want me to stay here with her tonight?" He glanced Stormy's way. She seemed almost caught in a trap, not knowing what to say. "I'll be happy to stay with Stormy."

"We will have an officer down the hall in that little alcove, in order to get here quick should there be any type disruption…"

"Wait," Stormy interrupted her voice low and thick. "I… thought…I thought…you had him…"

"Bonnie Bruce overcome the Police officer and is now at large. We know he's here in the city, but we don't know where. He can't go to his home. It's under surveillance."

"That's settled, then." Peter glanced at Devon, expecting the very expression on the man's face he was seeing. But to Stormy he asked, "Have you eaten? We will order up. How about you officer?"

"No, thanks, I'll pass." Devon's mind was on Anna Jane. How would she get home? "I have another task." He left the two studying the hotel menu. He heard them agree they'd not eaten all day.

"Does this bring back old memories?" Peter dipped a chunk of Italian bread into the garlic oil. "Have you had anyone cooking for you since I was in your home?" He saw she was slow to answer, the fatigue obvious as she was practically hunched over her plate, her elbows on the table she was barely eating. "Hey, eat a little more and I'll help you to bed, then I'll spread out on that fancy sofa in the sitting area." He glanced around the room. "Only the South would offer all this, and Haven is the south isn't it?"

She stumbled as she left the table, already oblivious to his presence, sleep the number one important thing on her mind, as she shrugged out of the oversized robe and climbed onto the bed. Her head touched the pillow and Peter pulled the sheet to her chin. She was groping for the blanket and he placed that over her, too." Curling into her favorite position, Stormy was asleep.

Peter pushed the dinner cart outside the door, wiped up the few crumbs and wondered if the Southern Comfort theme of the hotel afforded a blanket for him, and there it was top of the closet shelf. He was as tired as the next person but sleep wasn't coming easily. He couldn't turn off thoughts of the afternoon, the horrible stench had taken up residence in his nostrils, but food had helped, still he listened to unusual noises coming from the hall and was grateful for the officers outside the door.

Stormy had only been asleep an hour when the moaning began. Peter stood beside the bed, his hand gentle on the covers. "Shh. Shh." He whispered her name, "Stormy, it's all right. I'm here with you." When she was settled he returned to the sofa, pulled the blanket up to his ears and tried harder to sleep but Stormy's cries brought him to his feet as the door opened from the outside and the police officers stepped in.

"Is everything all right in here?" They gave Peter an accusing glance but realized he was making a mad dash for the woman's bed as they spoke and the lady was crying, a terrible cry the man was trying to suppress. "We'll leave you," they said, relief on their faces they weren't the ones to deal with the commotion. "We're going to lock this door, Sir. If Bonnie should come we don't need to make it easy."

"Stormy. Stormy." The cries subsided finally to a moan, tears still falling on the pillow case. Peter could only guess the whole thing with Bonnie this day had brought back the past full-fledge. Now he said a prayer Bonnie wouldn't try coming to the hotel and that the Police would pick him up through the night.

His voice wasn't doing it; he tried shaking her gently, not to frighten her more, but she didn't waken. She had been groggy since they'd returned and he wondered what Bonnie had given her to last this long. Her words had been thick and the fact she wasn't moving bothered him; the medication had overcome her ability to focus. Her crying continued as he glanced at the door, listened to see if the adjoining rooms were hearing her cries. Someone farther down the hall was knocking on the wall. A door opened, he heard voices and the tap on Stormy's rooms door. He stepped to the door, "Yes?"

"Sir," the ladies crying is disturbing the other room occupants. "Can you do something about it?"

"Like if I've not been trying," Peter muttered. He went back to the bed, the pillowcase beneath her cheek was wet, the front of her gown and where the sheet was near her neck. He rubbed his forehead, muttering again, "I wasn't going to do this. It always gets me in trouble." But he slid out of the second set of jogging clothes he'd thrown into his suitcase and climbed into the bed behind Stormy's sleeping form, one arm beneath her head, the other over her waist, Peter pulled her into the curve of his body. Soon the crying lessened to a snub that reminded him of a child's last crying bout. This woman needed to be held. Yawning, he closed his eyes and slept. Let the Officers do their work. He was doing his.

It was still dark of night though the clock said four a.m. Peter usually awakened to go for a run at that hour, but this day was different. He smiled to himself. He liked this day. He nuzzled her neck, but it wasn't her neck. In the dark, he couldn't see and he didn't know she had turned. His lips were on her lips.

"Peter?"

"I certainly hope so." He lay a hand on her stomach. "This certainly feels like you."

"I know it's you. No one else feels like you."

"Sleep with a lot of men, do you?"

She giggled. "No, I didn't mean that. Not intimacy, just how I feel in your arms."

"Your Cop Boy was here last night, do you remember? He asked if I was going to sleep in your room. I was a bit shocked, coming from him. Are the two of you a number, or not?"

"We were never a number."

"Are you hallucinating, or still under the influence of drugs Bonnie gave you?"

She snuggled closer. "This probably sounds too suggestive for our present predicament but I like sleeping with you." She yawned. "Your body is very comforting."

"Comforting, huh? Sixty year old men, eighty even, probably have comforting bodies."

She kissed his lips. "I have dreamed of kissing you for months now. How did you really end up in my bed?"

"I paid the two officers standing just outside the door. So don't get any ideas of anything more than kissing me…."

She felt his grin beneath her lips. "I won't. There has to be a few things settled before I go further."

"Hmmm. That sounds enticing. You know I've wanted to make love to you since the day we first met. I was a gentleman. I lay myself at your feet; finally I left because I could see I was going nowhere."

"So much had been drilled into me, Peter, in my heart I felt you truly loved me but what I had been through, I had to be sure and in that need I nearly lost you because when we were no longer in contact with each other I suspect the worst that you wanted to marry so badly you found someone else."

"My heart was in my throat the day I left, do you remember what I asked you to do?"

"I sent you an email, one word, the word you told me to send when I was ready and you didn't answer."

Peter set straight up in bed, beat on his chest and gave a Tarzan imitation. The rapping on the door began immediately and down the hall a deluge of knocks on the walls began.

"Are you nuts?" She pulled him back down on the bed. But with all the knocking on the walls, she covered her head with the sheet. "You just ruined my reputation."

He covered her, straightening the covers. Slipped into his jogging suit and said, "go to sleep." Then he answered the knocking on the door. "Sorry, officers, I turned it off. Shouldn't have left it on."

They glanced at the television, then to the sleeping form in the bed and him with a blanket wrapped around his neck. "All right, Buddy," one of them said. "Our next team will be here soon to relieve us."

"All right, then this time I'll throw the second bolt," Peter turned the knob, and went back to fall on the bed. "So you don't like my Tarzan call?" She turned to face him. "That meant I finally found your email. It was in my messages but to be certain I called my secretary. She said, "I copied it and deleted it."

"Oh, yeah, what did she say?" She raised up onto one elbow. "I thought you had found someone else."

""Mr. Storm said yes." He smiled. "That confused me. I was watching you scoot around on your chair deciding to leave while I was speaking and it came to me. Mr. Storm wasn't Mister at all, it was you. But then," He picked up her hand and kissed her fingers. "You were gone and I didn't get a chance to give my Tarzan yell."

"You wouldn't." She lay back down, her hair spread across the pillow.

"Oh, yes, I would. I've waited that long and the last months I just knew you were making plans with Damon." He touched the hair that had mused across her forehead. "I really thought that."

"Oh, no, I think from here on Devon will be seeing Anna Jane. That would be a beautiful match, two lovely people."

"You have no feelings for him? I seemed unable to understand why you didn't feel for me as I...."

"For Heaven Sakes, Peter..." She was interrupted by pounding on the door. "What is this place...."

Peter was hurrying. "It can't be good," he was muttering as he threw the bolt. "What is it?"

"Sir." The young officer was trying to control his excitement. "Bonnie Bruce is in this vicinity and he has Miss Anna Jane from the Weather's Pharmacy. The Chief says we're not to let you two out of sight."

"Do they know exactly where he is with Miss Anna Jane?" Peter asked.

"Oh, no, Peter, I know what you are thinking that you can talk him into giving her up."

"That's what I do, Stormy. If someone can get into Bonnie's mind, if there's something good left in there, he sees himself as a victim the world had mistreated and now it's his time." He looked the Police Officer in the eye. "Where do they think he is?"

"That's the part of it, Sir. He's out front. He's got a hold on her, standing in the hotel drive and he has a gun."

Stormy's eyes were luminous. "Please, Peter. We've just found each other."

"Stormy, I would never let anything keep us from being man and wife. You should know that." He gave her a lop sided grin. It was hard, seeing the tears. "Promise me, you'll stay right here in this room."

She nodded and Peter slipped out the door, taking the elevator down to the lobby where the Chief of Police stood talking to Devon Malloy . "Chief," he said, offering his hand. "Peter Daniels." He nodded to Devon.

Devon spoke up. "This is the man I was telling you about."

"It's up to you, Son," the chief was an older man, a father figure to his young officers and this one was no different. "Bonnies dangerous because now we've found he's been busy all these years right under our nose and he don't take it lightly, being found out, but that's our home town girl he's got in his clutches and we got to protect her. You see though," he paused, pointing, "The way he's holding her, shields him." He sighed. "We can't very well put a bullet in him for fear of hitting her. Killing her."

It took a few minutes to find a spot to call out to Bonnie. The officers surrounding the hotel drive in a semi circle, Bonnie in the middle, close to a car he'd stolen and access to the highway. An ambulance was parked in front of the Hotel, the medics safely behind it rather than inside, ready if needed.

"Bonnie, this is Peter Daniels. Why don't you turn the girl loose and lets you and I have a talk. You've been the victim long enough, Bonnie, carrying your grief and sadness, allowing it to make you do bad things, that's no way to end your life, some officer shooting you in cold blood in the middle of the street."

"What do you know about my life? Who says I'm sad and done bad things?"

"Has the young lady hurt you Bonnie? Does she deserve this kind of treatment from you?"

"I'm punishing her boss for what she did to me, this one was handy, I couldn't reach the other."

"What's her name, Bonnie? You need to know who you're holding and tell us why you'd hurt an innocent young woman."

"Step out here where I can see you." Bonnie motioned toward the pavement in front of him. "You think you can talk me in? It won't happen." To Anna Jane he said, "I know where you work. I don't know you. What's your name?"

"Anna Jane Smith."

Bonnie laughed, "Ain't it always that way? I figured you to be a Smith."

"No Sir, that was to have been my married name, but my fiancée got killed."

"What'd he do rob a bank?"

"No Sir, he was in the Military, I was going down for us to be married when I got word he was killed in some kind of military maneuver they were doing on base." Anna Jane noticed the lines in Bonnie's face. "Aren't you tired, Mr. Bonnie, wouldn't you like to sit down and rest?"

Bonnie gave her a hard jerk, "If you are trying to soften me up, forget it. I don't know what we're going to do to get out of this, but I ain't sitting down and neither are you. So stop the chit chat." He stared hard at Peter Daniels across the street. "I know your voice. "You ain't no doctor, you're the one came to my house. What kind of game you playin, you know I could've gut you and left you layin."

"I think you're tired, Bonnie. I think you want this all to be over. Turn the girl loose. Give yourself up."

"And go back to prison?" Bonnies laughter had a maniacal sound in the air. "You have no idea what that's like. Put a young man in there, don't give him medical treatment, let parts of his body rot off, then whose going to see to his medical needs, you think I want to get even? You got that right."

"They need you, Bonnie, down at the morgue, someone's killed an older lady, some say it's your mother, you need to identify her, Bonnie.

There's a young woman, blonde hair, no one knows who she is, but you might."

"I didn't hurt Holly. If she's gone it's that good for nothing she lived with and her with a baby comin on."

From that moment, Anna Jane felt the life going out of the man with the stronghold on her arm. If he went down she knew he would kill her and she was tired from standing on the hard pavement. She dared not talk, he seemed to be growing more nervous by the minute, tired and nervous. By the erratic murmurings he uttered now and then it seemed he was trying to consider if his daughter had been hurt and if she had who had hurt her, was the man telling the truth or was it a ruse to make him give up?

It can't be Momma," he muttered, "She's restin in the wall, all stuffed in and sealed away. Now, maybe Holly will take notice we're gone, me and Momma, who's gonna pay her bills now?"

It was four in the evening, they had been on the pavement over four hours now, the sun beating down, no water and no end to Bonnie being held in the sight of every armed policeman. She was his protection, if he turned loose of her they'd shoot him. If they shot first, chances were he would take her life before he fell, his finger seemed frozen to the trigger.

"Mr. Bonnie," she whispered through parched lips. "I think I'm going to fall. I wish you the best and I'm sorry if I cause you to get shot but I've stood as long as I can."

He felt her slump forward and the next feeling was a burning pain in his shoulder. The gun flipped out of his hand and her weight demanded he turn loose of the girl's body. He knew men were running toward them as she slumped to the ground. All the while he was reaching for the knife in his boot.

Daniel saw the glint of metal in the sunlight, "he's got a knife," he screamed. "He will slash her throat," he cried out, remembering the knife held to Stormy's. But the knife went up, one swift draw across his own throat and Bonnie crumpled to the middle of the street bleeding. "Get a medic." Daniel was running to the center of the street, stooping down, the girl was all right she had fainted. Bonnie's eyes were staring sightlessly up to the heavens. There was a gurgling sound and Daniel knew he was gone.

It was draining, Peter felt the loss. He heard the comment, "There lies a good for nothing, never amounted to a hill of beans." But Peter in his chosen profession knew, once there had been a child someone should have loved, nurtured, and guided. Possibly no one had set an example and as many this one had never known what love was about? Prison hadn't helped Bonnie Bruce, he was already to far gone when he landed there. Whatever he'd endured, no doubt he didn't intend to return to that life, he'd take his own first…and that's what he'd done.

Sometimes he wondered that his own thoughts balanced the scale, private and sealed within, because Bonnie had hurt Stormy and his heart had ached with the knowledge he'd gained from her journal. He had known then Bonnie Bruce deserved punishment. Today he feared for Anna Jane's life. It was times like this, the calling that claimed him to return to hourly appointments listening to people's problems caused him to question how could it be? You knew someone deserved punishment and yet you understood where that person's behavior was bred.

Weary, he returned to the room where Stormy waited. She arose from the sofa by the window and came to him, putting her arms around him, waiting for his to close around her and she lay her head on his shoulder. "You tried," she said. "It was so long ago, he hurt me, did I tell you it was Bonnie? I can't remember right now. Surely I did. But to die in the street…"

"There's more," Peter replied. "Let's not talk about it today." He drew her back to the sofa. "Do you have to stay here while the Pharmacy is replenished? Your home?"

"No, the company will come in and completely rework the Pharmacy, update it in the process and as for my home; I have to remove personal belongings and anything dear, other than that I have a friend whose husband is a carpenter, I will have to get on his list but in the mean time they will board up the windows and lock the doors. What do you want me to do?"

"I want to take you home to my parents. They will love you, Stormy and help you forget all the ugliness you've known in your life." He studied her, serious appeal in his eyes. "Could you do that? Go with me for a week… or two would be better. Get to know the folks, be sure I'm not taking you down the wrong path."

"You look so troubled, are you having second thoughts, Peter?" A spasm of alarm was racing through her veins. She thought they'd come so far these last twelve hours.

"No, no." he pulled her to his side, his lips against her cheek. "I see things like we just witnessed and it makes me all the more certain one person does not have the right to expect another to travel the road together unless they are one hundred percent in agreement."

"I thought I'd lost you, Peter, with my old fashioned ways." She sighed. "I admit I did so many things wrong when you were ready to give your all, even on such short acquaintance, but now I know I love you. Wherever you go I'll go with you. Once the Pharmacy is completed, the house built back, I'll sell and we can do whatever you want. If you'll let me return once or twice a year to visit my son's grave, that's all I'll ask of you."

"I would never keep you from that." He seemed unable to turn loose of her. "So, do we sit here the rest of the evening or go to your home, pack up whatever is necessary and head out tomorrow?"

"I'll have to talk with the employees and set up papers for their unemployment or salaries if their help is needed. Then, Peter Daniel's I'm ready to begin this journey with you." She stood, stretching out a hand, "Come on, fellow, let's move it. Move it. Move it."

"Seems this car needs gas," he said, leaning in to give the dash a better look, "Yep, almost empty." They pulled into the nearest gas mart. His phone was ringing as he got out, "It's Mom," he said. "Why don't you talk to her. "Hey, Mom, it's me," he said, "Here's Stormy, we're coming home. Talk to her."

Laughing, Stormy took the phone. "Yes, yes, I am happy. Yes, I think he is, too." Peter was listening through the open window until a diesel stopped at the air station with its motor left running. "So how did that conversation go?" He asked when he was pulling away from the station. "What?" Her smile was intriguing. "Are you keeping something from me?"

"Only the fact I think we are going to be one tired set of Twinkies by midnight."

"Somehow, I don't think that's the right answer, but if you're keeping something from me, it better be good."

Leaving town was not easy. Packing was a major chore.

"I don't know what I would have done without you." Stormy wiped sweat from her brow. "The air is on and I'm stil in melt down." She glanced at Peter, little by little he was stripping. The shirt went first, then the tennis shoes, then the long pants were changed for an old pair of cut offs.'

"I knew just where to find these." He grinned, "I can't go much farther with your carpenters on site." He spread his arms and spun around. "Put a little music on and I can work all day. Hear that?" In the background Frank Sinatra was spinning on the old machine, Strangers in the Night. "Come here, my little kitty," he wagged a finger at Stormy, taking her into his arms to dance across the room."

"Uh, Sir, I don't believe this is a tango."

"No?" His eyes lit up in pleasure, "But it's so much fun. I love dancing with you."

She tapped her wrist. "If we are going to your parents, we are going to have to bring this to a close."

"Yeah?" He fell back into one of the high backed chairs. "I think we can leave in the morning, you got everything squared away at work, this morning. So, are your bags packed?"

"Like the Thanksgiving turkey. It's a wonder the zipper is holding. I had to keep one item in a garment bag, on second thought I should put in what I'll need at your Mother's, because when we open that suitcase it is going to be like an explosion…but I had to get those clothes out of the house for the Carpenters."

"It's fine. My mother had large closets built in each bedroom and if I know Mom she is right now in there lining the drawers, leaving some kind of fragrance and setting your bathroom up like a spa." He shook his head. " I only have one regret."

"What's that?" When she stepped closer he pulled her down on his knee. "I always feel my heart jump when you have regrets, due to our past history."

"Never fear. I had intended the next time I took you home to my parents, we would be married."

"So…let's go down to the Courthouse and get a license. It will be good in Springfield, won't it?"

"I don't think so, I think the license has to originate from the same court system as the county where you marry." But his face lit up in smile. "I'm just blown away that you finally decided to marry me."

They were like two children leaving their respective rooms the next morning. The hotel staff joked with them as they ate breakfast and then followed them to Peter's car wishing them a safe trip.

"You are happy," She said, smiling. "I am too." They were passing the church with the famous organ. "I think I was in the greatest turmoil when we left church that day, afraid you would leave and you did."

"There's a church behind the folk's business reminds me of that one." He paused, thinking, "We could marry there, if you find it pleasing. Do you want to be married in a church?"

"That would make me even happier. So much in my life has been arranged by others and now that we have truly found each other, Oh, yes, Peter, it wouldn't have to be fancy, but in a church…."

"I know it would add more meaning to have our friends present, but…" Stormy smiled.

They drove into The Blue Willow lot to find a huge banner stretched across from the entrance two light poles, one on each side of the drive, WELCOME STORMY WEATHER AND PETER. Stormy was laughing at Peter's expression, "Already, I'm second place." His smile showed he didn't mind at all. "Come, on, let's find the folks."

There were hugs and exclamations over the recent events and the fact the two were engaged to marry, "But, tch, tch, tch," Peter's Mother was dismayed, "No ring, my darling, you must give Stormy a ring." She saw his expression. "You have one, but you are waiting for the right moment."

"Mother." He practically moaned as Stormy found the two amusing. "You ruin my plans, Mother."

"Tch," she said, "Eat lunch and then go, a grown man, a mother tells go get a license, we have plans too." She reached for Stormy's hand. "All is as we discussed. Now, eat and then, my Son," she said turning to Peter, "She must have a nice ring. We plan to keep her forever. There will be babies to bounce on our knees." Peter's father merely smiled and kissed Stormy's cheek saying he had to return to work, someone must run the shop, but he kissed his wife unabashed before all within view.

Peter was shaking his head but Stormy felt the love between the two in their banter. This was something she had never had, the frivolity of people who loved precariously. All she had known was the stiff and controlling love between Mr. and Mrs. Weathers. She was going to enjoy this new journey of life.

"I'll just hang out with Dad a few minutes," Peter said. "Then, we'll go see about a license." His smile was infectious. "Don't get my bride in trouble, Mother," he warned. "I don't know whether…."

"Come, my darling," his mother was leading her to the ball room just beyond the dining area, where she and Peter had danced that one time. Sliding the doors enough for the two to enter, "What do you think?"

Stormy gasp in delightful surprise. "Oh, it's beautiful. How did you do this on such short notice?"

"For you and my Son, I would work all night." She laughed good naturedly, "I had help and it was a pleasure. Now, as agreed, I called your person, Anna Jane, and she was most enthused to be a part of your surprise for Peter, she said she knew exactly who you would enjoy having present for the reception and I have contacted the friends dear to Peter's heart. It will be a surprise for him. I am so pleased, Stormy that you want to make him happy. Peter's friends mean so much to him." She turned toward the outer working area of the establishment. "So now, come, hurry my son down to get the license and whatever the time between, this room remains closed until the two of you are wed."

"It's beautiful. Thank you." There were tears in Stormy's eyes. "It is a dream come true."

"Mother, we are leaving you and Pop for an hour or two, I have a place I want to show Stormy."

"This is another little college hill town," he explained as they rode along. "But there are many quaint little areas, almost as though lost in time, the winding creek, those limestone boulders and the greenery, isn't it something?"

"Beautiful," she agreed. When he pulled into a suburb that seemed to allow more than the usual acreage around each home she leaned forward taking in the beauty of the terrain. "Oh, Peter, how peaceful." He had come around to open the door and was reaching for her hand.

"We could follow the concrete road, or I can show you from the back side of the street where the homes are built. I don't know how it was missed, perhaps the buyers thought this little plot of land was part of a different development. No one asked to buy it, and I'm relieved as I purchased it before the housing project began," He took a deep breath, as if needing to explain further, "I had almost given up, Stormy, when I came home after the casts were off … I was terribly disappointed that I had left you behind. In the back of my mind I invisioned the two of us here; In my despair I almost turned it in to the realtors and yet, I had this tiny thread of hope you'd change your mind and send me that one word." He led her through a winding path with a pattern of trees that lapped overhead, and the promise of a stream as they could hear the trickle of water and then it was as she expected, white boulders, a small bridge across the stream and a bench time had bleached white.

"So you own this?" He was motioning she could sit. "I like your bench. It's comforting."

"Like I said, I heard many people say what an attractive spot this was and wondered why no one had purchased it and I kept quiet, hoping I'd hear from you and that you would like this little respite from the world." He smiled, laughter forming, "just off the path of activity, and yet peaceful and quiet."

"It is. I feel at peace. It's lovely, in it's own way I compare it to how I felt sitting in the church by your side listening to that magnificent organ music. And yet, that day when you left the peace I'd felt drained from my body and my mind as you drove away."

Peter drew a small box from his pocket, going down on one knee, his expression serious as he took her hand. "Stormy Weather's, here before God in this beautiful setting only He could provide, I'm asking you to marry me. Stormy, will you be my wife?"

Tears welled up in Stormy's eyes. "I will, Peter. I have not been any other's wife, nor have I known the love that I feel for you. Yes. Yes." He was standing, pulling her up, the ring on her finger and then the wonderful embrace. Their kiss was full of promise as their tears mingled together.

This was the day. No one was happier than the bride and groom but his parents beamed with satisfaction and Angeline's happiness and pride were infectious. "The Momma, has done her magic at the church," Peter's father explained. "Wait until you see, our pastor is ready to perform the ceremony and the surprise Stormy requested is on the way."

"Mother made her famous wedding cake," Peter guessed but his father only laughed.

Overhearing, Peter could only wonder what the long awaited surprise might be. And then it was time.

He knew Angeline would be sitting on the front seat on one side, standing in for Stormy's parents, and across the aisle, of course, his parents. But when he walked in from the back to stand with the Minister, there in the pews he had regretfully known would be empty were his friends and Stormy's.

Devon and Anna Jane sat on second row. Anna gave him a shy wave as a smile wreathed her face. Then there was Gerald, the Pharmacist and family, and he suspected every employee of the Pharmacy. On the groom's side were his fraternity brothers, their wives and a few children. With close friends of the family invited by his parents, Peter's heart settled into a gentle rhythm. It was a very pleasing gathering. These were the people they held dear and no one could ask for more.

The first chords of the organ rang out. His mother hadn't missed a thing if she helped in the arrangements. Here they were, his mother and dad, walking hand in hand up the aisle, seated on the front row seats then Angeline ushered in by Billy, seated on the other side, and the music settled softly as the words to How Great Thou Art brought Stormy down the aisle, so beautiful his heart caught in his chest and he wondered if it would quit thumping by the time she arrived to stand by his side. The first song ended and the second began, a voice as pure and strong as Andrea Bocelli sang, "When I am down and oh, my soul so weary…"

Peter and Stormy turned to face each other as the words closed around them, their world, this moment it was theirs, "I am strong when I am on your shoulders…You raise me up to more than I can be." With uplifted faces and hearts overflowing they listened to the Minister's words and said their vows.

"I now pronounce you husband and wife," the Pastor said and the congregation of people cheered. "Mr. Daniels you may kiss your wife, Mrs. Peter Daniels."

Peter couldn't resist, "Stormy Weathers is now Mrs. Stormy Daniels." While everyone was laughing Peter leaned in for the traditional kiss and then took his blushing bride in his arms.

When the kiss lasted a bit longer than expected, the pastor turned his attention to the guests. "A reception follows in the Blue Willow ball room. It is with great anticipation and expectation you are welcomed to come congratulate the happy couple."

Within fifteen minutes of becoming Mr. and Mrs., Peter and Stormy were photographed in the church setting, her off white dress arranged professionally as the photographer directed each pose, and then followed them to the reception area to catch more candid shots. It was Peter's expression made it worth every effort applied.

"Whoa." He exclaimed, seeing the ball room filled with people; for the room had taken on a happy surreal atmosphere. "You and mother collaborated on this? When? This would take days to do. It's wonderful! I thought the church was pretty…and you are beautiful…. But this?" He was like a little bo y with wonder in his eyes. "Thank you little wifey." He was kissing her again. "I am so happy, Stormy. Seems I'd almost given up and here you are in my arms."

They were to do the first dance, waiting for the floor to clear they were observing Billy and his new girl, Billy seemed genuinely happy and there was the fact Devon seemed quite smitten by Anna Jane. Stormy reflect on Anna Jane's sincerity wishing them the best in life, a solid rock, Anna Jane was always sweet and caring. She and Devon were perfect together; two wonderfully decent people finding each other.

Though he would never reveal his thoughts, Devon had sit through the ceremony, bits and pieces of the investigation of Bonnie Bruce teasing his mind. Facts were coming together and he was sifting through the fog of years past, to believe perhaps he had been drawn to Stormy for more reason than he had realized, it was possible Stormy was the one in the room Bonnie and the BOyz threw him into that fateful night of years past. If it were true, she had borne his child…there was a sadness he could not share with her…now Stormy would find happiness and as he glanced down at his and Anna Jane's entwined hands, perhaps he would too.

"How do you feel?" Peter whispered as the music swelled and they were beckoned to the dance floor.

"It is my dream come true, Peter." Her breath caught, "The dress your mother found for me so it would all be a surprise for you, how could she know, except her heart was in it for both of us. I described one I'd seen, sent her a photo and she mysteriously came up with it. How does she do these things? The church, the music I requested and now this….it is more than a fairy tale, Peter, it is love most obvious. Your parents are exceptional. And you are my handsome Prince Charming, my dear-dear husband."

"God bless us, always," Peter whispered. "We must never let him down for the gift he has given us."

"Each other." She replied as Peter reached for her hand.

The orchestra began to play. Peter took her in his arms, "Stormy Weather," he sang……..."This gal and I are together…All I ever wanted in life is here to stay……"

The End